# The Perfect Partner

A Chadilaine Manor Regency
Book 2

by Elaine Lyons Bach

ISBN: 978-0-578-59239-8
Published by Mary's Lamb Press

*Dedication*

*I dedicate this book to all the wonderful, caring authors who use their valuable time reaching out to help others achieve their writing goals by sharing their expertise in a plethora of subjects in the world of writing and publishing.*

*I want to thank the members of The Beau Monde, a chapter of the RWA for all their help with historical accuracy, especially researcher Nancy Mayer, who never fails to answer promptly and completely, citing sources.*

*Thank you to members of the ACFW who present gratis the monthly tutorials, and those who traded chapters with me to critique my manuscripts, and who reviewed me on their blogs.*

*I particularly want to thank author April Kihlstrom for the insightful lessons in her excellent Book-in-a-Week class which pushed me over a writer's block halfway through this book.*

*Thank you to the members of the Catholic Writers Guild for their help and guidance through the online conferences and Facebook pages. Kudos to author Michelle Buckman for her intuitive suggestions for structuring and improving the story. Gratitude and blessings to the proprietors of Full Quiver Publishing: graphic artist, James Hrkach for beautifully interpreting and achieving my vision of the book cover, and author Ellen Gable Hrkach for all her support with the publishing side of it.*

*I could not have accomplished The Perfect Partner without the encouragement and help of all of you.*

# CHAPTER ONE

*March 1, 1817, Surrey, England*

Lady Diana Ashton surveyed her realm from her vantage point high in a Chestnut tree half-hidden in the wood. Capability Brown had redesigned the park a few years ago to make it appear as if created by nature alone. She could just make out the imposing castle-like outline of her beloved Chadilaine Manor. Wreathed in morning mist, it seemed enchanted. She hated having to leave home for so long. She was free here. Free to roam the grounds checking on the fox's dens, the badger's hole, and the rabbit warrens. She was free to climb into her treehouse and spend the day reading, or wade in the lake and feed the swans spent bread, and especially free to ride the wooded trails on her favorite horse, Satin Cloud.

If she told her brother Colin or sister-in-law Eden where she would be on the estate, she need not take an escort along. That was important. There were times she needed to escape the closeness of family. Eden's mother, two sisters, and a brother were invited to live in the empty dower house after Diana's governess had married Colin. Eden's family could be chatty and opinionated. After her years of solitude, chattiness could be exasperating.

Her trip to London this time would be for the entire season. She would make her come-out and officially enter the marriage mart. Diana shivered. She wasn't ready for this. Marriage meant bending your will to another. Marriage to a lord meant she would be expected to produce an heir and a spare at least. Children were a joy; she would love to raise a bevy of them. But, childbirth terrified her. Fully one of every three women died in labor or shortly after. Her own mother had died days after she was born. Marriage must be put off as long as possible. She wanted to live before she died. But she did want to experience a *grande passion* like those in the novels. She wanted to be wanted.

Raised on their vast estate by her often-absent earl father, Diana was frequently lonely. On his death, her only sibling, Colin, had taken on the responsibility of her. But he took his new position as earl seriously and was often away from Chadilaine as well. She longed to be a triumph and make Colin and Eden proud of her. She owed them that much. They'd been so devoted to her. Whatever she put her mind to she could achieve, could she not? She would find a way to accomplish all her goals by the end of the season. But she would have to pretend to be someone she was not. She would have to sparkle, to become fascinating to the young aristocrats of the bon ton. Diana drew in an extended breath and released it audibly. She would approach this dilemma like a soldier preparing for battle. Eden's sisters would be brought out into society along with her. They anticipated the adventure. She dreaded it.

******

Colin Ashton, Seventh Earl of Edmunds, was seated in his office with a list of names in his right hand. He tossed the paper across the immense carved cherry desk toward his countess and leaned back against the plush leather of his chair. "I'll not tolerate that man in my house, Eden! He must not be found within a ballroom's length of Diana or your sisters or any other innocent in England. There's nothing more to be said. I'm adamant about this." Hidden beneath the desk, resting on a buckskin-clad knee, his left hand curled around a different, crumpled note. "Nor can I believe that you, knowing what you do of him, would even consider it." Gradually, Colin allowed the concealed warning to fall into the waste bin at his foot. Concern for his entire family clenched his heart. They deserved security. *Who wrote that threat?*

Lady Edmunds glanced at the list of names. Her generous mouth curved into a knowing smile. She absently rested a hand on the growing curve of her belly. "I understand your anxieties about him, Colin, but Diana will not. We told her nothing of that night. She recalls Major Bradley fondly, as a family friend."

"Please, love, do not speak his name in this house! And annihilate it from the guest list post-haste. Make up a new one without the offensive name and consign that thing to the fire!"

"What reason—?"

Colin's elbows hit the desk, and he growled, "Does one need greater reason than what transpired between him and you?" He could never forgive himself for not being there for Eden when she was in jeopardy. He would guard his sister closer.

"I was about to say what reason do I give to Diana?"

He ran a hand through his curls. Contrition pricked his heart. How dare he take it out on his tender, *enceinte* wife? She knew nothing of the menacing note. He gentled his voice. "No reason. You are inept, my candid countess, when it comes to dissembling. Leave that to me."

Eden chuckled as her eyes sparkled with amusement. "Dissembling? Leave to you? Surely, you're as bad at that as I."

Colin hung his head in mock shame. "The explanations, if it comes to that."

"We have time, my love. Maj–ahem–the 'persona non-grata' is greatly altered. His wounds from Badajoz will interfere with any spryness. Surely, he's matured in the last five years. At least, that's what I'm told."

"What you're told and what I know are two disparate things. No more mention of him. The very thought of his existence brings the taste of bile to my tongue. You'll be preaching forgiveness at me in a moment, and I'll not have it. The incident concerning you should be enough to give anyone a disgust of him. He's a thoroughly unsavory creature. It is I who has the splinter in my eye, and he the plank in his!"

She laughed. "At least you admit to a splinter. But how are we to ... His family–we cannot strike them from the invitation. It would be political suicide."

"Let me sort that out."

"This is merely the first tentative record of guests. We haven't decided on a date for the ball. Names will be added and dropped as Diana makes new friends and recalls old ones."

"Nonsense, my sister will want the entire populace of London to come to her debut. She'll want a crush. And hers is to be among the first of the balls. I heard our little flock of females planning it."

Eden came close to her husband. She held up an index finger for him to examine. "I'll twist Diana around this little finger. She'll forget a certain unmentionable person ever existed."

He grasped the hand, kissed the finger and said, "See that you do. And don't attempt to twist me around that particular part of your anatomy as well."

"Oh? Is there some other ...?"

"Hush, wanton! Desist from putting ideas in my brainbox this morning. I have appointments all day. I cannot be anticipating us together as I entertain matters of state." He pulled her down onto his lap and kissed her soundly. He would now have the devil of a time putting her from his mind.

To Colin's frustration, Eden untangled herself after one lingering caress, crept to the massive oak door, and peeked out. "I thought I heard footsteps." Closing the door tightly, she wandered back. Her eyes avoided his. "Could there be another reason you don't want Diana to speak to...'the name?' "

His shoulders stiffened. "To what do you refer?" *Had she also received a threatening message?*

"Merely that there was ... an intimation ..."

The earl went to Eden and gently tilted her face up. "What intimation?

To whom have you been listening? What do they say of her?"

"Not they. Not now. Just the one time–when first I came to Chadilaine. Nurse Warren told me some circumstances of Diana's birth. I heard nothing more, but there are times when Diana does look almost exactly like... If I say it aloud, and it's not true, love of my life, merely speaking the words could cause–irreparable damage."

Colin grasped her hand to his heart. Eden bowed her head. His chest rose and fell against her. "Cause damage to...?"

Tentatively, her eyes met his and held fast. "To the quality of our relationship. Still, I think you may know of what I speak."

"I'm aware, considerate wife, your circumspection is such that I need not ask you never to repeat Nurse Warren's suggestions–even if there is the least possible foundation for them. As that female has now gone to her reward, I no longer fear she will spread further rumors."

"Of a certainty, my tender husband, you may depend upon my discretion."

"And never think that complete honesty between us could do other than strengthen the quality of our relationship." Hearing himself promoting honesty as he consciously hid the contents of that missive mortified Colin. Heat suffused his cheeks. *Hypocrite—Speaking of honesty while hiding that threatening note.* He smiled brightly at his wife to disguise his shame.

Since his grinning mouth was now awfully close to hers, Eden pressed her lips to his in answer.

Colin returned her kiss with force but broke off quickly. "Off with you, baggage," he said, eyes gleaming. "And have Perrin send Mrs. York to me. I have a little matter to discuss with her."

"At once, my husband," Eden parried as she scurried toward the door, snatching up her book on the way. She paused to turn and tease him. "Could you be hiding way back here in your office to avoid seeing my mother?"

Colin lifted his brows and playfully clapped a splayed hand to his chest. "Bless me, has your dear mother come to call so early?"

"You're safe now. She and her companion have tottered back to the dower house."

"So sorry to miss them."

"Had the staff not alerted you, you would not have managed to."

Colin waited to be sure she was gone before he bent to retrieve the crumpled note from the waste bin. He unfolded it to study the hand again. *"If you dare bring Diana out this season, your family will suffer certain tragedy."*

## CHAPTER TWO

Colin stood in the housekeeper's parlor addressing Mrs. York. "There was an unsigned note among the letters on the salver Joseph brought to me this morning. Joseph could not say where it came from. It had not been there when he received the post and arranged it on the tray. He said he sorted the letters and delivered Lady Edmunds' and Lady Diana's to them first. He left the salver on the hall table while he did. He went back for the salver and brought it to me in my office, failing to notice a folded paper had been stuck between the letters."

Colin searched the housekeepers' expression–nothing there but wonder. He must be more direct. "Are you aware of anyone not part of the family or the staff being inside the manor any time before twelve this morning?"

Mrs. York's eyes looked heavenward as she searched around in her mind for an answer. She shifted her hefty form on her small feet. When she discovered an idea, she punctuated it with a bobbing pointer finger. "There was the one boy, milord. But he was only in the kitchen as I recall, and only briefly."

"To whom do you refer?"

"Why, Billy Bryant, milord, tenant farmer's boy. Brother to Daisy, one of the parlor maids."

"Bryant? Not one of my tenants."

"No, milord. His family farms on the Bradley estate."

The skin on the back of Colin's neck tightened, and the hairs bristled there as if an icy breeze had blown across it. His voice tensed. "Why was he here?"

"His father had an awful accident chopping wood for the fire. His hand slipped, and the ax hit his leg bone. Tore him up bad. Billy came to ask if Daisy could come home a bit to help her mother nurse her father and do the cooking. I said, 'Of course.' I hope that was alright, milord. Since the family is repairing to London, we could do without her while you're gone, and they looked so worried, the both of them."

"Yes, fine. Might Billy have entered the hall?"

The housekeeper thought and shrugged. "Anything is possible, milord. I followed Daisy to her cell to help her get ready and gave her a few pence in case of a need. He was in the kitchen when we got back. They left right away to ride home in his dogcart. I portioned Daisy's chores among the other maids."

"You did well, Mrs. York. Don't fret. I'd appreciate you mentioning to the staff I'm wondering how the note got there. It's unimportant, truly. I'm merely curious."

******

Lady Diana Ashton stood before the cheval glass, scrutinizing the newest addition to her debut wardrobe. Turning this way and that to get the best view of her backside in the mirror, Diana concluded, "I look like a stuffed sausage; do you not agree?"

"I think it quite pleasing to your figure, milady," her maid answered.

"I liked the style and the material when I saw the pictures, but the color, does it not wash me out?"

"Not at all. It enhances your complexion."

"I'm not so sure. Everything must be perfect if I'm to attract the perfect beau."

"I have every confidence in you, milady."

"Good to know someone has. I certainly don't." All eyes would be on her. Society would expect her to make a brilliant match. She would be in competition with the newest *crème de jeune filles* for the notice of the latest crop of unattached noblemen. Around promising young men, she was a newborn foal–all gangly and awkward and stupid. She was too used to blurting out the first thing that came to her mind. They'd laugh at her. Suitors preferred a miss who was demure and circumspect. If she was to be a politician's wife, she must be able to mince her words and mind her manners. "If only I were certain my brother's Eton chums would be there, Major Bradley and Mr. Blake. They know me well, and they can always make me laugh."

"There was a time you were quite sweet on them both, I believe."

"Truth be known, I still am. Though poor Major Bradley I've not seen in years. His injury in the war seems to have kept him from rising in rank. That's unfortunate for him. He had such hopes of advancement. He prefers to stay in London now." Diana paused to observe her lady's maid. "It occurs to me you'll need new dresses to wear when you accompany me. And this color and style will flatter you more than me. Please take it. Eden had so many others made up for me to choose from."

"What are you giving away, Diana? Is that a new dress for the season?" Eden's youngest sister, Hope, entered Diana's open door without invitation. "Let me see how it looks." She grasped Diana's wrist and turned her. "Tsk. Only a friend would tell you, but it makes you look fat, truly. Lilac is a poor color for your complexion. The style does nothing for the things that matter. In fact, it flattens you even more up there." Hope laughed, pointing at the offending bodice area. "Lord, I wouldn't have that thing."

Diana narrowed her jade eyes but cooled her reply. "You needn't worry, you won't."

Continuing to poke fun, Hope added, "If the Mantua maker made some tucks in here and there..."

"But that would not be the style. Martha, help me out of this."

As the maid lifted the dress, Hope pressed on. "It looks well enough for a crush. Have you chosen the material for your court costume?"

Diana revived at the change of subject. "I care not a fig about fashion, but the presentation dress for the Queen's Drawing Room is perfect as it must be. It's of ivory silk lama with seed pearls sewn to it in drapes around the hem and a train of silk. It's an angel's attire, restrained as I hoped it would be. I wish we didn't have to wear the ridiculous hoops, but Mrs. Bell assured me there's a new flexible one out this year that makes it much more comfortable. We must practice our deep curtseys as soon as it arrives."

The maid held up a morning dress, and Diana nodded. Martha helped her mistress don the outfit. "The ostrich feathers for my hair have been ordered. I do hope they find the feathers on the ground as we do peacock feathers here. I'd hate to think I'm wearing something a bird was murdered for."

Hope laughed her false little tittering laugh. "What things you think of, Diana. Your court dress sounds divine. But why would anyone prefer restraint in a dress? The more frips and lace and jewels and gathered material, the better."

"Madame Danet has devised a stunning court dress for you."

"My new frocks are well enough. Madame Danet does have a certain flair. But truly, Eden has instructed her to keep the *décolleté* at a modest height, and I cannot convince her otherwise as I hold no purse-strings. The pin money they give me is parsimonious. I ask you–how am I to attract a man with my two best qualities hidden behind muslin? I shall be so *outré*. I could dampen the material a bit... But Eden would have me sent to bed. I cannot wait to get out from under her thumb and have my own husband and household."

"Take care what you wish. That could be exchanging a light thumb for a heavy one. And the second one you can never get out from under. Madame La Croix is working on the gown for my ball as well," Diana said, steering Hope away from her endless complaining. "She says it will make me appear to float along the floor as I dance. I think it hides my stomach charmingly. I wish I could control my eating better, but I get so hungry."

"As do I. But mother tells me extra flesh on the limbs is attractive to men. It proves you are healthy. Incidentally, who is Major Bradley?"

Baffled by the abrupt change of topic, Diana answered without missing a beat, "An old family friend who was injured at Badajoz. He lost a leg. His elder brother is Lord Richard Audley. Their estate abuts our seat here in Surrey. Have you heard something of him?"

"Only his name spoken as I passed by your brother's office door."

"At the back of the house? What took you out there?"

"If you must know, avoiding mother by playing with the kittens in the mews."

"Certain you weren't listening at keyholes? Mine, perhaps?"

Hope forced a chuckle. "How else is one to find out what others are saying about one? Or how discover *on dits* to spice one's conversation?"

"One with your talents can always make them up."

Hope twitched her *retroussé* nose. "But you're the one with the imagination, Diana."

Diana drew herself up to full height and turned slowly to face her adversary. She mustn't descend to scratching Hope's eyes out. She had to live with the girl.

A knock sounded, and they both jumped, turning their heads to the door. Diana beamed and waved the welcome visitor in.

Hope's elder sister, Faith, smiled broadly at her. "Diana, how lovely that dress is on you." Entering one step, she continued, "I declare you can wear any fashion and show it to best advantage. It only needs your hair styled up and a jaunty bonnet to complete it. When does the hairdresser come? I cannot wait to see what you decide upon. Will you have a cluster of 'follow-me-lads' bouncing upon your shoulder? I think they are so feminine."

"The coiffeuse comes Wednesday, but I fear the styles that are the rage will only increase the squareness of my jaw. My face will look even more like a horse's."

"Please, Diana, cease self-effacement," Faith said. "Either you fish for compliments, or you cannot possibly know how pretty you've grown."

"That's merely your sweet nature speaking. You think all God's creatures are beautiful, including beetles, and stoats."

"Well, they are, especially stoats." Looking mildly offended, Faith turned to her sister. "Hope, Madame Danet awaits you for the second fitting. She brought the latest copy of *La Belle Assembly*. I am to tell you, Diana, there will be visitors at tea. Eden would not say who, though she was smiling mysteriously as if it was a good secret."

"Thank you, Faith. While you two shop, I suggest you choose more cloaks, muffs, and parasols in matching colors to your wardrobes. It looks as if the cold and wet will continue this year. I pity the farmers. It bodes a repeat of last year's poor crops and rising food prices." Diana took up a small book from a side table and curled into the cushioned window seat. She glanced out over the lawn to the willows that overhung the lake. Their long cords of branches were just showing the pale green promise of leaves. Too soon, there'd be no more roaming the woods pondering the great questions of life. She yearned for the solitude the grounds afforded to commune with her Creator. In London, she would be constantly chaperoned and kept too busy to think.

Faith asked, "A new book, Diana? What now?"

"*The Conversationalist's Companion*. It has the rules set out by Cicero. And suggestions for dialog starters and what not to bring up in polite discussion. My first defense in my campaign to attach a worthy gentleman by the social season's end."

"May I borrow it when you've finished?" Faith asked. "I can never think what to say to strangers."

"Oh, pooh," Hope said. "You merely comment on something they're wearing or the color of their eyes or their wit. All people love to hear themselves complimented."

"Certainly, you may borrow it, Faith," Diana answered. *When had Hope ever uttered a compliment?* "I'm nearly finished now. It's the last of the books we ordered. We must make up a party for Hatchard's once we're in town."

"The very thing!" Hope chirped, heading toward the door. "The perfect place to see and be seen by members of the less gentle sex."

"I hope to find a few books on art and poetry..."

"La, Diana!" Hope rolled her eyes. "The ton will deem you a bluestocking. You'll frighten all our beau away. No man wants his wife cleverer than he."

As apple red suffused Faith's cheeks, she pushed her sister out of the room and followed her.

Diana held the closed book in her lap. How shallow she'd sounded. All that prattle about clothing. Who was she trying to fool? She hated making banal conversation with people she didn't know, especially men. But she must succeed in attaching an estimable beau. Anything else would be disaster. She'd be an object of pity among the ton. Possibly even ridicule. Colin and Eden treasured her. She wouldn't let them down. But it was daunting. How could she find in a few months the one person she'd want to spend the rest of her life with? Daniel, Fourth Earl of Eversley, was a possibility. She'd once been able to talk with him candidly about anything. But they were children then, and children make friends easily and chatter on about the oddest things. He'd not been back to Chadilaine in over five years. His situation had changed enormously. Had he changed as well? Would he even remember her?

Diana sighed and read aloud, "Deal seriously with serious matters and gracefully with light ones." *How does one do that?* She imagined frowning and looking sympathetically at a young lord as he spoke of the recent death of his mother. She tossed her head back and allowed a tinkling laugh to escape lightly rouged lips while she listened to a poetic-looking young man's assessment of the garish ensemble the Countess of Dover wore to an event at Carlton House.

Allowing her glance to fall again to the page, Diana yawned and read another vague stricture. The print blurred and faded from the page, and she closed her eyes. A splendid scene burst forth. She was at Almack's first ball in a glorious gown. Her hair was done up with a cluster of tresses gathered to one side and falling forward over a bare white shoulder. The Ashton Emeralds to complement her eyes graced her neckline. She was attended by no less than seven handsome young admirers with adoring expressions. They were gathered about her, importuning her for the privilege of bringing refreshment or for her hand in the next set of dances. One young man asked Diana her opinion on his little ode to her. She said something witty, and all the young men laughed heartily. The entire assembly hushed; all turned to see who had amused these young men. Then it happened. Daniel's striking cerulean eyes arrested her glance from across the room. She was forced to withdraw her gaze from his or give away her unruly interest. He must not know the lure he held for her. If he did, he'd have power over her she was not yet willing to allow him. He must prove himself worthy of her first.

He'd taken the bait. Meticulously dressed, Daniel carved a path unerringly to her through the throng. His hand extended toward hers. "My lady, you are magnificent. Is it possible you remember your old comrade from childhood days?"

Lightly placing her artistically curved, lace-encased fingers upon the gloved palm he held out to her, she parried, "Most assuredly, Lord Eversley. What carefree times we spent that summer. I remember it with fondness."

"Will you not, then, grace my humble self with a turn on the floor this evening?" A gleam in his eye, he teased, "I recall you dancing most elegantly with your governess as you practiced your steps at Chadilaine."

"Eversley, it would seem the musicians are just now beginning an open waltz; let us indulge for old times' sake."

"Surely childhood friends needn't be so formal in address. You used to call me Daniel. Allow me to hear my Christian name upon the downy petals of your mouth again, and I shall not need the music of an orchestra to dance to." Thus saying, Daniel's fingers curled possessively about hers as he placed his other hand at her waist. Warmth invaded her flesh there. Masterfully, he led her around the ballroom floor in the mesmerizing circles of the waltz. The entire company stood about the edges of the floor gazing with envy at the perfectly matched, fortunate, and deliriously happy couple.

Diana opened her eyes and snorted in laughter. Daniel would die before speaking such flowery phrases. He was shy, forthright, and to the point. But he would try to be gallant. And they would dance until dizzy with the exercise. Surely, he'd learned to dance. Whatever she hinted she wanted to do, Daniel would join in. Or would he? Had he become a domineering male like so many others?

Father always said, "Take control of your destiny or it will control you." Eden told her to leave everything in God's hands, but God helped those who helped themselves, did he not? Or had Algernon Sidney made that up? Hadn't God placed her in this high position in society so she could accomplish greater good for his people? She'd had precious little choice all her life. Her father ordered her about, and now her brother told her what to do. She'd take command this season, her debut as an adult. No one could tell her whom to love. It was she alone who would choose. She must choose wisely. With an estimable man at her side, she could change the world. Daniel might be that man. Her memories of him were tender, but they were memories only. And memories could play tricks on you. Her first contest in this war of independence must be to secure the perfect life partner. Laying her head back against the pillow, she bit a fingernail, breathed a deep sigh, worried, and strategized.

# CHAPTER THREE

Daniel drove his curricle slowly past the Ashton Townhouse. The knocker was not yet installed for the London season. The family were not at home. Disappointment tugged at his gut. He'd felt more of a sense of belonging with them that summer at Chadilaine than he had his entire life. He'd looked forward to seeing them again. Happily, they must arrive soon. Parliament met next Monday. He could stand to wait. Lord Edmunds' MP friend, Jeremy Blake, had invited his family to a balloon ascension. Jeremy had said with a wink he was off to visit Chadilaine and invite Colin's family as well.

Daniel hated crowds, but Thomas was excited about the party. He'd go for his adopted brother's sake. He hoped Father would beg off the excursion. If Father went, it would be to talk politics with his cronies and drag him into the conversations. He'd parade him around as his eldest son, just home from the Grand Tour. He would leave out the information that Daniel had studied art and architecture. His father was forever drilling into his brainbox the responsibilities he must shoulder for the family name. It was a great deal to take in. If that woman hadn't abducted him all those years ago, politics and diplomacy would probably be second nature to him now. As it was, he knew only what he'd learned these past five years in school. But whenever government, military, or politics was introduced as a subject in his education, his mind had promptly wandered off.

******

Diana preceded Hope and Faith into the main salon. Her face lit with delight when she spied the mop of bright red curls. "Jeremy!" She gathered herself to run to him but hesitated, noticing the children. She drew her frame into a regal posture. "You've brought me your little Sandra to play with." She crossed the room, plucked a pillow from a chair, and tossed it on the floor next to the flaxen-haired toddler. "Hello, my friend." She plopped down upon the cushion. Lord Aaron, Colin and Eden's four-year-old, approached her with his blocks. The children's nannies looked on as Diana began to build a castle with him.

Hope sat on the sofa with Jeremy and smiled at him. Faith chose a seat across from them. He nodded to the young ladies, then turned away to address Diana across the room. "For a moment there, I thought you were about to run and leap into my arms as you used to."

"I considered it. But I am a grown-up lady now, so my station excludes such behavior," Diana said, chuckling.

"Yet sitting on the floor is permitted?" Jeremy teased.

"When the only guests are a very old friend and a very young one."

"Don't care for the way you stress the 'old' in 'old friend,' " Jeremy scowled comically. She cast him an arch smile. "I thought you would not."

Little Sandra took that moment to kick the block castle apart. When Lord Aaron complained loudly, the flaxen-curled little girl shoved the boy before any could intervene. Jeremy stood and walked across the room. "We must leave now, Sandra, if you cannot treat Lord Aaron better."

Sandra puckered her brow and protruded her lower lip prodigiously, saying, "Then who will play with me?"

"You should have thought of that before you attacked your friend."

Little Aaron took Sandra's hand in his and said in his sweet, high-pitched voice, "I'll play with you, Sandra."

Jeremy told Sandra to tell Aaron she was sorry, and Aaron promptly said, "I forgive you."

Chuckling, Diana said, "Would that adults could make up so easily."

Standing over her, Jeremy taunted, "I see you are grown, Diana, in wit and beauty as well. Why, your pug's nose has reshaped itself quite satisfactorily. And all those red spots you used to sport; whence have they gone?"

"You mean to torment me mercilessly, though your smile remains only in your eyes these days. Does that happen to all old persons?"

Jeremy glanced at the others in the room. His smile faded. "Only the worldly-wise and weary old persons, Diana. What think you of my daughter's new frock? She chose it herself."

"This sweet little tyrant has grown a full hand taller since Sunday last," Diana said. "Turn around, Sandra. Let me see your new dress."

As Sandra twirled, Diana poured compliments upon her.

Faith asked, "Any adventures this week, Sandra?"

"I pinched my finger," the girl said, running across the room to Faith. Little Sandra held the offended digit up to her friend for perusal.

"Did you really? Oh, I see. It's pink right there. Did you cry?"

"Yes, but I stopped."

"What a brave girl—honest too! May I kiss it to help it heal?"

Sandra nodded and stuck her finger up to Faith's lips to be kissed. Jeremy's eyes beamed as Faith administered the kiss to his daughter.

Sandra scurried back to Diana, poking her finger up to her. "You kiss it."

Diana kissed the offended digit. "Isn't your birthday soon, Sandra?"

The child's face shone. "Yes, yes! I forgot. You are to come to my *fete*. You, too, Miss Barrett. Lord and Lady Edmunds cannot come; they have appointments. You both must come."

"I think you forgot Miss Hope Barrett," Jeremy prodded.

Sandra turned to Aaron and pulled a face. The little boy laughed.

Jeremy turned toward Hope, cleared his throat and blushed. "You are invited also, of course." Turning back to his daughter, he said. "Tell the ladies what we will see at your party and restrain your voice, please."

"A giant balloon with a man in it!" the child screeched.

"A grand atmospheric voyage, no less," Jeremy explained. His eyes were wide with exaggerated wonder. "An immense aerial vessel will ascend to the clouds before our very eyes with a man riding in its basket."

"I want to ride in the basket, too," Sandra demanded.

"Much too dangerous, love."

The child folded her chubby arms in front of her and stamped a foot. "If the man can go inside, I want to go inside too. It is my *fete*."

"The man knows what he's doing. There've been bad accidents in balloons. I'll not risk my dear girl's safety. I love her too much."

Sandra's eyes reduced to slits. Jeremy commanded, "As I say, or no party at all, Sandra. Change your attitude instantly, or we leave now."

Eden distracted the child. "Aaron's nurse is ready to take you both to the playroom, Sandra, but only if your father allows it. Aaron has new picture books to show you and a toy camel with real hair."

Jeremy extracted a promise from Sandra to play nicely and saw her to the door. As he turned back, he extended a hand to Diana, helping her stand. She asked, "Have you mastered any new magic tricks I can help you perform after supper, Jeremy?"

"I'm afraid not, Diana. No time these days for my little hobby. I hope you're not too disappointed."

"I am a little, but I'll survive."

Turning to Faith and Hope, Jeremy announced, "Before you young ladies entered, we were speaking of a certain bachelor who may be of interest to you all. Someone I'm certain you recall, Diana. He stayed here at Chadilaine five years ago. It's Lord Eversley of whom I speak."

Diana schooled her expression, giving no hint of how mention of Daniel's name affected her. Jeremy loved to tease, and she refused to provide him with ammunition. There was a time before Jeremy married Cassandra that Diana had cherished a fascination for him. She had treasured Cassandra like a sister too. Her death had devastated her. Imagining herself wed to Cassandra's husband felt a great deal like betraying his late wife.

"You may not know him, Miss Barrett and Miss Hope Barrett, or know how very rich and handsome young Eversley is," Jeremy said, "but he's accepted an invitation to Sandra's *fete*. You'll have a chance to meet him there."

Hope fidgeted, all dimples and attention.

"You provoke our curiosity by speaking of his face and fortune, Mr. Blake." Faith lifted her gaze toward Jeremy. "What are these compared to a man's beliefs, values, hopes, and dreams? What does Lord Eversley aim to accomplish? These will tell more of the manner of a man and whether he is to be considered."

Jeremy gave her his full attention. "So, it's a beau's principles which attract you, Miss Barrett. I really cannot say about that. However, Lady Edmunds tells me she receives missives from him." He leered at Eden and waggled a single auburn brow.

"Colin receives the letters from him and reads them to the family, Jeremy. Why must you torment with ridiculous intimations?" Eden quelled.

"Why must you reward me with that little knowing light in your eyes when I do?"

"You dally with me in my husband's presence because you know I am his alone. Do you practice with another in mind?"

"Forgive me—habit," he said, his expression instantly apologetic, then morose. "You know I could never entertain thoughts of anyone other than Cassandra. Her loss is too fresh. Though it has been above two years, it seems moments ago. Let's change the subject, or you'll find me poor company indeed."

Diana asked Jeremy for the date and time of the balloon ascension and the party. The girls plied him with questions about where it was to be held, how the balloon was inflated, how one managed to maneuver the balloon, how it got down again, and—the ever important—what one wore to such an event.

After the visit, as Jeremy and his daughter were boarding their carriage for the ride home, Colin took the MP's elbow. He furtively handed him the crumpled message. "Hide this."

Using his magician's skill, Jeremy deftly palmed the paper and slid it into an inner coat pocket. He lifted a questioning brow at Colin.

"That was in my mail this morning, no address, no signature. Examine it on the ride home. See what you can determine about the handwriting or the full meaning of the message. I've shown it to no one. I don't wish to alarm the family unnecessarily. Advise me at our next meeting. What do you make of it? What should I do about it? I have a few ideas. You and I know the real circumstances of Diana's birth; Eden once heard a rumor of it. I've never told Diana. I have a dread this note refers to that situation. If it should get out, it could destroy her, and thus the family. Should I warn Eden? Diana?"

## CHAPTER FOUR

A bright yellow landau barreled downhill toward the parade grounds where the balloon ascension was to be held. White strings of lather covered the four horses. Lady Diana, Miss Barrett, Miss Hope Barrett, and Colonel Matthew Barrett fought to stay upright inside the bouncing carriage.

"La, Diana, if you'd chosen your hairstyle last night, we'd not be late and need the coachman to crack the whip so. All our coiffures shall be ruined before we even arrive–if we arrive with our lives intact."

"Must I say 'sorry' once more, Hope? I've never had my hair cut before."

"You never will at this point."

"I fear the wrong decision. Hair grows back slowly. Recall when that chimney sweep attacked Eden and cut her hair off? It took her three years to grow it back."

Hope held a palm up to silence her. "Her hair was shorn by a madman, Diana. The hairdresser only wished to trim yours up to the small of your back so it wouldn't be so heavy and need so many pins to keep it up."

Matthew cleared his voice. "It's a monumental decision. Your hair is your crowning glory. If left to me, young ladies would never cut their hair except for comfort or ease of drying."

Diana wrinkled her nose. "There is that. It takes hours to dry."

The carriage slowed, and John Coachman chose a spot on a ridge to halt the horses. When he hopped down from the driver's box and pulled out the steps, the family spilled out *en mass*. Diana promptly scanned the horizon for Jeremy's barouche among the sea of vehicles and spectators. A large gaudy ornamentation of various colored ribbons and flowers for the party made it easy to find. Wending their way in the wind toward Jeremy's group, the girls tightened the bows on their bonnet ribbons to protect their hairstyles.

"Look, Diana! Surely that can't be the balloon we're to watch ascend. I thought it was to carry a man in a basket," Hope cried. "Tell me we're not too late and missed it! It's your fault!"

Faith said, "That was the pilot balloon sent up to assess the wind direction."

Hope clutched her bonnet. "La, I need no balloon to tell me that in this gale!"

Diana consulted her watch. "There is but half an hour yet. For Sandra's sake, I pray the wind ceases soon, or the entire aerial show shall be abandoned."

Matthew halted. "Ladies, have a heart for a wounded soldier. I cannot keep up with my unruly leg on this sloping ground."

"How thoughtless of us, Matthew. We're too intent on being at Mr. Blake's party on time." Diana turned back, matching her stride to Eden's brother's as he started ahead again. He so rarely complained of anything that she was truly contrite. When he first invalided out of the army five years ago, it seemed the tall, handsome blond would make a stellar career for himself in the war office, but he'd some sort of falling out there and didn't shift himself to anything else. He seemed content now to rely on the good fortune of his elder sister in marrying so well. His former bright and breezy mien had slowly disappeared, leaving him with a perpetually drawn expression. His leg still hurt, but surely it had ached even more when the wound was fresh. She knew he took laudanum for the pain, but laudanum couldn't be a bad thing, could it? Not if mothers were encouraged to give a tincture of it to their babies for colic or teething.

Diana saw Faith turn abruptly to see where they were and lose her balance on the incline, sprawling face down in the grass.

Jeremy noticed the girls since Hope was shouting and waving at him. Seeing Faith fall, he ran to her, right past her younger sister. Diana and Matthew arrived before him and helped Faith up.

"My new dress," Faith groaned. "I hope it's not spoiled. Grass stains are the hardest to get out."

Diana cried, "Faith, you've bit your lip. There's blood!"

Faith touched her mouth and gasped. Bright crimson dripped along her glove.

Jeremy pulled a handkerchief from his pocket, pulled her hand away from her dress and dabbed at the wound. "Blood stains can be trickier than grass stains. It'll stop in a moment. Blood flows freest from the face; the cut is not deep. You may have a purple lip for a day or two."

Faith's brown doe-eyes widened.

When the group was satisfied that Faith was whole and the bleeding stopped, they started on toward Sandra's party.

Hope arrived at Jeremy's side. "Look, Mr. Blake, the balloon is half-inflated. How much longer will it take?"

"The aeronaut has completed more than five and twenty ascensions before this; He estimates the flight time to be at three-thirty–a half-hour from now."

As the group reached the decorated barouche and greetings were expressed to Sandra and her nanny, Jeremy touched Faith's elbow to draw her aside. "I'm ashamed to admit I must ask for the handkerchief back once you're through with it. The initials were embroidered by my dear Cassandra's own hand as her first token to me. I must hold tightly to such keepsakes. There'll be no further gifts from her." Jeremy's Adam's apple bobbed as he spoke, and his eyes shone with a surplus of brine.

Faith's chestnut brows furrowed with distress. "Would that I'd dabbed the hem of my shawl on my lip rather than ruin such a precious token with my blood."

"Nonsense, merely have it washed with cold water. I stress cold water, not hot. It has seen blood before and come out quite new."

"Oh, I imagine there's a story in that."

"Yes, but an epic too long to tell today."

"How may I return it?"

"Will you be with the family when they come for the season?"

She nodded. "Lord and Lady Edmunds have been so good as to offer me a second debut. When they brought me out three years ago, circumstances forced the family to repair to Surrey early."

A sparkle invaded Jeremy's eyes. "I recall. I also recall you were causing somewhat of a stir."

Faith blushed. "Drivel. I was a wallflower of the palest kind."

"I think not, Miss Barrett. I hope you're not one of those misses who denies the existence of her finer points to attain the appearance of modesty."

Faith waved the thought away. "I, too, hope I'm not like that."

Matthew approached them, bearing a plate of delicacies from the fully appointed picnic table. A rare smile twisted the corner of his mouth. "Diana jokingly tells me I must ply you with food, Faith, so you will be fortified enough to stay upright when the balloon at last ascends. Can your lip allow you to eat, do you think? I chose only what I thought might not cause it to sting."

"You're too kind, my brother. I'll try," Faith said. She nibbled a biscuit cautiously.

Jeremy nodded to Matthew. "As Miss Barrett is cared for by another champion, I reluctantly leave her side to see to my guests. I also fully intend to disparage Diana for that taunt about standing upright. I bid you *adieu* for the moment, Miss Barrett, Colonel Barrett."

Circulating among the party of friends, Jeremy stopped to speak to Diana. "I regret your party came so late. There was one here not half an hour ago who asked about you."

Her interest piqued. "And who might that be?"

"Why, Daniel, Lord Eversley. He stayed a time, looking for you, I think, but was forced to make his apologies when his father, Lord Darrow, called him away. Unfortunately, I didn't elicit a promise of return from him before he left."

"Thank you, Jeremy. I'm sure I'll meet him at some point during the season. It'll be nice to see how he has grown." She yawned.

Jeremy left her side, adding over his shoulder, "Oh, he's grown very nicely–I daresay a handsome fellow, if not a little Bohemian."

The food on her plate suddenly lost its taste. It was too soon. Diana had hemmed and hawed, choosing just the right outfit, bonnet, and gloves in case Daniel did appear at the party. But she'd planned his first sight of her to be at Almack's, in evening attire with her hair perfectly coiffed, wearing her jewels and perhaps a touch of kohl about the eyes. She wanted Daniel's jaw to drop when he first saw her.

The ribbons beneath her chin obstructed the turning of her head to look for him. The wind had died, so she loosened the bow and removed the hat to check the condition of the cloth flowers on its crown. She attempted to adjust her long hair, which was causing the pins to hurt her scalp. Giving up, she crammed the bonnet back on her head and tied it loosely. A headache was coming on.

Jeremy noticed Matthew furtively scanning the crowd and stopped beside him. "Looking for a lost love?"

"Looking for someone I hope not to find."

"Sounds mysterious."

"Colin has charged me with a commission. I'm not to let any of the girls out of my sight, and I'm to keep a certain Major Bradley from approaching them."

"I know something of that. I've not seen him here, but there's quite a crowd."

"Colin told me of some of Bradley's more revolting deeds and that Bradley has a number of scores to settle with him. He suspects Bradley may go so far as to waylay one of the girls in order to get back at him. I hope to raise Colin's regard for me."

"Is that needed?"

"It was he who recommended me for my sinecure, and I who embarrassed him by falling asleep at work once too often. My commanding officer understood. So many wounded soldiers are in my position. But one cannot have an officer on duty snoring."

"If I am not being too curious. What made you so sleepy?"

Matthew slipped a small vial out of his vest pocket and flashed a glimpse of it to Jeremy before shoving it back in its hiding place. "The Black Drop. I've tried everything to wean myself off it. I took less this morning so I could stay awake. But I'm beginning to sweat already. I know the signs. I'll not be able to contain myself much longer. I prefer not to have to resort to taking it in view of the girls."

At the appointed time, the festively colored aerial vessel rose in the air, and the wicker basket was attached. The aeronaut mounted the steps, threw a leg over the side of the basket, pulled his other leg in, and yanked on a rope. A loud rush of heated air resulted. The silk ark ascended silently and hovered above the earth a few minutes. The final cord holding it to Earth was detached. The balloon lifted higher in the air with exclamations and applause below to encourage it on. Then the winds on high caught it, rapidly sweeping the merrily decorated airship westward.

The servants began to pack the picnic paraphernalia when a drizzle misted the crowd. Some attendees opened umbrellas, and others dispersed. Matthew hinted he was not feeling entirely well and would like to start for home. The young ladies made their excuses and began to head for their landau.

Diana caught a glimpse of cerulean eyes in the crowd, and her breath halted. She strained to see the eyes again—Daniel's; they had to be. A gust of wind ripped her bonnet from her head and tormented her hairstyle until several loosened pins gave way, and her hair tumbled half-way down. Diana bent to retrieve the bonnet and slipped on the wet grass. She scrambled to stand, saw the mud and grass clinging to her clothing, and ran to the carriage.

Safely ensconced in the landau and on their way home, Diana yanked out the rest of her hairpins. Was she right? Was that Daniel? The owner of those blue eyes was not familiar. His hair was darker than the platinum of their youth, and his height was not as tall as she thought he would be. Still, there was something about him, the artistically slim build and the relaxed style of his clothing, not shabby but not starchy. Since Jeremy first mentioned his name, she seemed to see Daniel everywhere. Her heart was pounding, but that was probably from running. Had he seen her run away?

She hoped not. She must meet him and determine his present regard. Would she still be fascinated by him? She thought she would die that day long ago when his finger touched hers as they carried the charity basket of food. She'd laughed when he brandished his stick sword at the dragon that looked suspiciously like Sean, her brother's mahogany setter dog. There were tears in his eyes when he had to leave with his newly-found family. He'd wiped the brine away with his forearm and blamed it on a stinking cold.

But five years was a long time. His letters to Colin proved him to be an earnest and thoughtful young man. She would take the initiative. Her strategies must be intricately plotted to ensure she didn't miss a single opportunity to encounter Daniel. How was she to go about doing that?

******

On the parade grounds, Daniel stood dazed, holding the leads of his curricle horse and ignoring the increasing rain. He could have sworn he caught her eye–that for a second, she saw him. Then the wind snatched her bonnet, and she ran to the carriage. Did she recognize him? Was there something wanting in him? He knew his shoulders and back were still somewhat stooped from the hours of work in the chimneys when a child. His straight hair embarrassed him, for it refused to conform to any fashionable haircut. But Diana judged people by their qualities, not their appearances. At least the Diana he had known did.

He almost hadn't recognized her. But when her hair tumbled down her back, he knew. Only she had that glorious waterfall of spun gold ending in a froth of curls. He'd anticipated seeing her. She'd been so easy to talk to years ago. She'd listened with reverence to everything he had to say. She made him feel his thoughts were important. She helped him understand himself better. He needed that badly right now. He needed someone he trusted to help him make the right choices. He'd see her in town as soon as propriety allowed.

# CHAPTER FIVE

"Who'll paint your portrait, Diana? Have you chosen?" Faith asked from her seat at the pianoforte in the ballroom.

Hope stood lounging with her elbows on the polished instrument. She followed Faith's gaze toward the floor-to-ceiling windows, where Diana looked out at the last sprinklings of snow in the rose garden.

The melted water in the ornamental pool swirled in the center with the movement of a trout Diana had placed in it ten years ago. She'd caught it while fishing and felt sorry for it. Dining on table scraps had fattened it enormously.

Her eyes remained fixed on the view of the garden as Diana answered Hope. "I refuse to have a portrait taken. One has to devote hours to it: choosing the setting, dressing for it, sitting still—so confining, artificial, narcissistic." *Who'd want to see a portrait of plump, thin-lipped, pug-nosed me?*

"But it's the thing to do, Diana." Hope's mouth quirked with her anticipated jest. "You must have a portrait to hang with those of your ancestors. One to show your children how you looked before they spoiled your waist."

Diana shuddered. A portrait would begin the marriage mart.

"When do we leave for London?" Hope's face glowed with excitement. "Surely after Easter. Is that why your brother came home? Do we leave Monday? The roads should be free of snow by then. I cannot wait to begin receiving invitations to ride in Rotten Row or to balls and performances. The opera—it sounds magnificent." Hope whirled about the empty floor, miming receiving flowers, elegantly extending her hand for a salute, accepting invitations, seductively fluttering her fan, smiling and nodding. "I intend to turn my charm upon every male I meet. I'll not fish with a line, but cast a wide net, draw in all it encompasses, and toss away the rotten ones as I detect them." She gestured wide to indicate the casting, drawing in, and tossing away of phantom beau.

Faith turned a page of the music in front of her and suspended her hands above the keys. "Surely, if one encourages all her male acquaintance, there will be resentful gentlemen when a favorite is revealed. Best not to cause pain in anyone." She promptly fingered the keys, effectively drowning out Hope's response.

Hope tilted her chin higher and took a seat in one of the chairs along the wall. "Better them than me. No matter what idea I express, you take exception to it."

Diana glanced at her nails. They were torn and ragged. She must stop biting them somehow. But she didn't realize she was biting them until it was too late. "You must admit, Hope, your declaration does sound mercenary."

The muscle of Hope's jaw swelled as she clenched her teeth. "The entire season is mercenary. Mommas study Debrette's for the family and fortune of suitors until they can tell at a glance who is moneyed, who a mushroom, and who a hanger-on. Your Aunt Chadwick in London seems particularly good at that. We must consult her when we visit."

Faith shook her head. "Lady Chadwick considers you and me a pair of those mushrooms. Tread gently there. Your venal streak is showing."

"Your way doesn't sound the least romantic, Hope," Diana said, turning her eyes to the room at last. "Some of those fish in your net may be dissipated old widowers looking for a young mother for their existing brood. I'll cast my lures only at the one or two who appeal to my tastes and make friends of the rest."

"Why not make friends of them all and allow the gentlemen to do the wooing?" Faith's expression was enigmatic.

Diana sighed. "That would comprehend I am wooing material."

Hope jumped up from the chair, whirled in circles to the row of windows, and looked out at the collection of dormant sticks standing in the slush. "Romance is not in the male mind. Mother says men have no need to marry except for money or to set up a nursery of brats to leave their money to. The woman must convince the man he cannot do without her. Oh, where is this dance master? I need to practice the steps of the Scottish Reel and the cotillion. I get confused about when to clasp one hand or two and with which partner. With all this practicing bowing and exiting backward for our presentation at court, it's been months since we danced."

Diana sighed. "It's been a week, Hope, and we arrived early for the appointment. Mr. Headley will be punctual. He always is."

"He's a dear man," Faith said, "so patient and genuinely adept at all the steps: The perfect dance partner."

Hope scoffed. "How can you say so, Faith? He's a toad. The perfect dance partner must be taller than one to show you off, especially if the step calls for one to go beneath his arm. And it would do no harm if he were young, with a pleasing appearance and manner."

"Do you describe your potential husband or a dance partner?" Diana asked.

Hope's face puckered in a scowl. She refrained from answering.

Faith softly began to play a Celtic melody. "Finding a husband is rather like searching for the perfect dance partner. It's best to dance and converse with an assortment of young men so you may make an informed choice from the more varied experience." She stilled her hands and glanced at Hope. "I advise you, little sister, to dance one set per gentleman at first, though two are allowed. Thus, you show no partiality and stir no unfounded hopes or unwanted interest–something learned by experience at my come-out. Some young men mistake playful humor with flirting or genuine interest. They may become possessive of you, to the detriment of other more suitable beaux. It's best to wear your heart on your sleeve only when your heart begins to beat faster. Be open about where the butterfly of your favor rests, but do not allow it to alight too soon."

The applause of a single pair of hands announced the arrival of the dance master. A slender, pasty-faced man with thinning yellow hair and no apparent neck entered the room. He was followed by the pianist, Mr. Miller. Mr. Headley nodded to Faith. "Most poetically expressed, Miss Barrett. Allow me to add further the perfect partner may not be the one you would typically think, not necessarily the one whose views match yours, for where is there room in that for growth?" Mr. Headley approached the seated Faith and placed leaves of music on the pianoforte sill, arranging them in the order he wished Mr. Miller to play. "The perfect marriage partner is like the perfect dance partner. He must be attentive to his companion's every nuance of thought, able to predict what her next move will be, revealing of her strengths, considerate of her inadequacies to the point of making up for them. He must not allow a false step to occur on either party's side by the gentle strength of his powerful arm."

"You describe an angel, Mr. Headley." Faith's smile lit her eyes. "That sounds impossible for a mere human."

Diana bit the inside of her lip to strangle the giggles that threatened to give her thoughts away. The dance teacher was a bachelor and such a macaroni, he couldn't personally know of what he spoke. He was so thin she doubted the strength of his arm as well. How long had the gentlemen been near the door? Had Headley heard Hope call him a toad?

Headley tapped his ornately carved walking stick loudly on the glossy wood floor. Diana and Hope moved to the center of the room to the spot the instructor indicated.

"You may be right, Miss Barrett," Headley said. "I've been accused more than once of being idealistic, but I consider that a virtue."

Mr. Miller assisted Faith in rising from the piano bench, holding her fingers just until she needed his help no more. She joined the other girls. He abruptly seated himself, breathed deeply, and slid his fingers gingerly onto the keys where hers had lately rested, careful not to make a sound.

Diana cleared her throat and asked to practice Mr. Beveridge's Maggot first. The accompanist found the correct music, and they began. The girls were forced to imagine their various partners. As decorum required, Mr. Headley stood a distance from the girls, calling the steps and beating out the time for each dance with the metal tip of his stick. When Diana asked for the waltz, Headley balked. She chided him that since the Prince Reagent had given the formerly scandalous dance his blessing by including it at a formal state ball the year before, who were they to cast aspersions on the dance? Besides, Countess Lieven had introduced it to Almack's and danced it with Tsar Alexander several years before. The dancing master told the girls to be seated a moment while he conferred with Mr. Miller. Diana and Faith lowered themselves gracefully on the chairs closest to them. Hope collapsed onto her seat.

Headley stepped closer to the pianoforte to finger the sheet music, rifling through it, apparently choosing the music for the next dance. He bent to whisper to Miller. The pianist murmured something to Headley, and Diana noticed the men casting a quick glance Hope's way. One corner of Mr. Headley's mouth hesitantly turned up, and he nodded slightly. He approached the girls so purposefully Diana thought he intended to remonstrate with them. He merely told them to let him know when they had rested sufficiently, and they would begin the less scandalous open form of the waltz. It was to be their last lesson for the day.

The girls revived quickly, and the simple steps of the more refined waltz were begun. Headley stressed the first beat of the measure with his stick as the ladies moved in line with their phantom partners.

"Down, up, up. Down, up, up. With grace, Miss Hope Barrett. You move very like a milkmaid with two overfull buckets on her yoke."

Hope glowered at Headley and tripped.

"No. No. Back, side, together. Front, side, together. Right, left, right. Left, right, left."

Hope stopped and balled her hands into fists. "This is ridiculous. I'm weary of dancing sans partner. If you think it's so simple, let's watch you do it, Mr. Headley."

Headley let go of his stick. It clattered on the floor. He stepped forward to

Hope, who cringed but stood her ground. "Lady Diana, Miss Barrett, placate me and leave the floor, please." The dancing master took the tips of the fingers of Hope's gloved right hand and bent over them in an exaggerated, chaste salute inches above her fingers. "With your permission," he said.

Without waiting for her permission, he lifted her hand and clasped it, while fitting his other hand at her waist. He held her out as far from him as his arms could reach. The pianist began to play, and Headley masterfully whirled the girl about the room. Hope's feet barely touched the oak planks. Beads of sweat formed on her face. When the music stopped, the instructor's hands left her abruptly, and he stepped back. Hope tottered and fought for her breath as she clenched her eyes and placed her fingers to her temples. She mumbled, "Yes, now I understand. Thank you." She turned and wobbled out the ballroom door. Headley bent to retrieve his walking stick, and Miller stood and made a tidy bundle of the sheet music.

In the blue salon, Diana related Mr. Headley's metaphor of a dance partner to Eden. Lord Aaron's nanny had just taken him up to nap, and the two were left alone. Her sister-in-law beamed. "Ah, I like that. But one must endeavor to be the perfect partner to attach the perfect partner. It's not an easy task. Indeed, it's a life-long effort. Refine your virtues, and they will allure your soul's mate. People may forget the witty things you say, or even your acts of charity, but they'll always remember the way you make them feel. Make people feel good about themselves, Diana."

The tall build of Eden's younger brother appeared at the open door. He hesitated. Eden raised her face to him. Her smile clouded slightly. "Matthew, how nice to see you. Come in; come in. We are speaking of ways to attract a proper life's helpmate: a subject of interest to all unmarried ladies. As a representative of the prey, have you any suggestions?"

Matthew limped forward a step, eyes inspecting the floor. He shrugged. "Take your time. Don't be impatient to give up your freedom. Once you tie the knot, your life's no longer your own."

"Excellent advice." Eden blinked. "I see you heed it yourself."

"I'm poor husband material at present. Much too sullen these days, and I'd need a home to take my wife to and an occupation to maintain us."

"You see, the prospective beau has his responsibilities as well, Diana."

Matthew cleared his throat. "I thought to speak with you, Eden, about a private matter. I'll return at a more opportune time."

Diana leapt from her chair and darted to the door. "No. Don't leave on my account. I want to see Mr. Stagg at the stables to discuss how my horse is to be moved to London. I'll stop by the kitchen for apples for the horses and one of Cook's Banbury cakes for me."

"Diana," Eden called. "There's really only one perfect partner. You know of whom I speak?"

"I imagine you mean God."

"You know me well."

"You mean I should become a nun?"

Eden laughed. "No! I mean make him your partner, your closest friend for life, and he'll never disappoint you. That's impossible for a human partner. Think on it."

"Yes, Eden. He already is my constant friend. Good-bye for now." Diana disappeared through the door.

Matthew watched the girl leave. "Am I invited to go with you to London?"

"That's up to you, Matthew. There's room in the townhouse. My only caveat is there'll be no family left here to be with Mother. Her rheumatic joints cannot bear the rigors of travel."

Eyes aimed at the carpet, brows creased tightly together, Matthew grumbled, "She has her companion. With the family removed, the servants here will have no one to wait on but her. She'll revel in the attention."

"True. Still, she prefers one of her children in attendance."

"It's time she grew out of that. We're adults with our own ways to make in the world."

"She knows that. But after that episode of getting lost in the park, Mother is fearful. I think she sees the end of life approaching and hopes to keep one of us nearby as security against dying alone."

"She'll live forever. That kind always does."

"As I say, it's your decision. Mary may want to visit her while we're away. But she's *enceinte* now, too, and a little further along than I."

Matthew audibly expelled a breath of air. "I'm sorry, Eden, but Mother and I haven't seen eye to eye for years. I try to find some bond between us purely out of duty. It's drudgery to sit with her. We've nothing in common but my childhood, and I tire of living it over and over through her eyes."

"I know you try. You're right. You've been patient. You deserve amusement."

Matthew brightened and began to lumber about the room. "It's not for amusement I hope to go. I thought to visit the Horse Guards and make amends. Perhaps I can find a sinecure there more to my liking than the last. I've managed to lower my dose of laudanum by a respectable amount. I cannot go any further on my own. I need help. I thought if I looked up some of my comrades who took an interest in medicine, one might know of a permanent cure."

"I know you struggle. I pray to God you achieve both ends for your sake. If I can help you in any way, I will."

## CHAPTER SIX

"Chris? Christopher Black?" Colin called to a stocky, corn-silk-haired boy of twelve standing on the walk above the Thames where the river flowed past Somerset House. The youth was talking to a boatman on the muddy banks below. Chris turned at the sound of his name. Recognizing his savior, he waved good-bye to his friend in the boat, saying, "Later, Jake. It's Lord Edmunds." He removed a pair of leather gloves from his breeches pocket and pulled them on as he approached Colin. "Pleased to see you, your lordship."

"And you as well. How are things? Is your brother here?"

"He has a cold and lessons to do. I finished mine early. Me muv–my new mother is over there with a friend: Mrs. Clancy. We are to see the exhibit in the Great Room."

"Partial to paintings, are you?"

Chris made a face. "Mrs. Clancy tells me m-other it's class to see the showings. She wants me here to help her up them steep Nelson stairs. Someun wasn't thinkin' when they put the paintings up there. It'd be just as easy to have the show on the bottom floor, and old people won't have to climb."

"I believe it was to take advantage of the bright rays from the skylight in the dome that influenced them to hold it on the upper floor."

"Oh. Sensible like."

"Are Mr. and Mrs. Goodstock treating you well, Chris?"

"Ever so good, milord. And I likes the harbor and the sounds of the boat whistles and the water slapping against the dock. It lulls me to sleep nights. Me new mother is a good cook, too. Me-my new father says I grow like a weed 'cuz he's had to buy me bigger clothes and shoes twice this year. But he ain't complainin'; he says it proud like."

"I can tell you've learned much about grammar and deportment. I'm proud of you. Might I ask? Do you keep in touch with your companions from the foundling home these days?"

"Some, milord. There's Stumpy Collins and Jimmy John. They work on the wharf. And Turtle Stevens is on a barge that goes up the Thames to Oxford and back."

"What about Big Bill? I saw him at Tattersall's last I was in town. He was leading the horses to be auctioned."

"Yes, he does that, and he works with a blacksmith. He's learning to shoe horses. He gets to stoke the forge and pluck out the hot iron to be hammered." Christopher waved at two matronly ladies dressed in their best. "Me maw is lookin' for me."

Colin moved toward the ladies and greeted them, teasing one about her cooking causing Christopher to grow like a weed. "Is he minding you, ma'am? Is he a help?"

"Mercy, yes. You were a Godsend, Lord Edmunds. When you brought those two boys to my husband and me, we had no idea how much we needed them to brighten our lives and lift our hearts. They both try to help Mister G on the harbor, but we tell them getting a good education is their work right now. Learn sums so none can cheat you, and learn to speak with quality, so you can do well in trade. That's what we tells 'em."

Colin turned from the ladies and spoke quietly to Chris. "I'll let you go then, but I wish to meet with you and as many of the old foundling home boys as you can gather at my townhouse. I have some work to charge you with. There'll be ready in it. Just send me a note with the time as soon as you've arranged it. You know my address?"

"Remember well, milord—the gingerbread, too."

They both smiled at that and nodded good-bye.

Colin walked around the edifice to the street entrance of Somerset House at a brisk pace and made his way up the stairs to the dome-shaped Great Room at the top of the building. He glanced swiftly over most of the paintings displayed there. It'd be quite a task to find what he was looking for amidst the morass of paintings hung closely together from floor to ceiling. For moments at a time, he lingered in front of one painting or another consulting the catalogue he'd purchased. He was examining a canvas high above him when he felt the touch of fingers on his shoulder.

Turning, Colin found himself face to face with the slender, grave aspect of a young man with a head of over-long, wispy, ash-blonde hair. "Eversley! Delighted. Must have the family to dinner at your earliest. Catch up on the news. How did Italy and your host family of master painters strike you?"

"Amazing," Daniel answered. The young man spent a few minutes colorfully describing his adventures in the warm country along with the quirks, dignity, warmth, and generosity of the Gandofi family.

When his conversation began to wane, Colin prodded him, "Is Thomas with you? Is your family here?"

"The family's in town, yes, but not with me at the moment. Father and mother have seen this showing with Serina. Thomas and Serina chose to ride hell for leather in Hyde Park this morning to beat the crowd. I love riding, but alas, I slow them down. It makes me feel like a frail old man."

"You're far from that. Dispense all negative thoughts. Keep the mind young, and the body will follow. Oh my, I lecture like an old man."

Daniel asked, "You spend your second day in town alone at an exhibition? Are you a patron of the arts, Edmunds?"

"I'm on a mission. I felt I could dispatch it quickest alone. I hope to commission an artist to do a portrait of Eden and little Aaron, a conversation piece. If Diana will sit for one, which I doubt I can get her to do, I'd like to have her portrait taken as well—a gift for her eighteenth birthday. I came here to determine what might make good poses and scenes for each sitting. Perhaps it would be best to allow the artist I choose to make suggestions as well. What do you think? I do like Madame Vigee-Lebrun's paintings of mothers with children."

"Yes, she's exquisite at rendering natural-appearing scenes. One could hardly guess they were posed. They're a frozen moment in a family's daily activities. And the expressions of love and delight on her sitter's faces reveal true family feelings. Kauffman was quite good at that as well. I'm presently enamored of the paintings of Caravaggio, but that may be the warmth of Italy yet clinging to my shoulders."

"I need an artist residing in England and one who still lives. How did you go on with Gandolfi? Were you able to improve your own skills? I relish seeing your portfolio if you have any portrait studies. I still have that watercolor you did of Eden the summer you were with us. I had it framed and hung on my dressing room wall to remember the day. You do have talent. Is it possible you harbor leanings toward portraiture as an avocation?"

Daniel's eyes lit, and his expression became animated as he spoke. "The human face and figure are my favorite subjects. They are the most challenging. If one paints a house or a boat, it is all about line. If one paints a dog or a horse, each subject looks much like any other of its breed, varying only in color. In the human face alone, the variety is endless. An eyebrow askew can spoil the likeness completely. The expression is all-important. I find I rise to the challenge."

"Perhaps I'll give you the commission, but I warn you only if I deem you a rare talent."

Daniel chuckled. "I must admit, I once imagined painting Diana as a sort of modern-day Goddess of the Hunt. I know she despises the idea of the dogs tearing the fox to pieces, so I thought I might have a background scene of the Quorn with Diana astride Velvet Cloud in the foreground. On the side of the viewer, unseen by the hunters, the face of a fox will be seen peeping out of a pair of pistol bags tossed over Satin Cloud's withers for the purpose. Diana looks slyly at the audience. She's hiding the fox, you see."

"Enchanting! Sketch it, Daniel. We must make an appointment. Have your secretary and mine carve out a suitable date in our calendars as soon as possible. I must admit to being pressed for time today, but I intend to bring the family for a call. When is your family at home to visitors?"

"Fridays from one to three. We look forward to gathering with your delightful clan again. How changed everyone must be from the last time I saw them."

"You've yet to meet our Aaron," Colin said. "We attend Almack's the Wednesday next. Shall we see you there?"

"It is in our plans to attend. I'm impatient for the evening."

Colin extended his hand to clasp Daniel's as he added, "I wager you're impatient as well to be called to your seat at The Lords?"

Daniel blinked, and a doubt-filled smile hesitated upon the young man's mouth, leaving it quickly. "My Father anticipates that far more than I. I look forward to our next meeting."

Colin left the Royal Academy and crossed the street to Hatchard's Booksellers. Walking up to the familiar, dark wood-encased windows displaying the most recent book acquisitions felt like arriving home at a little outpost in the city. He was speaking with a colleague about a recommendation for an abigail for Diana, when his sister and sisters-in-law arrived as arranged and all moved inside. Almost on the hems of the ladies' walking dresses, as if serendipitously, Jeremy Blake entered the store.

After greetings all 'round Lady Diana addressed her brother's best friend, "We're getting up a party to attend Almack's this week, Jeremy. Will you appear?"

"Lord, no, imp. I've done my time there. The repast of dry cake and drier toast and butter cannot tempt me. I get better tea and lemonade at home. Have you your vouchers yet?"

"Our Royal Summons from the Lord Chamberlain arrived yesterday. Eden and my aunt, Lady Chatworthy, applied for them weeks ago. We attend the Drawing Rooms Monday and expect to receive our vouchers for Almack's Tuesday. That's if no one manages to upset any of the ruling ladies before then." Diana chuckled as if joking but glanced sideways to indicate to Jeremy the present company who was capable of distressing behavior.

Hope's eyes pinched into slits of odium; she said nothing.

The party began to peruse the books, and Jeremy meandered to a table of tomes on spiritualism. He had opened a large volume and was scanning it with interest when Faith came to his side with a copy of Fordyce's sermons open in her hand. "What think you of this phrase, Mr. Blake? Is it not astute?" Faith held the open book up to him. Upon the pages, she had placed Cassandra's washed and folded kerchief with his monogram neatly facing him.

Jeremy pretended to read from her book as his left hand retrieved the cloth and stowed it in his inside breast pocket in one smooth movement. The warmth of the cloth momentarily disturbed him. "Yes, Miss Barrett. A wise saying. One I must commit to memory," he said grandly.

Faith looked at the book in Jeremy's hand, and her smile faded. "Necromancy, Mr. Blake? I should not have thought it of you."

Jeremy clapped the book closed. He glanced at its spine. "Is that what I have in my hand? No, no, too many spiritualists are charlatans. Most of their phantasmagoria are mere magician's tricks. I myself have unmasked a few fakes." He gently tossed the book on the table.

"You attended séances to reveal the malefactors?"

"Yes, a friend was being led astray by swindlers. I felt her money would be better spent on necessities. As one who has amused himself with learning the illusions of magicians, I was able to spot the tricks of the spiritualists' trade."

"Chancing seeming a prig, I fear for your soul, Mr. Drake. Deuteronomy 18 strictly warns against consulting with ghosts or spirits or seeking advice from the dead. For one as august as you to attend one of these spiritualist parlors is to give credence to what they do, and lead others astray." Her right hand ventured to stay his arm. He glanced down at it, then to her face. A wrinkle of genuine concern marred her brow.

"It's also to put yourself in danger, Mr. Blake. To dally in the occult is to trade your privileged intimacy with Our Creator for mere fascination with the prince of liars." Faith's left hand found its way to her chest and was poised there as if to keep her heart from exiting its home. Her expression of entreaty was troubling. "I assure you I only speak boldly out of concern."

"Your distress is misplaced, Miss Barrett, although appreciated. I'm in no danger of being led astray by a professed telepathic. I exposed her as the sham she was. I don't seek advice from the dead. That's what our good God warns about. There are evil spirits as well as good, and one has no way of knowing which he is speaking to. But there have been visits of the dead recorded by saints during their lifetimes. These were unsought, but genuine. I believe it is the making of money on such things that God frowns upon." Though he smiled, Jeremy managed to look ashamed at the same time.

"You've given this thought. That consoles me. Be careful. Fallen angels are powerful and quite good at disguising themselves."

"Lucky for us, there are twice as many faithful angels." Jeremy lifted a finger and tapped her nose. "You need not have gotten that pert little nose all out of joint."

Faith's eyes widened. Her breathing halted.

He grinned at her, expecting a retort, but none came. He'd gone too far. "Be at peace. It's merely that I...sometimes wish...that one, in fact, could..."

"May I be bolder, Mr. Blake? Who would you have visit you from the other world, if...?"

"You understand me. My dear departed Cassandra, of course."

"And what would you ask her if her spirit were to materialize?"

"Not ask, tell. I'd tell her how dearly I love her. I was too glib when she was with me. I teased her so, and the word 'love' was rarely upon my lips. I would tell her now how awfully I love her and always will. I'd say it over and over to make up for the times I failed to when she was alive." His voice faltered, and his eyes grew bright with liquid.

Faith squeezed his arm and looked into his face, securing his gaze, bringing it outward again. "She knows, Mr. Blake. She knows everything now. She knows how much you loved her."

"Love her," he corrected, clearing his throat.

Diana came up to the two. "So serious you both look. Ah, Faith is boring you with Fordyce. No wonder. I have a question for you, Jeremy."

Bowing from the waist and unfurling a hand, he said, "At your service, my lady."

"Have you an opinion of Mesmerism?"

"I've not investigated him enough to form an opinion. I've heard stories of Mesmer's philosophies and techniques effecting interesting cures. Still, there are those who swear the foul-tasting waters of Bath are a panacea and others for whom they make them wretch. Why do you ask?"

"I was reading a novel on the trip to town and wondered if people really can be Mesmerized."

"I'll investigate it for you, if you like."

"Don't go out of your way. I thought you might recommend a book on his techniques."

Blake shook his head.

After purchasing a few selections for his library, Colin joined the little group. “Diana and Faith, if you and Hope will allow me a moment of privacy to talk of boring politics to Jeremy here, I make you a promise of hot chocolates for all as soon as we have concluded our business.”

Hope joined the group and chimed, “Shall we be anywhere near St. James’s Street?”

“What do you wish to visit there, Miss Hope Barret?” Jeremy asked.

“Why Berry Brothers and Rudd.”

“Are you in need of tea or spices or perhaps twine?”

“Silly. It’s all the rage to go there to be weighed on their enormous scales. Even Beau Brummel was there.”

Colin chuckled. “We’ll do what we can to accommodate you, Hope. Off with you now.”

Diana and Faith smiled and sauntered off arm in arm to the opposite side of the store.

As soon as they were out of earshot, and Colin had determined Hope’s whereabouts, he began, “What were you able to make of the note?”

“For one, it’s enigmatic in several ways. The lack of signature may mean the author refused to be known, or that he believed you’d know who he was.”

“So, you think it was a man.”

“I merely use the literary ‘he.’ The hand is at once forced and unsteady. It seems the writer has had penmanship lessons but is either attempting to hide his true identity or is writing with some difficulty, perhaps caused by pain as in gout.”

“You’re no help at all, Jeremy. What of the message itself?”

“Even that can be taken in at least one of two ways.”

“How so?”

“Why as a grim threat or as a warning from someone who possesses facts the family is unaware of and hopes to steer you away from disaster.”

“In that case, I think the author would have been more specific and would have signed it. Do you have it on you?”

Jeremy removed the folded slip from his watch pocket.

Colin unfolded it once more to reread the words: *If you dare bring Diana out this season, your family will suffer certain tragedy.* “I see nothing here but threat.”

“Then I suggest you keep your wits about you and double up on those who attend your household. Always travel in a group with strapping servants guarding you.”

“I take measures as we speak.”

## CHAPTER SEVEN

On the steps to his rooms near Portman Square, Major Dorian Bradley handed the slender youth who served as his tiger a pouch of coppers. "This is for the girl. She's to spend it on a clean outfit from a street vendor. Nothing showy. Tell her to make herself as presentable as time and circumstance allow. The rest you will use to get the two of you to this address. Don't let yourself be seen near her. Once she enters the servants' entrance, you race back here and report to me." He handed the boy two thick letters. "Give these to her the moment you reach her. Tell her to give them to the master of the house only. They're letters of character from The Winchester Female Asylum and from a doctor at Guy's Hospital, saying she worked in his house as an abigail. Tell her not to worry because they're forged. If Lord Edmunds questions the doctor, he'll vouch for them, saying he hired her from the asylum. Now, do you have all that?" The boy nodded vigorously, his raven curls bobbing. "What did I say?" The boy repeated his commissions almost word for word. "Good. If you're back here in two hours' time, there's a chop house meal in it for you." The boy sprinted.

******

The aromas of warm crusty bread in the oven and a rosemary-coated leg of lamb rotating on the spit over the fire permeated the kitchen. A clockwork mechanism turned the roast; a heavy weight on a chain inched upward each time the spit turned. Each blob of fat dripping from the meat made the fire sizzle, and a flame burst upward. On the long table in the servant's hall, Mrs. Fitzwarren briskly laid out a repast of cold sliced tongue, cheeses, pickled vegetables, and the innumerable muffins leftover from breakfast. Around it in various poses were gathered five young men of several sizes and ages. They were dressed according to their trades as boatmen, wharf stevedores, and one hefty blacksmith. In their company was a young lady who looked as if she might be able to take on any one of the boys with her bare hands if the occasion warranted it. She stood stiff against the wall, her glance darting about the room.

As food was brought to the table, each boy took a seat and nodded to Mrs.

Fitzwarren. The girl hesitated until the cook indicated a place for her. When all were settled, they bowed over their meal. The housekeeper said, "Thank you, Lord, for this food and for gainful employment." Those seated said, "Amen," and tucked in.

When Colin entered the servants' dining hall carrying a tray with five plump leather pouches, those eating caused a thunderous sound of heavy wooden chairs scraping the floor as they jumped to stand in greeting. "No. Be seated. Finish your meal. Listen while you eat." Colin set the tray on a side table. "First, I want to thank you for coming. It was a long and difficult journey for some of you, and you had no idea what I wanted."

A slender young man with a large gap in his teeth and unruly red hair said, "I'd a gone further for you, milord. Nuttin's too good for you." The others murmured in agreement as they reseated themselves and picked up their bread again.

"Bless you, Jimmy John. Let me lay it out for you." Colin turned to his housekeeper. "Thank you, Mrs. Fitzwarren. Do me the goodness to close the door as you go and guard it until we complete our meeting." Once she left, he began in a quiet voice, "I trust you not to let a word of this leave this room. Simply, I've had a threat of harm to the family."

Mutters of "No!" and "Who dares?" drowned Colin out. He held his hands up palm out and slowly lowered them, effectively quieting the crowd. "I've reason to believe the Honorable Major Dorian Bradley wrote it, though I may be wrong. Memorize his address. Get to know his face, his habits, and his haunts and get word to me immediately if you hear anything of interest. I'm leaving Christopher in charge to get a schedule to you of my sister Diana's appointments as she accepts them. She is the one in most danger. Chris also knows Bradley's tiger, Noah. He'll point the boy out to each of you when he can. Noah's not entirely happy with his circumstances and may inform on Bradley for a little coin. I'll speak to each of your employers, explain the situation, and arrange for substitutes for any time I might need you. The schedule will change each day as the family makes its plans.

"Here's some ready to carry in case you need to use a conveyance, send a messenger, get a bite to eat, or anything else at your discretion." At this point, Colin turned around and picked up the drawstring bags and deposited them in front of each of the boys sitting at table. "These coppers should start you off, and if you find yourself in need of more, don't hesitate to ask."

"Judith, these young men know each other from a foundling home of which I am on the board. I'd like you all to take a good look at Judith. Remember her face and help her guard Lady Diana. Judith will accompany

Diana anytime my sister goes outside the walls of this townhouse. She'll look for one of you if she needs to contact me. Any questions?"

As a cacophony of questions rose to a crescendo, Colin knew he'd not be able to extract himself from his guests for some time.

******

Diana sat at her dresser, pinching her cheeks and placing her curls just so. The longer she looked in the mirror, the more distorted her face seemed to her, so she stuck her tongue out at the image. Raising her hand to her tresses brought the exquisite scent of the orchid corsage Daniel sent Diana for her first night at Almack's. Surely, he remembered how she liked to shove her face into the blossoms in the orangery at Chadilaine Manor and inhale the orchid's delicate sweetness into her lungs like a gourmand savoring a favorite pudding. It was proof he loved her. Or at least, that he liked her. Or he was thoughtful. Or he was merely polite and politic. Or he had no one else he cared to send flowers to and thought he might as well send some to her. Or had he sent a larger corsage of even more costly flowers to a miss he truly admired?

When Colin knocked at her open door and entered, she stood and turned. "Where've you been? I've been dressed and awaiting you above half an hour." Since her brother carried two brown paper packages, Diana clenched her teeth to stop further complaints. Were those gifts for her?

"Thank you for waiting so patiently, Diana. You're a vision. Martha has coiffed your hair beautifully. Your mantua maker is a genius. I know you chose this dress and I approve it. Your court dress was a success, but I think you look more composed in this ensemble. It may lack a refinement or two, so I took the trouble to bring you a few accoutrements for your perusal. You may wish to add these ... or not."

Colin offered Diana the larger of the two packages. "This belonged to our mother. It was her favorite. As I recall, your pet color this year is turquoise; I thought you might like it."

The paper was ripped off, and a fine, long paisley shawl spilled out. Diana exclaimed at the softness of the weave and the play of the four shades of blue-green on a white background. Colin draped it around her neck and gently turned her to face the cheval glass, leaving his hands on her shoulders. Diana's right hand went to her mouth, and her eyes swam in brine. "Oh, Colin, it's stunning. I don't deserve this. It's so silky soft and warm. I'll feel like Mother has her arms wrapped about me, approving me, giving me confidence."

Diana had never mentioned her need for her mother before. Colin's glance fell away. His Adam's apple bobbed, and the muscles at his jaws contracted.

"Do you not think the color too bold for a neophyte?" Diana asked. "I must wear only shades of white to dances."

"You'll fold the shawl and have your maid hold it while you dance. I'm reminded I engaged a young lady to serve as abigail for you."

"I thought Martha would do that. She'll enjoy the parties and shopping." Diana glanced at Martha, who averted her eyes. It seemed this was news to her, too.

"She will. Do you realize how tiring it is for a servant to sit in the hall waiting all night for you to appear so she can undress you and freshen your clothing and put away your things before she finally catches a moment of sleep? Then up again to help you with your morning's ablutions. I thought Martha could use some help during the season. You'll be changing clothes more often in town. More to the point, Judith, the young lady of which I speak, is in dire need of employment since her father, brother, and sister depend upon her for their very bread. Humor me in this, Diana. As your lady's maid, Martha will be included in many entertainments. Do not worry."

Diana glanced at the smaller package her brother still held. At least he thought enough of her to explain things. She kissed his chin and told him, "You know best."

"I see your eyes are pinned to this package. The shawl was not enough?"

"It was more than enough; more than I dreamed since I was not even aware something like this of Mother's existed."

"I thought you might like something new to set you apart, to give you poise. Doing the season for the first time can be daunting. I felt guilty for not allowing you to wear the Ashton Emeralds at the presentation. Young misses don't want to appear money-mad, Diana. Some suitors look askance at a prospective wife who would throw their fortune away on jewels. Most *jeune fille w*ear either a simple cross of precious stone or a strand of pearls or elect to display what nature has given them." He chuckled. "I'll not voice my preferences."

"Colin."

"Hmm?"

"Are you giving me the bundle or not?"

He laughed and placed it in her hands.

The paper was ripped and allowed to fall to the floor as it revealed the exquisitely carved mother-of-pearl guards of a fan. A brilliant blue tourmaline was embedded in the rivet. Diana slowly opened the spines to display a pastoral watercolor scene of a garden with deer grazing by a pond with swans. All was done in glorious greens and blues complementing her mother's shawl. Again, Diana's hands went to her mouth; this time with the fan clutched in the fingers of one hand. Her moist eyes shone. "Oh! This is the most glorious thing I've ever seen or hoped to own. You're too, too good to me, my dearest, sweetest brother."

"I was informed by spies that you've memorized all the little sayings of the Language of the Fan. That is one reason I chose it for you. The scene reminds me of Chadilaine, and I thought if you were missing home, you might open the leaf to see it. But I warn you, I too know the Language of the Fan, and if I happen to catch you plying it, I'll read your messages as easily as any young swain."

"Then I must be sure to use it only when you're not looking."

Colin widened his eyes in feigned shock. "See that you do."

"I've noticed Eden often signals you at parties with her fan. I couldn't interpret all the signals, though."

"Eden devised a few signals to help me know whether a certain Lord may or may not be in an approachable frame of mind on a certain cause. She's often more adept at probing such subjects as she's less daunting than I. She appears to have no ulterior motive when conversing with an irascible Lord whom I hope to steer to my way of thinking." Colin turned from the all-seeing eyes of his sister. He feared he was blushing. He would warn Eden that Diana was aware of their private messages.

Diana said, "Eden has been a great help to you in your career."

"Greater than I could have imagined."

"I'm so pleased you engaged her as my governess that day. She's been wonderful to me as well. Once you married Eden and her family moved into the dower house, Faith has been a great friend too. She's wise like her sister—though more didactic. Hope, well, she can be amusing. Eden's mother ... She has her good points."

"So, to Almack's ..." Colin held out a forearm toward her, and Diana placed her gloved hand upon it. They walked into the hall and caught up with Eden at the top of the stairs. In her full evening dress of lavender silk satin with white tambour-work at the hem and bodice, she looked like a queen. The glossy mass of dark curls weaving in and out of the tortoiseshell tiara completed the picture. Regally, Eden took Colin's other arm, and they descended to where Faith and Hope stood waiting.

Colin laughed and stepped forward. "I shall be the hit of the season with all these exquisite ladies hanging upon me and clustered about me."

As they approached the street door, Colin introduced Diana to the large young female with the scowling expression who stood there. She smiled graciously and nodded to the girl. *This is Judith? La, I shall be the on dit of the season with that person following me about.*

# CHAPTER EIGHT

A bevy of young hopefuls in white sat poised with their patronesses on benches along the sides of the assembly rooms. A collection of black-coated young bachelors clad in black pantaloons held down with shoe straps were gathered together at one end of the pale aqua room. They discussed the races, the boxing matches, bull-baiting, the latest way to tie a cravat, and anything other than the hoard of spotty-faced, insipid females. Their mothers had forced them to come to this farce to consider wife-bait to reign-in their high spirits. At the other end of the vast room, a quite different group of men who preferred to wear the traditional white breeches gathered. They knew each other from seasons past and were determined to attract a young lady with fortune for their coffers. Or they were lonely, earnest men who'd decided the life of dissolution was not all it was cracked up to be. They felt an understanding wife might be nice to fill the nursery, run the house, and sit at the other end of the table to entertain guests. Lastly, they might be men who lost a wife and needed a mother for the children already in their nurseries.

Musicians took their seats in the minstrel's gallery, and the disparate groupings of men wandered toward the center of the room. The couple who would lead the dance was agreed upon. The remaining gentlemen positioned themselves to attack the most promising young ladies. Since it was fashionable to arrive late, but before eleven, those dandies and men in the know would gallant the hopefuls now there but reserve choosing favorites for later in the evening when the rooms were full.

As Lord Edmunds' party arrived and entered the grand ballroom, Diana searched frantically for Daniel. Not seeing him, she marveled at the magnificence of the central chandelier, the height of the peach marbled columns, and the intricacy of the frieze of festoons.

Faith looked to see if she could find any friends she'd made at her abandoned come-out. She found one forlorn female face, which brightened when it saw her. Getting permission to greet the girl, Faith went to her.

Hope commented on the clothes and jewels the fashionable ladies of ton were wearing this season.

Eden quickly took Diana to Countess Lieven, knowing Diana's wish to dance the waltz. It must be one of the patronesses who would give permission for a young lady to dance it, and Countess Lieven had been the one who introduced it to Almack's.

It was almost as thrilling as Diana hoped. When she repaired to the dining room, three promising young swains gathered about her. At one hand stood a slender, curly-haired, self-styled poet, Lord Montcrief. He admitted to admiring Byron. Diana didn't care for that poet, but she was gratified she'd read enough of him to offer an opinion. On her other side was a muscular young man, Lord Fildes, who was enthusiastic about the sport of racing. He held a remarkable conversation with Diana about bloodlines and fetlocks and pasterns and training methods. He invited her to his estate to see his cattle, and she demurred. "I must confer with my brother about any such arrangements."

Now speaking before her was a promising scientist, Mr. Rhodes, who'd already been called to the Royal Academy. His voice was soft. His large brown eyes were most often aimed downward. They did lift and light when Diana made a comment here and there that showed she was listening, understood, and was interested in his theories. He'd been holding forth on a lecture by one of his colleagues on the need for trust in the word of the physician and the placebo effect.

Diana supposed Rhodes doubtful of her intelligence when she regaled the young men with her knowledge of the Language of the Fan. The other two passed her gift among themselves, marveling at its beauty and testing her on the various messages, showing they, too, had studied its secret language. The scientist was obviously repulsed by such fluff and was about to wander off when Diana mentioned Mesmerism. He told Diana he'd heard a student of the deceased Mesmer speak in the lecture hall only the week before. The man claimed to be able to bring about miraculous healings, and he was received with respect. Rhodes found the man's science a little confusing, but coupled with the current lecturer's talk on the placebo effect, it made a tad more sense now.

Diana's expression grew serious. "I was thinking such tactics as I read of in a book might be applied to illnesses of the mind."

"An astute idea, but the patient needs to be in full use of his faculties so he may participate in his cure," Mr. Rhodes said. As Diana looked a little crestfallen, he added, "Have you someone in mind?"

Diana turned to look away. She mustn't mention her neighbor's name. Talk of the late Lord Audley had quieted down, and she preferred to let it remain forgotten. His sons didn't show signs of madness, at least not yet. "I was thinking of the unfortunates of Bedlam."

"Oh dear, I think you're out there. What does one as innocent as you know of Bedlam?"

"My brother is newly on the board and mentioned some happenings at home. I'm so glad the hospital was moved. He tells me methods of treating the unfortunates are now more humane." Diana scowled. "At least they no longer allow young know-nothing bucks with a coin to poke them with a stick to laugh at their enraged reactions. I wager if I poked the bucks with a stick, they'd be doubly enraged."

Mr. Rhodes broke into a full-throated laugh. He shifted closer to her. The smile he gave her crinkled his eyes. The gleam there said he recognized a fellow philosopher.

The three young men in her court were all laughing when Daniel strode in. It was he, all right. Their eyes locked instantly. In a slow and obvious manner, Diana opened her fan fully, lifting it to touch below her lips while encouraging her young lord with a lovely smile. He started her way. His grin of recognition was hesitant, but undeniably there. The look between them was intense. She couldn't breathe. Those blue eyes bored holes in her brain. She dropped her gaze and asked the poet if he might bring her some tea. Lord Montcrief bowed and sauntered off in his best poet imitation to fill his commission. Good, this left a place for Daniel. Where the devil was he? What was taking so long? Diana tentatively raised her eyes. What a time for her brother to pull Daniel into discussion. Colin clutched the young man's arm in a vice grip and held him prisoner. *Lord, make my brother's conversation brief, though it rarely is.* Faith took the empty position by her side. *Bother. What next*?

******

"I examined the sketches you gave me, Eversley, and would be pleased if you can make the time to paint both. From what you showed me, I've every confidence in your abilities. The one in her ball gown can hang in the grand gallery at Chadilaine. Complete it first. I wager, though, she'll prefer the one of her astride Velvet Cloud. She'll laugh at the thought of rescuing the fox and then at the thought of her horse taking fences. That gelding is a beauty but no jumper. If you can finish the first in time, I'll present it to her at her ball. I know you want no compensation, but Eden used to paint quite a bit, and I know a man who supplies all the best artists."

"I'd be honored, and I have all I need." Daniel glanced briefly at Colin but continued to face Diana. His eyes absorbed her. His chest rose and fell nervously. *This is interminable.* "Please tell no one I'm doing this. I want

Diana to be natural in her reception of me. She can be a consummate actress. If she knew I covertly painted her, she'd strike stiff poses with her best side always turned to me."

Colin chuckled and agreed that was his sister to a "T". He excused himself, and Daniel was free. The young man took three more steps toward his goal when his father, the Marquis of Darrow, stepped into his path. Daniel bit his lower lip gently. If father introduced him to one more colleague who spouted off about the Whig Party ideals or the Tory party's lack of sense, he was going to run screaming from the room.

His father introduced Lord Partington. The young man asked Daniel if he would make him known to the collection of beauties near the punch bowl since he'd been told Daniel knew one of them personally. Lord Partington was handsome, intelligent, and well behaved. He expressed interest in the little bundle of energy with the yellow blonde curls–Hope, not Diana. Daniel nodded and strode toward the quarry. Partington had trouble keeping up.

******

Hope had made her giggling presence known and was complaining about her lemonade being tart. Diana frowned and tilted her teacup to her lips, barely sipping. How much longer could she make the drink last before she had no excuse not to go back to the dance floor? By her calculations, the waltz must be played soon and the musicians were picking up their instruments and sitting down again. The Countess was at the doorway, poised to give permission for the waltz. This would be her best chance to secure an invitation to the floor from Daniel. She'd danced with each of the other young men in her train. Diana consciously and deliberately set her tea down on a side table and moved toward the Countess and into Daniel's path. *Heavens, he brings Partington with him. The man had best not ask me to dance before Daniel does, or I'll ...*

"Lady Diana, well met. You look enchanting." Daniel reached out and playfully pulled one of Diana's long curls. "Stiff and sticky, my lady–unlike you to use sugar to curl your hair. I recall fondly your hair flowing freely down your back with the sun gleaming upon it. It was silk then."

"Not the style for a young miss at her come-out, Eversley. I'll keep your preferences in mind, however," Diana parried. He didn't approve of her hairstyle.

"Allow me to present to you, Lord Partington."

Diana nodded to the man, saying, "Pleased to make your acquaintance. May I present to you my sisters-in-law, Miss Barrett and Miss Hope Barrett?" When the girls were greeted, Diana introduced her court of *beaux*. The young men nodded to each other all 'round.

Partington honed in on the two sisters.

Daniel turned to Diana. His gaze unhurriedly encompassed her. For several moments, he appeared frozen. Finally, his chest rose as he inhaled deeply. "I glimpsed you in the last dance. You were delightful. Your movements natural, liquid." He pointedly glanced at his orchids on her wrist and grinned. "Are you perhaps fatigued and ready to sit out a set of dances?"

"La, I never tire of dancing. I intend to dance every set. I hear the strains of a waltz starting up. I adore a waltz, and no partner has secured me for this one." What more could she say without grabbing his hand and placing it on her waist? He must ask her.

Then the disaster happened.

"No partner, Lady Diana? We cannot have that for one so fascinating." It was Countess Sefton who had come close from behind her. "Please allow me to suggest to you the Marquess of Darrow for the next set of dances." Diana dipped her head to Daniel's father. "Thank you, Countess. Charmed." *Disgusted, but too well-bred to decline.*

"I admit I enjoy the waltz, but my dear wife does not dance these days," Lord Darrow interjected. "Will you do a kindness for an old man and consider this set with me?"

*Why do you cut out your own son? You must have seen Countess Lieven approached to present him as a partner. What can you be thinking? You know I cannot refuse anyone unless I'm ready to sit out the rest of the dances.* Diana glanced wildly, like a cornered cat, at Daniel. He said nothing. He looked bilious. She had to accept his father's invitation. This was a valuable political friend of Colin's. She preferred not to hurt anyone's feelings. She dared not give Daniel's father cause to dislike her. There would be other waltzes. "How can I refuse?" she said, making the question seem as if she were elated. Her gut clenched at being forced to mislead her spirits.

******

Diana was led away, and Daniel faced her friends as they glared at him with various puzzled and angry expressions. They wanted to know what had just happened. Clearly, the captivating Diana was fishing for an invitation from him. Obviously, he was attracted to her. Why did he allow the ambassador to step in and offer the invitation first? An explanation was required. Daniel clutched his gloved hands together, wrung them, then pressed them against the cloth of his pantaloons. "I'm sorry. I do not dance." *My asthmatic lungs do not allow me*. He almost said it aloud. But what if his lungs were as bad as he feared? She'd pity him and try to nurse him. He preferred she esteem him and feel she could rely on him. It was awkward enough admitting his incapacity to the Countess Lieven earlier when she suggested he partner Diana. He scowled at her friends, turned on his heel, and left Almack's, allowing himself to appear a fool rather than a weakling. There was nothing further here for him tonight.

******

Later that evening, Colin was leaning against a pilaster discussing with Lord Sidmouth the trials of the arrested blanketeers. Neither Bradley nor his family had appeared, and the doors were closed to any late arrivals. Faith sat with Eden. She rose and went to Colin. "Eden would like to go home immediately."

Colin's face blanched. He turned toward his wife to search her expression.

"She's fatigued and hot. She longs for the comfort of her bed."

By the end of Faith's sentence, Colin was at his wife's side, bending over her. "Can you stand?"

"Of course," Eden said. "I'm surprised you think me an invalid. I just need fresh air."

"We leave immediately. Faith, get your sister and Diana as we take our time walking to the entrance."

"Wait, Faith." Eden turned to her husband. "I asked Lord Darrow if he would convey Diana and Hope home. There's no need to deny them their pleasure. Darrow said there's plenty of room in his carriage. I hope that's alright with you. Faith wishes to leave with us."

Colin nodded, anything for his wife. "Tell your sister and Diana of our plans, Faith. Then meet us at the entrance." He encouraged Eden with a shrug. "At least we shall avoid the great carriage crush."

# CHAPTER NINE

The novelty of Almack's wore off quickly for Diana. She asked her partner to take her to Lady Darrow's side as the last steps of the Roger de Coverly were ended, bringing the evening to a close. Where had Daniel been the rest of the night? Her temples throbbed, and her feet burned. She was used to country hours, hearty supper fare, and sedate exercise. And she was used to getting her way. What had gone wrong? Daniel seemed to want to pick up the connection where they'd left off. His comment about her curls was merely Daniel letting her know his preferences. What did she care how she wore her hair? It was all for him anyway. She hadn't seen him on the dance floor or anywhere, but she'd been greatly occupied until now. At least she might question him as they waited on the steps for the coach.

Once outside the assembly rooms and waiting for Darrow's carriage, Hope was telling the group the dance had ended far too soon, when she exclaimed, "Mercy, don't look!"

"At what?" Diana asked, glancing everywhere.

A footman told Lord Darrow at least thirty carriages were ahead of theirs as they wound around the block. Darrow walked a few steps away to see if he could spy his family crest on a coach door.

"It's too gruesome," Hope wailed.

Diana's eyes rolled heavenward. "What is?"

"Another of those maimed soldiers," Hope said. Her mouth pinched as if insulted.

"We must be proud of our soldiers, Hope. They risked their lives for our country, for our families, for our very selves."

"Yes, yes, but it's still shocking when you see one with a missing limb. Why does he not don a wooden one and cover it with boots and trousers?"

Diana searched the crowd and spied the soldier. He was leaning on crutches among a group of other men. They didn't appear shabby, but they were not dressed in the attire required at Almack's. Perhaps they'd just come from White's or Brook's and were waiting to meet family members. No, more likely a gambling hell. Diana stared at the man with the crutches. He looked familiar. Then she waved. The man didn't notice her. One of his cronies tapped his shoulder and pointed her out. Major Bradley turned and saw Diana. For a second, his figure froze with his mouth agape. Then he closed his mouth, shifted on his supports, and brought his single leg forward, a step toward her.

Diana instantly closed the gap between them. Judith hurried to follow. Hope crowded closer to Lady Darrow's side, casting a pleading look at Daniel's mother.

"Lady Diana, is that truly you? Forgive my hesitation, but for a second, I mistook you for the ghost of my sister. I hardly knew you. You've grown quite comely." Major Bradley shifted his weight to stand taller.

*What a plumper! Cassandra was tall, slender, and exquisite, and I am... well, not!* "I'm so sorry about Cassy. I loved her deeply. Your sister's passing must still give you pain. It does me. I foolishly wish for a visit from her from the next world. Others have had spectral visits from their relatives. If only she'd let me know she's content."

"Oh, she's quite happy. My sister has haunted me more than once. She tells me eternity is all glorious, and I must mend my evil ways or spend it in hell without her. Very unlike her to chastise me so. Deuced uncomfortable her visits are. But you've greatly altered, my dear, and all improvement."

"Did you expect me to stay a child for five years?"

"The last I remember; you were eager to be grown. I recall you once asked me to wait for you to do so. How did you find Almack's? You were a success, I'm certain."

"I danced every set. I admit I was happy a few sedate dances were tossed in so I could catch my breath." Diana bit her lip. Why must she mention an exercise he could no longer indulge in?

"It's lovely to see your face glowing with pure joy at the thought of such employment, Diana. Sadly, I'll never be able to lead you out myself."

"Oh, but there was an Admiral there tonight with a wooden leg who danced the Minuet. He did rather well from what I could see. Are you unable to support such a device, Major Bradley?"

"My loss is above the knee, as you see. Admiral Sitcolm's is below the knee, much easier to navigate. I was fitted for a false leg, but it was cumbersome and gave me much pain. However, I've not given up hope. I've been to a man who's devised a lighter contraption. It has joints at the knee and the ankle. He's taken my measurements and is at this very moment making one up to fit me. You've perhaps heard of Mr. James Potts or his invention, the Anglesey leg."

"Yes, I have. Named after The Marquess of Anglesey."

"I hate to burden you with such gloomy conversation on our first meeting in five years."

"No, I thank you for being candid. I find it interesting and am heartened you take a positive attitude toward your injury."

"The next time you see me, I hope to be wearing the new leg. Then you'll not feel such pity for me, and perhaps your golden-curled friend will not be so dismayed at the sight of me."

Judith touched Diana's shoulder. "Lord Darrow is signaling for us, milady."

Bradley glowered at the intruding Judith. She stepped back.

"Yes, we must see each other again soon, Major. I'll ask Eden to invite you, your brother and your sister-in-law to supper one evening soon."

He lifted a brow and smirked. "I look forward to the invitation."

"I must leave you now. Thrilled to meet you again, Major Bradley."

"The pleasure was all mine," he said with an exaggerated bow of the head and a grin from ear-to-ear.

When they covered the few steps back to their group, Diana found the carriage still not there, but Lord Darrow scowling at her. "You left your party," he said.

"A few steps to greet an old friend of the family. I was within seeing distance."

"Not within reaching distance if someone had decided to attack you."

"Major Bradley is a neighbor in Surrey!" Diana snapped. "I've known him forever."

"Do you know his friends? Unsavory seeming fellows."

Looking back at them, Diana had to agree, but not everyone could afford the finery she could. She knew it too well from going on charity visits with Eden to tenant's homes. Military men were often more careless in their dress as Eden's brother had proved. How one dressed mattered less to them after seeing war. It didn't make them unworthy gentlemen. She chose to mollify the old grumbletonian. "You may be right."

"I am right."

"Do you wait for Eversley?"

"We wait for the carriage. I'm astonished you seem unaware my son left on horseback hours ago."

Diana gaped at the man, blushed, and consciously closed her mouth with a click of the teeth. The blood drained from her face. "I wonder he didn't take leave of me. I looked for him."

"In that case, I wonder as well."

"I'd hoped we'd have a dance."

"Well, as to that..." His lordship cleared his throat and appeared about to explain. Then he seemed to think better of it. "I trust he'll clarify all when he sees you. Your family is at home tomorrow. We plan to call. At last, our carriage."

******

The young men who accompanied Major Bradley leered at the lovely friend of their host long after she walked away. Bradley watched her enter the carriage. She was still young and eager and tender, much like his beloved sister had been. Cassandra had known his painful childhood, often comforting him as best she could. Diana was unlike the typical, self-interested, conniving, cold creatures in his milieu. *Too bad she lives with her contemptuous brother. He dares to judge me! He's always known his place in life. He's been loved and cosseted from the time he wore nappies. He had a father one could admire, and a mother who thought he could do no wrong.* His jaw clenched at the thought of the privileged Earl of Edmunds.

"Bang up to the mark that one is," a cohort said, leering.

Bradley turned and glared at his guests. "She's too good for your like. Scorch her from your lascivious minds."

The group hooted and cackled as one.

Shrugging his mood, the Major suggested, "Now, my fine fellows, who is for home, and who for an even more delightful hell?" As one, the young men opted to visit yet another gaming establishment.

******

When Martha drew the drapes at twelve, Diana growled to shut them again. Martha did so. "Thought you might like to know his lordship and her ladyship have had breakfast and your sisters-in-law are up. The house is brimming with flowers from the beau whose hearts you claimed last night. The housemaids would like to bring some up into your room as there seems no more space downstairs."

"Very well, open the drapes and lay out my riding habit." Diana remained supine with eyes closed. "I need to exercise my mount before we're flooded with visitors at three. You may tell the servants to bring the flowers, ask Cook to prepare me cocoa and toast, and send a message to Mr. Stagg to saddle Satin and have him ready in half an hour. I'll take my breakfast here." Diana forced one eye open. When the first eye did not slam shut, she opened the other one, sat up, stretched her arms wide, and swung her sore feet upon the floor. She clutched her head to contain the sudden throbbing. "May I never again dance the entire night."

Martha bustled out. A second maid knocked at the open door. Diana said, "Enter," and a footman carrying several arrangements of flowers stepped in. The maid told him where to place the bouquets, and Hope pushed in with exclamations of how lovely her own blossoms were. "Lord Melton sent me the hugest arrangement of long-stemmed roses. Mr. Jeremy Blake sent me lilies, and Mr. Blank sent me daisies, and that cheap Mr. Blankety-blank sent me a posy of violets."

Diana stood, stumbled to her dresser, and picked up her hairbrush, then set it down and unbraided her hair. When her tray was brought in, she asked the maid to set it on her bed. She went to her ewer stand, picked up the pitcher, and filled the bowl with water. Setting the pitcher on a small side table, Diana took a cloth, dipped it in the water, and proceeded to dab the sleep out of her eyes. *Good morning Lord, I have an awful head this morning. I hope the ride helps clear it. I'll talk to you then. But right now, could You please make Hope take her inane chatter off somewhere before I lose my patience?*

"Chocolate! Divine! Diana, do you mind?"

"Yes, I do mind! Go find your own food," Diana growled. "I haven't time to wait for more."

Hope huffed but left. Faith, who had come to the door, retraced her steps.

The hot cocoa helped. The sweet warmth of it soothed her throat and nerves. The buttered toast helped more. Diana opened the tooth powder and cleaned her teeth. A cloth to the entire face and a vigorous hair-brushing completed the revival. When Martha was ready with Diana's habit, Diana was ready to don it. It was too late in the day to have a satisfying run on Satin Cloud. Rotten row and the lady trail would be crowded with young people by now. Later, it would be clogged with fashionables dressed to the nines, walking, riding in their newest equipage, all to see and be seen. Diana wanted the wind in her hair as she raced her steed over the turf. She wanted to experience the blur of trees and sunlight and feel the power of the animal beneath her. She wanted to know the exhilaration of pure freedom, to become part of the universe. Just thinking of it stirred Diana's blood.

******

Her ride restored Diana's mood. Mr. Stagg, the head groom, had found an open space in the park to allow their horses to take their bits in their mouths and fly. Back home, she changed out of her royal blue velvet habit into a Galatea walking dress with long sleeves. She sat for the hairdresser's ministrations, then draped her mother's shawl over her arms. She thought if she could manage it, she would hint to Daniel there was something in the garden he might like to see. She must think up a plausible excuse. Once there, he could explain his disappearance last night.

The family, minus Colin in his room writing letters, had gathered in the grand drawing-room on the first floor. The chamber looked like a hothouse with the various bouquets sent to the girls from young swains who had danced with them the previous night. Diana had read the cards from the scientist, the poet, the horse-racing enthusiast, Lord Partington, and Jeremy Blake in her cell.

Eden motioned Diana over as she entered the salon. Diana bent to kiss her sister-in-law. "How do you feel this morning? You look well. I should not have stayed at Almack's had Faith not assured me you were merely tired and hot. I could certainly understand that."

Eden waived her fears away with a hand. "I'm resolved to take extra care of my health with this expected one. I'm re-energized now. I didn't want to get over-tired and irritable. I might end up saying things that would alienate one of your brother's colleagues." Smiling, she indicated the flowers displayed on the floor beside her. "Daniel sent you these. They were too large to move upstairs."

The glorious arrangement of pink tea roses, Queen Anne's Lace, lilies, and baby's breath stood in a tall vase of malachite. Someone's succession houses had been raided.

Diana opened the card. "Forgive me, fair siren. I promise to enlighten. Daniel"

She made no reaction but clutched the message and moved on to retrieve cards from smaller arrangements and posies. She found one from Mister Stevenson and wondered aloud, "Who can that be? I don't recall the face. I barely remember the last hour of dances. My poor muscles ached so. What sort of politician's wife shall I make if I cannot recall names?"

"Is that what you wish to be?" Faith asked.

"Is it not inevitable? Father and Colin have been so instrumental in getting valuable legislation passed. There's still much to be done. If one has position, one has power and is obliged to use it to better society. I cannot be a member of parliament, but I can be a members' wife and support his work. Look at Eden; she's an excellent helpmate to Colin. She comments on his speeches and entertains prospects for him. He's always crowing about how he can't do it without her."

"Thank you for the compliment, Diana. I do my best. But it's not without its stresses. Entertaining lords is no guarantee they'll vote your way. And some of them are more trouble than they're worth."

"I'm prepared to work." Diana moved about the brightly lit room, caressing the tips of the flowers and inhaling the sweet aromas. "First, I must make the perfect match: Someone who shares my values and ideals, so whatever we work on, we work together. I will entertain the cream of society: the statesmen and literati. I'll glide among my merry guests, covertly dropping suggestions to influence them to consider the worthiness of my favorite cause—the safety and health of working children. I intend to make a difference in the world. I refuse to live a wasted life spent in useless diversions, doing nothing for those in need. You and Colin have taught me that, Eden."

Eden refilled her cup from the teapot on the tray that sat in front of her. "They're worthy dreams, Diana. It's just that word 'perfect' you like to use that alarms me. I don't think perfection exists in this life, though we should strive for it. The numerous times you use the word 'I' worries me. 'We' is a good word, too. No one can achieve so much on his own."

Faith absorbed every word as she sat primly with her hands folded in her lap. "Your ambitions are further reaching than mine, Diana. But your position has always been advantaged. Call on me if ever you need help putting forth your causes. My perfect match will be a gentle man. One I can admire and share my little dreams with, who will provide for me and be proud of me, a man who will love children. I hope to have a nursery full."

Diana stiffened. She forced a smile at Faith. Filling nurseries was a perilous occupation.

Hope checked the state of her hair in the window glass's reflection. "I shall find the richest, handsomest, highest-placed lord I can. I'll make him so love me he can never say, 'No' to anything I want. He'll propose by the end of the season, and I will accept."

Eden brought a hand to her mouth to cover her grin. "I hope none of you feels pressured to secure a match this season. You're young yet. Think of making enduring friends, enjoying entertainments, and perhaps having an adventure. I'd like to see you allowing yourselves to know your minds and hearts better before you place them in the hands of a partner for life. Don't forget to pray about it. God knows and wants what is best for you."

The three girls looked wide-eyed at Eden.

Diana refrained from voicing her thoughts. *Eden tries to protect me from disappointment. She suspects I'll be unable to attract the perfect beau.*

"You're right about the others," Faith murmured. "But I've been out for several years now and should make a push."

Hope went toward the door and peeked out. "God made me pretty so I can catch a rich beau, and that I will do before the bloom is off the rose."

## CHAPTER TEN

Lord Montcrief, Mr. Rhodes, and Lord Fildes were the first to call. Colin came down when he heard visitors. Matthew graced the family with his presence as well. Lord and Lady Darrow and Daniel, Lord Eversley arrived with Serena, Daniel's sister, and Thomas, who'd been rescued along with Daniel and adopted by the Darrow's. The willowy thirteen-year-old Serena was self-assured and lady-like, aware of her beauty and exalted position. The gangly ten-year-old Thomas had a perpetual glint in his eye, which made him always seem to be telling himself a good joke. He was quiet but attentive to everything being said, and observant of every action or change of expression in all present. His eyes shifted from speaker to speaker like a silent spectator at a badminton match.

The first ten minutes was spent in reporting where and how everyone had spent their time apart, how everyone did health-wise, how awful the riots were, the plight of the cottage trades protesting new machineries, and the entire complexion of the lower classes. Even a little fear of revolution was tossed about. One was not required to spend above fifteen minutes at a visit, and Lord and Lady Darrow had other acquaintances they wished to pay court to. Since time was flying and Daniel had found a seat opposite her, Diana leaned toward him and asked if he was still interested in botany.

Daniel cleared his throat. "Why, yes, extremely so."

Lady Darrow gaped at her son. "I didn't know that, Daniel."

He glanced at her and away. "Why I, I'm interested in many things, Mother. I study flowers to paint in my backgrounds."

*Delightful,* Diana thought. *He joined in my ruse. We are yet in tune with each other.* "There's the oddest flower that popped up in our garden last night. I thought you might identify it for me."

"We shall all repair to the garden on our way out," Lady Darrow said. "I, too, am eager to see the flower."

Diana's eyes widened. *Were there even any flowers in the garden yet? My trick has gone awry. Have I completely lost my powers? How easy it used to be to wish hard for something to happen and find it happening!*

Diana glanced at Thomas. He stood. "If we're leaving, I don't wish to see flowers. Those in this room are sufficient." He walked toward the parlor door. "I hear you have one of those new gas-lit chandeliers, Lord Edmunds. I tried to get father to get one, but mother thinks they're too dangerous."

Colin glanced at Thomas, then Diana. "Yes, Darrow, you must see it. I had it installed in the music room. It's an amazing invention," he said eagerly. "There's the slightest odor at first, but that burns off. If you light it before guests are expected and open a few windows, no scent will be detected. That's the beauty of it: windows may be opened for air, yet it glows all night. I'm weary of having parties where the females faint due to the heat because one cannot crack a window for fear the candles will be quenched."

Darrow chuckled. "In that case, it would be a vastly different party, eh, Edmunds? What say we split up? Those wishing to see the chandelier follow Edmunds, and those wishing to venture out in the cold to see an odd flower which shall probably prove to be a crocus, follow Lady Diana."

"I'll stay here with Lady Darrow." Eden beamed at her husband. "I have a few more subjects to broach with her."

Daniel followed Diana with her abigail, Judith, trailing behind her as she raced through the hall.

Diana led Daniel quickly down the marble slabs of the staircase and out to the back of the garden where a bench sat beneath an arbor. It was cold to sit upon, but she tolerated it. Daniel offered his coat, but Diana put her hand up to stop him from removing it. "This shall be as short as your explanation of last night," she said. Diana looked at her maid, who was panting from running to keep up with them and had nowhere to sit. "You needn't stand outside with me, Judith. The garden is considered in the house as we're surrounded by walls on all sides, and it's too cold for you in that dress."

"I'm fine, milady. I never feel the cold. I'll just stand over there in the sun away from the wind and look at the statue and the trellises. This is a right pretty garden."

Diana jumped up and threw her mother's shawl around the girl. "Wear this then; I brook no refusals. I have long sleeves, and I'll reclaim this the moment we are within." She watched for a moment with satisfaction as Judith caressed the silk shawl and held it to her cheek, then she turned back to Daniel. "I think you know there is no flower."

"I wanted desperately to dance with you, Diana. I hate admitting weakness, seeing myself diminished in your eyes. Do you remember how awfully I used to cough when I lived at Chadilaine? It was from breathing the coal dust in the chimneys I'd been forced to climb. So much of it went down my lungs when I dislodged it."

"Your cough got better afterwards, even before your real parents came to get you."

"Yes, but it never went away. I'm fine most of the time, but if I exert myself: run or play sports or ride any faster than a walk... or dance, I cannot help but fall into a fit of coughing. The surgeon says it is asthma exacerbated by exercise. I didn't wish to embarrass myself and you at Almack's. I apologize sincerely. I managed to do just that by arranging with my father, who's aware of my condition, to dance with you. I'd only come hoping to sit one set out with you."

"Oh, I, I see. I thought the Countess Lieven had deserted my camp. I'm glad we could find this moment for you to explain. I care not a fig for dances. My feet were paining me last night, and the artificial conversations gave me the headache. The room was so warm that Eden and Hope felt ill. I truly much prefer the museums of sciences, history, and art. I'd rather a good play or musical evening than dancing. You must know that."

"You love dancing, Diana. You also love riding hell for leather on that horse of yours. That's another thing I'll not be able to enjoy with you."

"You're right about riding, but that shouldn't put you out. I prefer to ride alone with Mr. Stagg and pick my own spots and race as fast as Satin Cloud wills it. I don't ride for camaraderie, but for sheer exhilaration. Mr. Stagg can keep up. He raced horses in his youth. Come, let's go inside. I want my shawl back. It was my mother's. Is it not the most beautiful thing you ever saw?"

"I fear it is not, Diana," he said, his expression solemn.

Diana froze and stared at his face.

Daniel blinked slowly, exposing a light in his eyes. "I've seen something far more beautiful than that piece of cloth this day: I've seen your soul."

She relaxed and beamed but waived the tribute away. "Please, Daniel, no fulsome compliments. You know I have no use for them."

Daniel scowled. "You wound me. I meant what I said. I felt it." Before she could magnify her denials, Daniel added, "There was something else that drove me out of Almack's."

Diana gave him all her attention.

Daniel glanced away. "It was quite a crush last night, more than usual. I began to feel confined."

"Yes, the first warm Wednesday cramped the rooms with people. I recall you do not like being closed in. You told me once of fearing you could not escape the closeness inside the chimneys."

"One never knew when some bat or bird would fly in your face. And the rats..."

"You're forgiven, Daniel. Please forgive my tactlessness." She jumped up. "In we go now before they come looking for us, and I have no bloom to show them."

Inside the house, Diana claimed her shawl and wrapped it about her. "I'll purchase a warm cloak for you on our very next shopping trip, Judith." As the three traveled back toward the blue salon, Diana turned to Daniel. "You were quiet today when the riots were discussed. I was eager to hear your opinion."

"I was afraid to speak. My father and your brother are quite decided and well versed in their opinions. I'm barely informed. I've been out of the country for so long, and my interests have never been political, I fear. There's much to know, and I'm not the brightest fellow. I admit, Diana, I dread a seat in the Lords, though it is an eventuality, I suppose. I'm appalling at speeches. I have a poor memory at best. If I were to open my mouth, the points I had to make would surely desert me. I'd be standing with my mouth agape in that great hall with all the peers eyeing me while no sound came forth."

"You can write your speeches ahead of time and read them. You don't even need to make speeches right away, but your vote is all-important."

"Politics is far more than making speeches. It's flattering other members of your party and remembering who stands on the side of what. I have a difficult time remembering people's names, much less their ideas. Policymaking is a mystery to me. People overwhelm me. If I'd lived my entire life at home, it might be different. As it is, if it were up to me, I'd live as a hermit painting pictures until I die."

"Oh, pooh! You're more brilliant than you think. Find yourself a cause that resonates with every fiber of your being, and you'll recall all you need to write a bill and put it over—with fire and force. There are so many worthy causes in this age."

Daniel frowned and said no more.

The others were not in the blue parlor when Diana and Daniel came back. A footman told Diana the family was waiting in the hall. Once there, Daniel told his parents, "I intend to walk home. I have some thinking to do."

Lady Darrow made a fish-face at him. "But Daniel, we have other visits, and I wanted to show you off."

"Apologies, Mother. I'm not in a genial mood at present. I'd make poor company. I have a little project at home I'm working on and wish to get back to."

Lord Darrow rubbed at his nose vigorously. "I'm disappointed too, Son, but you're a man now and make your own decisions." He turned to Colin to make his farewells. "Delighted Edmunds. Bye-the-bye, a neighbor of yours in Surrey, Major Bradley, was outside Almack's last night. I've no idea what he was doing there at that time of the morning. We were on the street waiting for our carriage. Is Bradley not the younger brother to Lord Richard Audley, whose father died in Bedlam? Terrible thing that. I remember the senior Lord Audley, a charismatic personality, until his illness confused his mind. I recall it was once touted you were sweet on his daughter, Cassandra. Sad thing, her demise. Ashamed to admit, I stepped away from our party a moment last evening. A footman had confused our coat of arms. I returned to find your sister had walked over to meet Major Bradley among his questionable-looking friends." Eden and Colin exchanged looks that Diana intercepted. Eden blanched.

Colin glowered. "You spoke to him, Diana?"

"Undoubtedly; he's our friend. You should have seen him, Colin. You would have pitied him. He was so thin and sad. He leaned on crutches because his false leg gave him such pain he would rather not wear it..."

Colin interrupted. "We'll speak of this later after visits. I've something particular to say to you."

Eden added, "Actually, my love, I'd like all the girls to stay after. I, too, have something to discuss with them."

The Darrow family took their leave, but groups of visitors came and went for the entire couple of hours the Edmunds family was at home.

At the close of the visits, Eden and Colin rose and walked their remaining guests to the hall. Matthew pushed himself up from the couch with his hands and leaned on his walking stick. "I must say, you ladies were a success. I met many earnest young men today. I like your scientific friend, Diana, and the sportsman has his good points as well. The less said about the poet, the better. I think he believed his little "ode" to you to be more than it was. I rather liked your beau as well, Faith. I'm off to the Horse Guards to see if I can make myself useful."

Scowling, Hope watched her brother leave. "I wonder Partington did not attend. Matthew would have liked him."

"Mr. Blake didn't visit either." Faith stood and put her crewelwork away. "I thought he would. He didn't attend Almack's, yet he sent flowers and cards to each of us. Perhaps he comes to supper or on Sunday after church."

Diana stood and began to pace the room slowly. Faith tilted her head as she watched her. "I, too, feel the need for exercise after this."

Giggling self-consciously, Diana explained. "I imitate the movements of the panther we saw at the Exeter exchange. Do you remember? I studied him a long time. His walk was sublime: measured, powerful, but light, smooth, and graceful. Just the impression I wish to give as I glide across the floor to give my hand to a statesman in greeting."

Faith laughed heartily. "Would you care to join Hope and me on a shopping excursion after Eden and your brother speak to us? Then you can practice your slink in a more open area."

"I doubt I'll be allowed to go anywhere. Colin had his dictatorial brother look on his brow. I cannot know why, but I often make mistakes I'm unaware I am making until I have it explained to me. Don't worry; I think he's only unhappy with me."

******

As Daniel walked home, he thought over his confession's effect on Diana. He had to be frank with her. One should not develop a serious relationship with a lady without laying his cards on the table. *She must know the real you, and you must know the real her if you are even to consider spending a life together.* Daniel shuddered. He wasn't ready for ever after. He was far too unsettled in his own mind to take on the responsibility of another's happiness. But, what if Diana was the one created for him alone, and he let her drift while he matured? She could float into the arms of another man. He'd seen the look of admiration in that scientist fellow's eyes. Mr. Rhodes wouldn't stumble around, making up his mind. He was older and ready and appreciated Diana's intelligence and beauty. He was below Diana's station, but she would never take that into consideration if she loved him. And there was Lord Stillwell and several others who were eager for her ample dowry.

But what of Diana's regard for him? Had it not seemed to change when he told her he'd no interest in politics? Had she not seemed disappointed, even censuring? She would make a brilliant political wife. His own mother was only fair at that at best. She was good-natured but lacked the aptitude to be considered a raconteur. She left parties to others unless absolutely necessary. His marchioness mother was no Diana.

Diana was close to perfection. That was the problem. She deserved so much more than him. She was so bright and intuitive, so beautiful, so good-hearted, any man of worth would consider her a prize catch. Her dreams encompassed the world. His condition would surely limit her possibilities. The doctor had told him he had asthma, but he was not so sure. Doctors were not above telling one what one wanted to know. They could also be wrong about a diagnosis. He and Thomas had had a friend who'd been a climbing boy. He contracted a cancer of the lungs and died two years ago. The boy's symptoms had been the same as his: fatigue and a painful cough. If cancer and death were to be his lot, why burden Diana with it too?

He had no need of another tyrant to coerce him. She had no idea how difficult it was for him to muster the energy merely to carry out daily obligations. Marriage meant fatherhood. How could he consider it with his future in doubt? He needed to come to his own conclusions and lead his own life before he allowed Diana to lead it for him. But he was lonely in this world. No one understood him as Diana did. He could talk to her about anything, just as before. He could not imagine closeness with anyone but her.

When he told her he didn't dare dance, she was all-consoling, claiming to have had enough of dancing for a lifetime and saying she preferred museums for entertainment. What a plumper. Had she not said last night that she adored dancing and wanted to dance every turn? He was being truthful. Was she? She was being optimistic and reassuring, just as a helpmate should be. *I am more brilliant than I think.* Daniel snorted. *I think not.*

# CHAPTER ELEVEN

After the guests left, Colin told the footmen standing in the hall the family was not home to visitors until further notice. He suggested they take tea and rest their legs. He wanted privacy to discuss the situation with Eden and form a plan for their attack before they went to the girls in the drawing-room.

The footmen paced across the harlequin-tiled floor and pushed through the green baize door as Colin watched. He turned to his wife. In hushed tones so the words would not echo throughout the hall, he said, "All that can be done must be done to crush any friendship between Diana and 'the name I will not repeat.' "

Eden held her palms out and shrugged. "I doubt she entertains anything but a sort of hero-worship once removed and pity for his injuries. He lost a leg for our country. He deserves some recognition for that. Diana will love a man she admires, not a man she pities. Lady Darrow said the meeting was brief, with a wide space between them. She could hear them, and they spoke banalities. Major Bradley has fifteen years on Diana; I'm sure she looks at him as ancient."

"Nonsense, my love," Colin returned gently. "Diana is beyond her years. She thinks youths her age callow puppies to be ordered about. Men my age, she deems 'interesting.' She has always adored Jeremy, and she used to be quite foolish over the 'name' as well."

"You may be right there."

"I am right. I also have reason to believe he may use Diana's innocence to act in some spiteful way."

Eden's brow furrowed. She searched her husband's eyes. "What could he possibly have against Diana?"

"Only what he has against her brother. He holds me in contempt for effecting his sister's marriage to Jeremy, whom she loved and whom the entire Bradley family disapproved. Jeremy's station was not high enough for them, and his purse not as large as they required. You must admit I was actively responsible for their marriage. He also blames me for keeping him from rising in military rank."

"Did you?"

Colin shrugged. "Possibly. I sent one long letter to his commanding officer five years ago. His brother refused to advance him further money to buy his way up the line. He himself is to blame for his failures. I think in his demented brain, he also blames me for Cassandra's death, though that is far off.'"

"Is it not you who hold him in contempt for attacking me?"

"That goes without saying. But it's not my first concern with Diana."

"Is your first concern what Nurse Warren told me?"

Colin abruptly shut his jaw and drew up to his fullest height. "Exactly what did she tell you?"

Eden came closer to speak even more softly. She took her husband's hand, but her eyes failed to meet his. "She left it as speculation, but the substance of it was that Major Bradley's father may be ..." Her eyes darted left and right looking for anyone who might overhear her. "... Diana's father."

"I'm relieved I will not have to go into it myself, but it is ... possible, probable even. But few have any idea about it. Unless it were verifiable fact, known in society, and likely to get back to Diana, I refuse to even suggest it to her. I know well no child cares to be faced with the evidence his beloved mother was capable of betraying his father."

Eden drew an extended breath and let it out slowly. "I'm certain we can keep them apart. I'll speak to Matthew and Faith about him without mentioning—anything else. Diana puts great store in their counsel as well as mine. We'll do what we can."

"Nothing blatant. If Diana feels pushed, she'll push back to exert her independence. She's not above subterfuge. I'll endeavor to determine what entertainments he attends, and you must encourage her to accept invitations to competing venues. The debutante balls may pose a problem since you ladies try to arrange them so they don't fall on the same evenings. His reputation should keep him off the lists of many."

"Between the four of us, we'll contrive."

"This is Diana we speak of, Eden; she's not your ordinary miss."

"That's why it will take all of us to outwit her."

"Let's agree to warn all the young ladies to steer clear of him, even to the point of giving him the cut direct."

"Surely, not so dire. You say, 'nothing blatant,' yet the 'cut direct' is so. It could sabotage your political friendship with Lord Audley. You need his vote on the habeas corpus question. You need every vote you can get."

"I'll not put the ladies of my family in danger for the sake of votes."

"Then we are agreed. I'll exert myself more in counseling Diana. She's been protected and encouraged in her independence, yet she has a good head on her shoulders and a good heart. She usually heeds me, but I've not liked to reveal the evil in some men's minds for fear of dampening her positive spirit."

******

Colin patrolled the rug a few times before coming to an abrupt halt. He glowered at the three girls and commanded in stentorian tones, "Be seated, the three of you."

The girls huddled together on a yellow velvet couch and looked up at him with eyes like guilty puppies. He towered above them. His stern expression promptly melted. "I'm not angry, Diana. I know you think I am. Rather, I'm not angry at you. When Lord Darrow mentioned you met Major Bradley outside Almack's, I was mortified. I realize he is a neighbor who often visited Chadilaine as a friend in earlier years. However, he's no longer welcome in our home. He has not turned out well. A young lady guarding her reputation should discourage any acquaintance with him. He's dangerous. He's too old for any of you and too steeped in worldly knowledge. He has no consequence in society, though his elder brother applies himself to carry on the family name in better style.

"I'm asking you to be wary of Major Bradley and never approach him. If he approaches one of you, make certain there's a crowd of friends about you for protection. Never be out in public without your servants and in company with several others from the family. Will you promise me this and relieve my mind?"

Hope and Faith nodded their assurances with blanched faces. Lord Edmunds had never spoken to them so unguardedly. Diana's eyes were wide in amazement. Her nod was half-hearted. If Colin had only seen the poor man, he couldn't think him dangerous. In all the times she had enjoyed bantering with Major Bradley, he never overstepped the bounds of propriety in act or even a hint of suggestion. Yet she couldn't remember her brother ever speaking in such a caustic manner about anyone. He was obviously distraught. It made her curious to dig out the story behind their neighbor. Just who would know?

Eden took her husband's hand and led him to the door. Her brows were raised as she asked him, "Nothing blatant, you say?" She shook her head and chuckled. "Let me speak privately to the girls, Colin. Perhaps I can clarify things without alarming them if I carefully reveal his actions toward me. I'll lose my nerve if I attempt to do so with you standing here." He brought her knuckles to his lips, kissed them, squeezed her fingers, and left.

Eden turned to the girls, inhaling slowly as she approached. "I asked Colin to leave because I want to confess to you girls something I've never told you, something of which he is painfully aware. The summer after I came to be your companion and governess, Diana, your brother had a house party. I was invited to join in the amusements. On several occasions at that party, Major Bradley transgressed the constraints of decency in conversation and even upon my person. I admit I was inexperienced and foolish and may have given him the impression his advances were welcome. I thought we were harmlessly flirting. But it was no innocent attack he made upon me the night Colin left to continue the house party at a different venue. Bradley left on horseback before the others but hid in the woods. Once everyone had gone, I went to check on the estate agent's mother in her cottage. Major Bradley waylaid me in the wood and attempted to force me to lie with him."

At this revelation, Faith cried, "Oh, Eden!"

"By the grace of God, his attack was interrupted when the groundskeeper, who had been watching for me, called out. The baying of his bloodhounds sent Bradley scurrying. Nothing came of the occurrence but a headache and a sore jaw for a few days. I do not wish to go further into it, but Colin has since heard other reports of unsavory conduct by Major Bradley upon green young misses. Perhaps you can see why we both warn you so strongly to have nothing to do with the man." Eden watched Diana's expression. She looked drained, shocked, and bewildered at the same time.

******

In her room, Diana changed into a fresh gown and drank a cup of tea to revive. The day had been distressing. She recalled the house party Eden mentioned. That was the summer she, at last, had a friend her own age to play with: Daniel, the chimney sweep. He'd not known he was Lord Eversley then. She thought about the day after the house party when Eden did not come down to breakfast. Eden said then that she tripped on a tree root while running in the dark. Her face had a purple bruise on the right jaw. Was that the result of the attack she'd just spoken of? She couldn't believe it of Major Bradley. He'd been nothing but friendly to her. He complimented her when others joked about her looks. He had a ready smile and listened closely to her ideas. He was handsome or used to be. There were bright red veins about his nose now, and the hollows of his eyes seemed darker and puffier than she recalled. But he was older and had seen awful sights in the war. Even Eden's brother was greatly affected by the fighting. Matthew had nightmares about it still, and he'd been sent home to mend his injured leg years ago. If the occasion presented itself, and she could manage to keep within Colin's limits, Diana had a few questions to ask Major Bradley.

As to the problem of Daniel, he seemed obstinate about avoiding the political scene. There were Lords who did little in the House, visiting it rarely, and managing never to push forward an intelligent idea. They came only to vote with the party or a friend and to pretend to care. Some even stayed in their districts, shooting and fishing and racing and otherwise tending to their needs alone, neglecting the needs of their dependents. She despised such selfish people. Was that what Daniel had become? Painting was very well for a hobby. She admired talented painters, but paintings did nothing to permanently change the human condition. Legislation alone could do that. How could Daniel even consider shirking his responsibilities? She refused to understand it.

# CHAPTER TWELVE

Eden and the girls enjoyed a water party, floating on a barge down the Thames with stops to view the gardens along the way and a picnic at the end of it. Throughout the day, the younger ladies observed, with great delight, the rippling muscles of the twelve strong, young lightermen rowing their vessel. A musical evening after that and Exeter 'Change with Matthew next afternoon had the girls eager for a relaxing day at home. They began to wonder what all the fuss was about since the fascinating pariah, Major Bradley, had not appeared at any of these delights. Daniel and Lord Partington were not at the amusements either, but so much was going on, it was impossible to meet everyone. The next night, they attended a birthday ball for Miss Penelope Rivers. The entire ton was invited to Miss Rivers' family's townhouse on St. James's Square. Because it was one of the first of the year's come-out balls, many of those invited brought their visitors with them. It proved a dreadful crush with far more guests attending than had been invited. The Lords sat late into the night, so Colin was not yet there. Diana could not find Daniel. Might he be in the gallery at Westminster watching the proceedings and learning?

Lady Darrow and Eden found a comfortable bench among the potted lemon trees and claimed it by sitting. The scent of the lemon leaves refreshed the air of the great dance hall. Eden sat a lot lately. Her gown had been designed to expand around her middle, and it worked its magic. Matthew stood protectively beside her. He joked with the girls that if they found themselves missing a partner, he would happily sit one out with them. Hope made a moue at him and asked if he imagined she could not attract her own partners. Faith thanked him for the offer, saying she just might need his services. The girls gathered around Eden and Lady Darrow to wait for the dancing to begin.

Lady Audley and the dowager Viscountess Audley, dressed in mourning, waved to Eden as they arrived and made their way to her side. Eden and Lady Darrow greeted them with genuine smiles, offering condolences on the death of the former Lord Audley. The dowager viscountess protested, saying it had been ages since the former Viscount Audley had been mentally stable. His death had almost been a blessing. Eden forced herself to ask if Major Bradley was attending the ball this evening. Lady Audley said he had been invited, but as he stayed in his own apartments in town, they were not always aware of the comings and goings of her brother-in-law.

Mr. Rhodes came to Diana while her attention was preoccupied with the greetings and requested the first set of dances. Faith and Hope were applied to by their own beaux. These young men had no seats in parliament and were happy they could get their moments in with the eligible young ladies before the lords appeared and outshone them.

As they went to take their place, Diana questioned Mr. Rhodes. "Did you attend lectures today?"

"Indeed, though I doubt it would interest you."

"Indulge me."

"A doctor spoke of the dangers of prescribing opium for a protracted time. Taking it a brief span for insomnia or toothache seems beneficial. But, per him, there is a buildup of it in the humours which then exhibits certain adverse effects."

Mr. Rhodes ventured further when the steps brought them together again. "He warned if a person tries to stop taking it, he could suffer worse pain than that caused by the original complaint. He said the new derivative morphine was a sort of tamed version of the opium and much more reliable."

Diana noticed Matthew standing nearby. Was he eavesdropping? "The use of opium worries me," she said. "I've read advertisements for tinctures to administer to babies to soothe the ache of colic and teething. If it is harmful in any way, how can physicians recommend it? Many of the poor buy it to cut the stomach pains of starvation. Since the corn laws, bread costs more than opium pills."

Mr. Rhodes pulled up short and looked at her with astonishment. When a couple on the floor passed by him, he recalled where he was and moved. "I had no idea gently bred young ladies bothered themselves with such subjects."

"I read the newspapers and listen to my brother and sister-in-law complain of their frustrations with charities they serve on and causes they support."

As the second dance ended, Diana thanked her partner and reminded him she would need to return to her chaperone. They started to push through the crowd, but Diana spied a refreshment table in a little anteroom. "Lemonade would be lovely."

The two maneuvered their way as best they could through the river of guests and into the refreshment room. Mr. Rhodes led Diana to the protection of a marble column. "If you wait here, I will dive in and procure a glass for you." She watched him push and slide in and out of a crush of white dresses and black coats to the punch bowl.

"Lady Diana, you are a vision tonight."

Diana's flesh crawled at the sound of his voice. She turned to see Major Bradley directly behind her. He stood on two legs, steadying himself with a walking stick. He was dressed to the nines and looked younger somehow. Perhaps it was the close shave and the cropped hair. He appeared taller. Her misgivings swelled, but the crowd gave her confidence. She could not give him the cut direct without attracting undue attention, and she wanted an answer to her question. She glanced wildly for her brother. Nowhere to be seen. She braced herself. "And you look more cheerful than the last time I saw you. You must be wearing your new..." She smiled conspiratorially. "I shall not give you away." She moved closer and lowered her voice, "Tell me quickly, what is the bad blood between you and my brother?"

Bradley's mouth took a wary twist. "There was something back when I attended a house party before I rode off to war." He chuckled humorlessly and waived the idea away. "I was young and stupid and fooled by the glances Miss Eden Barrett tossed my way. She was gay and unpracticed, and I was confused by her arch smiles. I was in my cups and believed she cast lures at me. It shames me to admit I made some unsuitable advances toward her, but she was a mere servant then. She was on the grounds at night. I thought she came after me. I hope Edmunds no longer holds against me that I poached on his bird; after all, he bagged her. Is he here? Perhaps I should come and apologize."

"No!" Diana said. "Don't bring it up. You'll rub salt in his wounds. I merely wondered."

"He need never worry that will occur again. All the foolish urges of my youth were destroyed by the cannonball that took my leg and felled my horse on me." He shifted on his stick as his glance darted about the room. His forced smile spread across his face. "I'm a changed man, Diana. I ache for the love of a good woman in my life to turn me around and make a worthy person of me. But there are things I can no longer do for a wife, cannot give her... if you catch my meaning."

Embarrassed with the subject, Diana refused to reply as he seemed to want her to. The man must be in his cups to mention such a thing. She turned to look for her partner.

Bradley spoke to the back of her head. "Ah, now I recall. There's a secret I alone am privy to–knowledge which could ruin your family. I'll not reveal it, unless I have good reason to do so."

Diana's neck and arms prickled. Her heart trembled. *What secret?*

Mr. Rhodes appeared with the lemonade and held it out to her, "For you, my lady." She took it, thanked him, and sipped. Her heart had climbed up into her throat, and the sour drink caused her to cough and inhale it into her lungs. She coughed harder until Mr. Rhodes took the liberty to pound her back gently. She twisted to glance back at Bradley. He had vanished.

As she returned, shaking, to Eden's side, Diana was delighted to see Colin, Lord Darrow, and Lord Audley. Parliament had dispersed for the evening. Daniel must be somewhere about as well. Her brother was frowning at her. *What did he think he'd seen?*

Mr. Rhodes bowed to Colin. "I see you wonder what took us so long to come back. We stopped at the refreshment table and found it a push to secure a beverage."

His expression forbidding, Colin coldly nodded to Rhodes. "Thank you for returning my sister safely to us."

Diana greeted Lord Audley and Lord Darrow and glanced about. "Was Daniel in the Lord's Chamber today?" she asked.

"He was in the gallery earlier, falling asleep from boredom," Darrow said. "I admit, there are times when the minutia wears me out as well, but a law will affect a mass of people for years. It is best to get it right the first time, and that includes listening to every opinion, well expressed or dull."

Diana nodded, having heard similar sermons from her brother and father. Still, it seemed all the shouting, cane tapping, and jovial name-calling in the Lord's Chamber would keep anyone awake. She turned around to face the dance floor and possibly find a suitor there. Mr. Rhodes was still near her, but she'd already danced with him. He seemed to be trying to catch Hope's eye, as Faith was now nodding to Mr. Saxton and walking away on his arm.

Hope peered noticeably beyond Mr. Rhodes to Partington. The handsome lord was walking slowly and deliberately their way. Mr. Rhodes cleared his throat and repeated his invitation to Hope.

Lord Partington arrived and bent toward Diana. "May I have the honor of this set of dances, Lady Diana?"

"With pleasure," Diana said, offering her hand, and they were off to find a spot near the top of the room.

Hope was left to glare after them as she accepted Mr. Rhodes' request for the pleasure of her company.

As they faced each other in the line, Diana asked Partington, "Were you not aware Miss Hope Barrett anticipated your attention?"

"Did she now?" he smiled, looking amused.

"You sent her a beautiful arrangement of roses."

"Not so loud, or my other fair maidens will hear of it and become jealous." He waggled his brows at her to punctuate his words.

"Are you playing some sort of lover's game with her?"

"I hope not!" He sobered instantly. "Love has not entered my mind."

"What has entered your mind?"

"I admire that you stand up for your friend."

Diana was silent as the turns of the dance brought her away from him. An unwelcome warmth invaded her cheeks. She could barely tolerate Hope. The moment she was near Partington again, she said, "I would stand up for anyone who was being abused."

"Now I esteem you even more, although `abused' is a strong word in this case."

"What would you call it?"

"Instructed, perhaps."

"And the lesson you teach?"

"Do not be over-confident, and do not tie the affections of all until you have hooked your largest fish. It is not fair to the 'all.' "

"That is what you feel she is doing?"

He smiled broadly and cocked his head, "Thus the lesson."

"You've observed her only twice. You condemn quickly."

"But I observed closely and believe I judge rightly."

"You have a right to your opinions." What else could she say? He was spot-on.

"Thank you for so graciously granting me the right to my opinions," he beamed and winked. "I grant you yours."

Diana couldn't tell if the warmth of the room or the exercise was making her perspire. Surely it wasn't the friendly banter with this handsome lord. She didn't want to go back near the refreshments lest she be drawn into another encounter with Bradley. She glanced to see if he was in that vicinity and was surprised to see Matthew and Major Bradley with drinks in their hands, talking together cordially. As soon as she could get Matthew alone at home, she intended to interrogate him.

******

Lady Darrow stood up to accompany her husband to the dance floor for a sedate Boulanger. Faith promptly sat beside Eden. She flipped open the fan that hung from her wrist and applied it vigorously to her face. "I cannot believe my good fortune. In only two weeks, I've met two very sensible young men who seem promising prospects."

Colin, standing beside his countess in case she needed anything, looked down at Faith and smiled his little half-smile that was more in the eyes than in the mouth. "Only two, Faith?"

Faith glanced at him but couldn't bear to hold his gaze. He'd been so good to her family. He'd been sweet to her in so many of the little ways a girl remembers–ever gallant, looking out for her physical comfort, quick with a word of encouragement, a compliment, and a smile. And his teasing was always the pleasant kind, much like his friend Jeremy's. She dragged her eyes back up to meet his. "Only one is required."

"You glow tonight, Faith–glow with that inner something that is bound to attract the best of beau. You're genuine and gentle. I'm glad I didn't find you first," he said. Deep wrinkles at the corners of his eyes invited speculation. "In your sister, I have someone lively who gives as good as she gets, just what I needed to bring spirit to my dull self. You, however, will bring calm and order, peace and warmth to your husband's life and home."

Eden's mouth curled in a grin as she glanced back and forth between the two of them.

The tiny jealousy that haunted Faith raised its ugly little head. The only way to rid her soul of it was to confess. She leaned close to Eden and whispered, "I grow anxious of finding anyone as dear as your husband; truly, it is you who have found the perfect partner."

Eden kissed her sister's cheek. "You may be right. But despair not. There's someone out there who was created just for you. I'm confident."

The face of someone for whom she may have been made appeared in Faith's mind, but he was not on the dance floor. He avoided dances, and though he flirted with her, it was no evidence of ardor; it was his way with all ladies. He showed no real signs of returning her regard. Rather, he cherished a passion for his lost love. She'd probably have to settle for someone she took pity on. Someone nice and good. Someone she would spend her life trying to love. The thought of such compromise roiled her stomach. How could one enter the marriage bed with someone she didn't adore deeply, romantically? Unfortunately, it happened every day to other maidens, still... Faith consciously expelled the foul air of defeat and inhaled the invigorating air of resolve. The season had a long way to go, and melancholy was of no use. She would be more fervent in her prayers tonight and try hard to trust her future to God's design.

******

Diana and Hope were led back to Eden's side. Several young men stood near in hopes of just such an event. Matthew arrived with a gentleman in tow who wished to be made known to the girls: a second son of a viscount.

He presented the fellow to Colin and Eden first. Lady Darrow, who had returned, vouched for him. Lord Darrow tried to get Colin to join him in the card room, but Colin glanced briefly at his expectant wife and back at Darrow. He wasn't budging. Matthew offered to accompany Darrow, and they started off.

Diana stepped close to her brother, indicating with her fan that she had something secret to tell him. He took a step away from the group, and Diana stood on tiptoe to whisper to him. "Major Bradley is in the room."

Without changing his expression, he said, "I am aware. Thank you."

"Lady Diana Ashton, forgive me for being so bold." Diana turned to behold Lord Montcreif in all his sartorial splendor. He imitated Beau Brummel tonight even to the way he tied his cravat. "I must read you this poem I wrote in the first hours of this morning's light. You were my inspiration, of course. I'd been thinking of you all night." The diminutive poet bowed low, taking her unoffered hand and saluting the air above it. He didn't give Diana the opportunity to accept or decline his reading, but began:

"None is so rare as an original,
Yet Mayfair sports one.
The fair goddess of the hunt
Has arrived there with the sun.
Her figure so lithe,
Her demeanor courageous
Her wisdom so vast
It expands past the ages."

Montcrief smiled brightly, certain Diana would be pleased with his work. Diana searched her brain for a polite response that offered no encouragement. "It rhymes very nicely."

"Yes, I had wanted to use a word other than 'courageous'–not feminine, you know. I simply couldn't find one that fit better and rhymed with the next line. But once I got all of it down, I was quite pleased I'd chosen that word. I think it describes you well." The slender lord smoothed an imaginary wrinkle in his discreetly patterned waistcoat as he deposited the poem in his coat pocket. He removed his gloves.

*It is "courageous" to even speak to this fool.* "Thank you for your lovely compliments," Diana said. "If you make a copy of your poem for me to save in my remembrance box, I'd consider it a kindness." Was it possible to avoid deflating his ego without encouraging his fervor? This one must be allowed to slip silently back into the muddy pond.

Montcrief produced a beautifully enameled snuffbox and snapped it open. He took a pinch with the thumb and forefinger of his left hand, depositing it on the back of his right hand. Bringing it to his nose, he took a good whiff and sneezed explosively. "You may have my copy. I've committed it to memory." He wiped his nose with a handkerchief, replaced the snuff box, stashed the soiled handkerchief, drew his gloves back on, retrieved his ode, and handed it to Diana.

Diana gingerly took the paper from him. "It is agreeable to have young men pay one compliments, even if they are rehearsed. And it's amusing to have them seek one's approval, even though it may only be one's fortune and consequence they seek." She said it hoping to discourage him, but it was true. Was this why she could trust Daniel so easily? His title would be higher than Colin's one day. The Darrow estate was superior to theirs. He had no need to attach her. He'd been her friend since the day he met her, without knowing who his family was. Was she guilty of fortune-hunting as well? Frightening thought. No. She'd been drawn to Daniel when she thought him no more than a sooty climbing boy.

Diana held Montcreif's note out in front of her like a pair of soiled nappies. She turned and asked Eden for her reticule. Shoving the poem in the little purse, she grudgingly turned back. Her heart seized! Daniel was inches from her face. His amazing cerulean eyes held hers. Had she willed him there as she once believed she could? Had she regained her powers? Would the heat that radiated through her cool? Could she ever breathe again?

"My lady, would it be too much to ask? Will you sit this set out with me?"

"Charmed, my lord."

# CHAPTER THIRTEEN

They sat on a hall settee in full view of the guests and turned to face each other. The orchestra began the strains of a quadrille. Daniel searched Diana's face. She looked down and examined the mother-of-pearl sticks of her fan as she opened and closed it in her lap, stealing glimpses of him as they spoke.

"Let me begin by telling you how fascinating you look," he said. "This Greek goddess hairstyle is most becoming. Even your bearing is noble. Attending your old deportment master, are you?" The corners of his eyes crinkled with the teasing, but like quicksilver, they smoothed. He hoped it didn't sound as rehearsed as it was. "I wish to extend to you and your family an invitation to a premiere opening at Somerset House on the day after tomorrow."

"Is that the only day of the exhibit? We have plans to ride out to Deerdon Hall that afternoon to begin a little weekend house party."

"Are they plans that might be slightly altered? I've a particular reason for inviting you. We go to Mr. Blake's digs also but arrive late. I'd hoped to surprise you, but I see I must let the cat out of the bag. A painting I completed in Italy has been accepted. It'll be unveiled with a group of Italian works. A little ceremony with a light meal and wine is arranged for the opening."

"How glorious for you! In that case, I'll try very hard to carve out the time. Things must be explained to my family. I know they too will wish to take it in."

"I could drive you there before they're scheduled to leave, so you can see the painting and continue on with them when they arrive. It all depends on when they plan to depart for Deerdon Abbey. The gallery opens at noon."

"I'll discuss it with them and have Colin pen you the details. Speaking of galleries, I hear you were in the gallery of the Lords today."

He gave her a bland look. *Must she bring that up again?* He placed the tip of a finger to the knotted muscle between his brows and pressed the furrow straight, avoiding her gaze. "The entire political scene disgusts me. It seems each lord is there to protect his own holdings and keep the status quo. I can see spending time and energy getting a bill passed that would benefit the masses, but too many of the politicians seek merely to benefit themselves. Look how long it took Wilberforce to get the Slave Trade Act passed. Was any legislation more obviously right? I doubt I could stomach the abuse given Wilberforce for so many years for one bill."

"Much of the complaint against Wilberforce was against his Methodist frame of mind, and the fact that he sat in the House as an independent, sometimes supporting Whig causes, sometimes Tory," Diana argued. "Yet, he's the perfect example. He slogged on through, winning public opinion and slowly turning the minds of parliament until enough votes were amassed to pass the Act. Think how many people have been and will forever be affected by that one regulation. Dissension didn't stop him. He continues to support the campaign for the complete abolition of slavery. And my Aunt Chadwick works with him on her favorite cause: The Society for the Prevention of Cruelty to Animals."

Diana placed a gloved hand on his wrist. "It sounds as if you think you must do all this alone, Daniel, but Wilberforce had troops of people canvassing for him and giving him ideas of what to do next to get his point across. Colin doesn't achieve everything alone but works in concert with other like-minded men."

He was cornered. He clenched his teeth and gripped his knees. The movement dislodged her hand. She was right, but she was pushing him just like his father did. Lord Darrow insisted Daniel make his own life choices, simultaneously letting him know he would be deeply disappointed if Daniel didn't fulfill his dreams of a great statesman for a son. It distressed him to fail his father and Diana, but they were asking him to be someone he was not. They couldn't comprehend his condition. "I'll be my own man, Diana. I'll not be manipulated. I'll not be pushed into something that goes against my grain." The moment he said it, he wished he hadn't. He'd been too forceful in his manner and word choice. He saw it happen, though only he could have noticed it. The spark left her eyes. Not a muscle moved in her expression, yet where she'd been radiant, she was leaden. Had he damaged their connection with his stupid pride? *Blundering fool.*

Her voice trembled. "Certainly, you should determine your own course. I merely meant to encourage you in what you're destined to do." Diana stood and walked toward the ballroom. He noticed she neglected to slink like a panther or even hold her head proudly. She stopped at the doorway leading into the ballroom. Daniel caught up with her and shadowed her as she walked around the perimeter of the room to Eden's perch.

Hope shoved between Daniel and Diana. She addressed Daniel, "I can't believe Lord Chesterfield complained of a cramp in his leg and left me on the dance floor to find my own way back to the chaperones."

Daniel could believe it. Chesterfield was ancient and portly. "Is he recovered?"

"Do I care?"

"I see."

Hope asked Daniel if he might accompany her to the refreshment room. Daniel looked helplessly toward Diana. She sighed and shrugged. Placing a gloved hand on Daniel's outstretched forearm, she began to move that way. Hope followed closely on Daniel's left.

Major Bradley came into Daniel's view, but looked past him and slid away. Daniel felt Diana flinch and turned his head to see why.

Colin was there with a hand at Diana's elbow. "I feel the need for exercise and look for a suitable partner, Eversley. Pray, grant me the right to steal my sister for this one dance."

He glanced at Diana. Her face remained hidden from him. "If that is her wish."

Diana placed a hand on Colin's forearm. She seemed to grow by inches in his company. "With the greatest of pleasure, my lord brother."

Colin leaned forward to say, "Have I told you how proud I am of you tonight? You grace my arm beautifully."

"And you are quite the dandy yourself, young man. Were you free, every girl on the marriage mart should be jealous of me monopolizing your time. You are the dearest brother in the world."

"I'd not trade you for a hundred other sisters."

"That's not saying anything. You'd not know what to do with them."

"I yearn for the day when you learn to take a compliment graciously," he said, briefly crossing his eyes at her.

She laughed, left Daniel's side, took a position with her brother among the dancers, and the music began.

Daniel felt a tug at his left elbow. He glanced at Hope. Her expectant, merry expression brought a bad taste to his throat. The walls of the room closed in on him. He secured Montcreif's attention and asked the lord to please attend to Miss Hope Barrett in his stead as he was about to be sick. He skulked out of the River's townhouse without looking back.

## CHAPTER FOURTEEN

Standing in their library the following day, Diana spoke first. "I asked to see you because I have a question, Colin. Please, no flippant reply."

Colin's eyes widened. A smirk threatened to invade his expression, but he blinked, and it faded.

Diana placed her fists on her hips, elbows akimbo. "You and I are always frank with each other, so I ask you outright: is there anything Major Bradley might hold over your head that could affect the standing of the entire family?"

"Did he tell you that?"

"You evade the question."

"You spoke to him last night, did you?"

"It was he who spoke to me in a crowded room where I could not march my partner to the opposite end of the ballroom to avoid him. I didn't seek him out. If that's what you mean. I thought it politic for you that I didn't give him 'the cut direct.' I'm waiting for an answer."

"He's the prince of liars."

"That's the devil."

"I do not differentiate between the two."

"That's strong. He was your friend."

"Not for a long time...in fact, never. I put up with him for the sake of his family. Eden spoke to you about him, did she not?"

"Yes, but you may beat about the bush all you wish, I'm focused on my question and shall not leave without an answer."

"No, there's absolutely nothing he can know about this family that can adversely affect any individual in it in any way."

The way he said it sounded oddly dull to Diana, almost as if memorized. "Why did you not say that in the first place?"

"Then I should not have determined those things about you that I did."

"What things?"

"Nothing bad. Have you further reason for bearding me in my den? I have business..."

"You always have business. I'll be brief. We had planned an excursion to

Jeremy's home on Saturday. Might that be changed to the next day without fuss?"

"The girls and Eden look forward to the house party, and Jeremy has planned a gourmet supper and amusements. He'll perform a magic show. He even disclosed he's invited eligible *beaux* to escort the young hopefuls. What is it you wish?"

"Daniel invited the family to the Royal Academy of Arts for a luncheon and a showing of oils. One of his paintings is being displayed. I've seen none of his latest work."

"He has great promise as an artist. We'll see what we can do. Perhaps attend the exhibit early and briefly, skip the fare, then on to Deerdon Abby."

Diana was in her room before the thought niggled at her. Colin said Daniel had great promise as an artist. On what did he base that conclusion–the drawings and watercolors Daniel did when he was thirteen? Troubling her more was the way Colin avoided her eyes when she asked if Bradley knew some family secret. Just what was this incriminating information he'd hinted at? Did someone in the family make money illegally? Did someone murder someone? Was there a deserter in the family? She'd need to meet Bradley once more in private to quiz him. She chewed her thumbnail. She'd be disappointing her brother, but this was important. If Colin was right and Bradley was a bounder, what was to stop him from circulating rumors? Colin needed to remain above reproach in the public eye if he were to influence opinions. She must do all she could to keep the Ashton name pristine.

******

The family chose to view Daniel's painting before riding on to Jeremy's home for the rest of the weekend. Lord Edmunds' group slowly ascended the long spiral staircase of New Somerset House. When Eden halted on one of the decorated landings to appreciate the smoothness of the wooden handrail and gaze down at the mesmerizing curl of cantilevered stone stairs and wrought iron railings below them, Colin was the attentive husband. He hinted to Eden that none would take it amiss if she preferred to go back and remain in the carriage. "I'll go with you. We intended to hurry the viewing anyway. The young people can go upstairs."

Eden shook her head. "I merely stopped to take in the architectural flourishes. I'd not miss Daniel's showing for the world."

As they drew close to the painting Daniel indicated on the crowded wall of the conservatory, Diana squinted to devour the subject. Her imagination exploded. All breath was suspended as she examined it. The Italian back street scene was shaded and dark with a shaft of sunlight falling upon a small dirty boy in torn clothing sitting against a decaying stucco wall. He was holding a kitten to his face and relishing the softness of its fur. The eyes of the child were disproportionately large in his gaunt face. The expression might almost be shock. He seemed to look far beyond the viewer into an even more miserable world without hope. Still, there was innocence and beauty in the child as well. This little one, who should have been enjoying a game with friends on a sunny lawn, had seen too much and eaten too little to have the energy to move. Yet he'd found something to cherish, even if only for a moment.

Daniel stood close to Diana. "When I saw him huddled like that, I thought the kitten was his only friend in the world. I remembered how he felt."

A piercing wail from Diana brought Daniel's brows to his hairline as his head pulled up and away from the outburst. He began to babble. "What in heaven's name? What happened? Did I say something wrong? Are you in pain?"

Diana saw her brother staring in astonishment at her. What must he be thinking? She broke down and sobbed louder. Eden's arms encircled her. Colin handed her his handkerchief. Bystanders turned their heads from regarding the paintings to scowl at the girl.

After several choked moans and much throat clearing and nose blowing, Diana controlled herself and apologized to all present. "It struck me there are millions of children like the one in the painting, starving while I and the whole *bon ton* have copious amounts of the best foods served to us three or more times a day. I read in the Courier of a boy who was put on a convict ship bound for Australia for stealing two plain handkerchiefs. The child screamed and cried for his Momma as he was dragged in chains up the ramp." As she said this, her voice broke, and she had to apply the kerchief again. Lifting her eyes, she noticed other attendees gaping at her. She glared back at them and increased the volume of her voice. "How is this tolerated in a country of people who call themselves Christians? Would Christ hang a child for stealing two handkerchiefs to sell to buy bread? Dear sweet God, what have we done to your world? Dear Lord, why do you tolerate us?" Eden and Colin soothed her and walked her down the stairs and out of the building. There'd be no repast at this venue for the family. Jeremy would feed them soon enough.

On the steps of the museum, Diana hid her face in her brother's greatcoat. "Forgive me. I'm such a baby, Colin. It's not like me to bawl in public that way. I've shamed you."

"No worries about me. Crying is not a weakness; it's a sign of compassion, of humanity. Man's cruelty to mankind is something we all wrestle with, Diana," Colin told her. "Christ himself became frustrated with the selfish stupidity of mankind, asking, 'How long shall I suffer you?' Injustice is hard to fathom, and it's everywhere. Why do you think I so often neglect my family to serve on welfare boards and campaign for the causes I do? I could never find a moment's peace if I didn't feel I was doing my best to right the wrongs that I can."

Diana lifted reddened eyes to his face. "But news of my outrageous behavior will be bandied about. Eden's mother told me I must be careful not to cause comment in London. She said my behavior reflects on you."

"One cannot live one's life in fear of what others will think. I could never stand up to speak at Whitehall if I thought that. Knowing what you believe and standing by it is the far superior attitude."

"Why doesn't God destroy the evildoers with a bolt of lightning? Why does he allow evil at all?"

"Now that's a question for the ages, for people far wiser than I. I know we must trust God that he knows what he's doing, and that he wants only the best for us. He created us all out of love for a purpose. I recall a long discussion you and Eden once had about free will. That love cannot be forced. God will not force people to love him by loving others. And God can use adversity to cause us to question the lures of this world for the good of our souls. We must strive to determine his will in our lives, no matter what affects us. If we can do that, we can soar."

Daniel had followed Diana's family outside. He stood close by as Colin spoke with his sister. Diana turned to him expectantly, and her brother stepped away. Daniel placed a hand on her upper arm, gave a squeeze, then promptly pulled his hand back. "I wish I could console you, embrace you, but–propriety. I'm horrified it was my painting that brought all this out in you but pleased that you're so sensitive. My art instructor told me a good painting must evoke an emotion in its viewer. I certainly didn't intend to induce this torrent of feeling in you. Your brother's advice is sound, Diana. I was proud of your reaction. I thought you were brilliant."

Colin sent a footman for his coach and gathered the young ladies to continue to Jeremy's estate. Diana asked Colin if she might speak with Matthew privately as they waited. Eden's brother had elected to stay in London and had offered to take Judith home. It was Judith's day off on Sunday, and she had asked if she might see her family.

Diana drew near Matthew; Judith dutifully followed. "Do me the favor of being candid with me, Matthew. Is Major Bradley a friend of yours? I saw you speaking with him at the ball last night."

"I tolerate him, but he approaches me. I cannot admire the man–his values greatly oppose mine. I encounter him when I haunt the Horse Guards seeking commissions. Bradley lurks about pretending to sympathize with young fellow officers, but he has some hidden scheme. I don't trust the man. I overheard Lord Audley tell Eden he refuses to give his brother money since Bradley is a wastrel. He gambles for high stakes regularly at White's. Yet, he constantly sports some new acquisition: his high-flyer Phaeton and pair, a jewel-encrusted snuff box, a solid gold toothpick, and he's seen at all the clubs. Where he finds his blunt is a mystery. The man insinuates himself on me each time I try to pass him on the street." Matthew halted his words and glanced beyond Diana. "Was there something you wanted, Judith?"

Judith blushed red and stepped back, "No, sir. Pardon me, sir. I was too close."

"No harm done," Matthew offered, though his expression remained guarded.

As the family boarded their carriage, Mr. Rhodes arrived with a group of young lads and one lady. Diana waived, and he closed the distance between them. "Lady Diana, well met."

"Mr. Rhodes, have you come to see Eversley's painting?" she said.

"The very reason. I bring my Academy chums as well, though they may be more drawn by the banquet than the artwork. Students are ever hungry."

Diana chuckled, tilted her head and asked archly, "The charming young lady attends the institute as well?"

"Don't look surprised. Women are welcome to visit the Science Academy for lectures and demonstrations, though they're not allowed to comment or ask questions–something I don't agree with. I've met several females who hold forth very shrewdly on matters of science, present company included."

"Have you now? I should adore to continue this conversation, but family awaits." Diana took the gloved hand of a footman, deftly avoided a particularly fresh horse dropping, and stepped lightly up into the Edmunds' barouche.

Matthew approached Rhodes and asked him to remain a moment to discuss something before entering Somerset House. Mr. Rhodes nodded and waived his comrades on into the exhibit. Daniel left with them. Matthew waived to the street boy who held the ribbons of his horse to bring his curricle closer. He turned to Judith. "If you will do me the goodness to wait patiently in the carriage, I'll take you home presently."

As Judith climbed up, Matthew led Rhodes a few steps away, out of hearing. "You're a man of Science, Rhodes. Diana speaks well of you. If you hear of a lecture on a certain subject to be held at the Academy, might you get word to me in time for me to attend?"

"Unquestionably, Colonel Barrett. The subject?"

Matthew cleared his throat and glanced away but forced his gaze back to the kind brown eyes of Mr. Rhodes. "I'm interested in anything to do with opium, especially how to withdraw from its spell."

"Always a timely topic, I would think," Rhodes answered, no hint of censure in his voice. "I know of nothing soon. A man spoke a few weeks back of the dangers of trying to stop the habit on one's own. Cannot recall his name at present. I'm sure it's in my notes. He was fortunate to find an Indian doctor who had knowledge of the powers of opium. The doctor and a very burly servant stayed with him in a secluded cottage by the sea, which he rented on the doctor's advice. His amount of the black drop was slowly curtailed. The two men attended him unceasingly to encourage him, talk him out of falling back, observe him, and restrain him when necessary. He believed he never could have left the stuff off without their help."

Matthew nodded. "I'd be most grateful to meet that man, if it could be arranged."

"I'll do my best to discover his whereabouts. I've seen him at the school once or twice since," Rhodes said. The men shook hands and parted. Rhodes ran up the steps and through the bricked arcade entrance of New Somerset House.

******

In the curricle, Matthew told Judith he would not mind dropping her at her personal home. "As the family is to be at a friend's estate for the next three days, you will not be needed."

"I thought I would only get my Sunday half-day off."

"Lord Edmunds felt you might enjoy extending the visit to your family."

Judith demurred, telling Matthew she'd fear for his life if he were to arrive in her neighborhood in the open carriage in his stylish clothing. "Too many people there blame the quality for the high price of bread."

Matthew smiled conspiratorially. "I'm willing to take my chances, and it will save you a deal of walking."

"I'm truly concerned for your welfare, sir, but also admit Cook promised to make me up a basket of stale bread and remainders to bring home."

Matthew offered to stop at the shops in Covent Garden and pick up groceries.

"I can't afford that, and I'll not have you pay for it, sir. Take me back to the townhouse as agreed if you please. I ..."

"As you wish." Entering the streets of Mayfair, Matthew thought he caught a glimpse of Major Bradley and a titian-haired light-skirt turning a corner out of their sight. He noticed Judith's chin rise as she also watched the couple.

"An acquaintance of yours, Judith?"

A pair of frightened brown eyes turned to him. "Why do you say that?"

"The length of your interested gaze and the fact that you stopped speaking mid-sentence."

"I could swear that was Lissa. A bosom-friend who once lived on my street. I only ever seen one girl with that long, curly, bright red hair, and that was Lissa. Looked like her shape, too. But the clothes was too fine for her. Last time I seen her, Lissa could barely find food enough to eat. She could only dream of a outfit like that. I always wondered what happened to her after the typhus took my ma and Lissa's ma and pa. I once heard..." Judith clamped her mouth shut as her cheeks flushed.

Matthew pulled the ribbons back to allow a mail coach to cross the intersection. He noticed Judith's hands wringing. "You heard..."

"I only heard, and Pa says gossipin's a sin."

"Yes, but you seem worried. At times, we need to share the burden with one other to lighten it."

"Someun' tol' me Lissa was took in by a kindly woman who turned out to be a abbess that kept her prisoner and sold her to men to entertain in her cell. I've prayed it's only rumor. A sweeter child I never known."

## CHAPTER FIFTEEN

Mrs. Fitzwarren and Cook packed a basket with a few things that wouldn't spoil. There were jars of preserves, loaves of bread, fresh apples, sweet biscuits, and a chunk of fresh meat from the ends of a roast.

"You're certain the family won't mind?" Judith asked. "This is too much."

"His lordship'd most likely tell me to add to it," the cook said.

"Hope I can keep this hidden from them who'd take it from me afore I get home." Judith lifted the heavy basket with effort and put it down again.

"Wait a minute, dearie. Perhaps I can get you a lift." Mrs. Fitzwarren sent a footman with a message for a tumbril owner she knew. The man happened to be delivering a pianoforte across the street. After hearing the address was in Little Ireland, Thurgood said he'd be pretty worn out after the job was over. When the footman told Thurgood tea and cakes awaited him, he sent word he'd be only too happy to take Judith to her home once he concluded his work. It was not too far from his own digs. It was late afternoon by the time he finished getting the apparatus in the house and where the family wanted it. More time was spent visiting with Mrs. Fitzwarren and helping himself to four pastries and three cups of tea with sugar. Then they were off to Judith's home.

A half-mile away, the area of St. Giles announced its whereabouts with its distinctive smells of open cesspits and sewers and the everlasting mildew and uncollected garbage. As the tumbril approached the maze of close alleyways and gin shops, Thurgood shifted the ribbons to his left hand and reached below him to grab a sturdy piece of lumber he kept for protection. Judith saw the action and approved. She wished she'd thought to remove her redingote when several slatterns called out to her they'd "give some pretty pence for that there fancy clothing." Judith thanked Thurgood endlessly for the ride and told him to halt only long enough for her to jump down at the next corner. His carriage was too large to get down her alley. He did as she said, leaving her off by a two-story crumbling brick building. The minute her feet hit the cobbled stone; she ran into the darkness of the rookery.

Judith set her basket down in front of her and hefted a rotted wood door on its hinges to open it. She called out, "It's me, Judith." Violet crept out from her dim corner, and Toby lifted the sack from his face as he lay on his pallet on the floor. Little Violet's blondish hair was sparse. Inscribed by the dark half-circles of worry, hunger, and loss of sleep beneath them, her eyes appeared twice their size. The two children looked with wonder at the food treats peaking from the basket.

Judith set the basket on the only table in the room. "Where's Pa?"

Toby shifted on his side and propped his head up with a hand. "He got extra work guardin' a new grave tonight."

Judith tore a baguette in half and placed the halves on two slabs of wood the family used for plates. On the bread, she portioned a small amount of the beef. "Eat only this much now so your stomachs won't ache from stretching. The meat must be eaten by tomorrow so it won't rot. I'll give you more of the roast later before you go to sleep. I need newspaper or a rag to wrap a bit of meat and cheese and bread in to take to Pa."

"Must you go now? I gets scared at night," little Violet whimpered.

"I won't be long. Toby's here with you."

Violet looked at her with a trembling lip. Toby lay on his mattress of leaves stuffed under rags. He could barely stand. He'd be no help defending her. She'd have to defend her brother if a thief or worse burst in. "Times, we hear people yellin' somethin' dreadful. The men sound so mean. They get drunk and sings too. Then we try not to laugh, or they'll know we're here. Once I heard a woman scream and scream. It was awful."

"I know, Violet. I wish I could help you. I used to keep that big, heavy skillet by me for protection when Papa had to work nights. Can you lift it?"

Violet tried to heft the iron pan, but it was unwieldy in her thin sticks of arms.

Judith pulled a dusty rag out of the window, saying, "I'll bring this back as soon as I gets the dinner to Papa. I don't have to go home 'til Monday morning, so I can stay here three nights with you. You'd best put the basket in the darkest corner with that board over it to keep the rats off it 'til I get back."

Judith rushed back out the door to avoid hearing her sister's whining complaints. As she made her way to the graveyard, she wished she could give little Violet and Toby something warm to wear like her new wool redingote. Her ladyship had bought it just for her on their first shopping excursion together. Judith had marveled at the thickness and softness of it, but especially at the cherry red color. Lady Diana had told Judith the color would make her easier to find in a crowd. If she gave the coat to Violet, her ladyship would notice and think she wasn't grateful or that she was careless. She might have her turned off for it. Judith approached the rusted iron entrance of the graveyard, crossing herself several times for luck. She was not afraid of the ghosts who hung about it. She feared the resurrection men who haunted it. They were often the lowest forms of life. But hunger made people where they couldn't think straight sometimes, and it made them willing to do things they wouldn't normally be willing to do.

A burly figure moved among the graves. Judith's heart lurched before she recognized her father's shape. He came close and took her bundle as he closed his arms about her for a hug, saying all in the action. He held up the parcel and raised an eyebrow in question. Judith nodded. Mr. Leeds lifted a corner of the rag, walked back to the fresh mound of dirt he'd been hired to guard, and fell into a seated position on the clipped lawn. After stuffing a wad of the beef into his maw, he mumbled, "If you stole this food or that cloak there, don't tell me. I'd not want to think bad of you."

"I didn't; I swear. Cook gave it to me since I was to be home a few days. 'Twere her suggestion. She packed it. The family is at a house party and don't need me. And her ladyship as I's guardin' give me the cloak. She said she don't want me to catch my death, and the color would be easy to spot if I got away from her in a crowd. Be alert, Papa. I heard her ladyship's uncle tell her he suspects Major Bradley of wicked dealings. He says Bradley keeps coming up with extra money for fine things from somewhere and it's not the card tables and it's not his brother."

"We know where it's from," Mr. Lees grunted. "I'll get word to 'im. Never seen 'im meself. Cutter says Bradley told 'im to find him a different place 'further away from town to hide the bodies in before they're sold,' so he means to keep the business goin'. Seems some gangs is claimin' his spot near Guy's. Peculiar thing, though: Bradley told Cutter he wanted it close to town, but far enough from neighbors so if somebody screamed bloody murder, 'twouln't be heard.' Is he thinkin' a corpse can scream?"

Great bumps of gooseflesh bristled Judith's arms. "If it gets out what Bradley's doing, you'll be involved too. I don't care if that man goes to jail, but what'll become of us if you do?"

"He's quality. They're above the law. And it ain't a jailin' offense, Judith. Pillory, maybe. It's the fam'ly takes it out on resurrection men. Anyway, Bradley works through Cutter an' others. Don't get his own mits dirty. Now I'm thinkin' if I warn 'im, an' he stops sending his brutes out here nights, he'll not be handin' me part of a cut that isn't. Better I keep that message to meself."

"But I'm supposed to report to him all I can about the family's goings on."

"I'll tell Cutter about them bein' out of town and such. Bradley don't need to know everything."

"He give me the characters that got me my position at Lord Edmunds' place. He told me what to say. He give me the money for the clean clothes and had his tiger take me there. If I don't deliver, he'll get me sacked. I likes the family. I likes my position."

"Don't worry. What he don't know won't hurt 'im. I gotta keep 'im happy, too. Your brother's medicines and the rent for that pit we sleep in is costing me more than I earn as a gravedigger. These extra grave watching jobs is fewer an' fewer what with them cast iron coffins and markers sellin' so good now. Most people here can't afford 'em at least. I hates leavin' Violet alone at night, but helpin the resurrection men is the best I been able to do. I prays the whole time I'm here God'll forgive me and protect my innocent babies."

"As soon as quarter day comes 'round, I'll give you everything they pay me. They feed me and clothe me and give me a bed. Don't really need money." Judith watched her father eat awhile before she got up the nerve to say, "I'll keep my ears open for a job for you with the family or their 'qaintances. I'll never quit worryin' 'bout you 'til you don't have to dig up bodies no more."

Leeds shrugged a shoulder. "Stiffs don't bother me. They don't feel nothin'. Left where they're planted, they'll just rot to slime. Usin' 'em for science this way makes 'em worthwhile a little longer. The medic students learn all about a body's insides by seein' and feelin'. Can't learn no other way. An' if the body's still sportin' a bit of jewelry, why that'll feed a number a deservin' poor mouths."

"What about the family of the dead man? What if they find out he's gone?"

"Not likely. They takes 'em the same night they're planted and fills in the hole right then. Family that does come back to visit don't usually come for a time. All they see is a nice mound a grass."

"What about them that puts trip guns around the site?"

"They slows us down all right. An' if family posts watchers till the corpse is too far gone to use, we can't dig any near it till there's no more guards. It ain't all diggin'. Bradley knows a guy at the workhouse who tells him when a pauper dies that ain't got no fam'ly. He tells Cutter to get some'un to show up and claim the body afore it's buried, sayin' their kin to it."

Reaching for the emptied rag Leeds held out to her, Judith promised, "Next time, perhaps I can bring more bread from the house and maybe more things in jars, too. The housekeeper put a jar of apricots in and a jar of pickled feet. The other would have been thrown out. The bread is spent, and the meat was from last night, so it'd go off before the family returned.

Cook don't resurrect the bread with water. Just bakes new every morning."

Her father nodded. "Get back to your brother and sister. Leastways I won't have to worry about them bein' alone tonight."

## CHAPTER SIXTEEN

Jeremy still wore a black armband, though it'd been three years since his wife's death. Lord Partington stood beside him while the guests arrived in the great hall at Deerdon Abbey. "It's past time, Jeremy. None would condemn if you dispensed with that band."

"I'd censure myself to forget her so quickly. Nor do I wish to raise hopes in any maiden's hearts."

Lady Chadwick, whose ears always pricked up when a person's voice was lowered to a whisper, injected herself into the gentlemen's conversation with her braying voice. "Do you not wish to give little Sandra a new mother?"

Jeremy gave no indication of annoyance at the masked advice. "Sandra thrives with her nurse, her nanny, the staff, and me."

Faith swallowed the sour taste that rose to her throat. Standing behind Lady Chadwick, she heard all. Mr. Blake was such an honorable and sensitive man, wise and gentle. He might never get over his first wife. There were men who didn't. She was seven and twenty. Three more years and the bloom would be completely off the rose; she would take her place on the shelf. Would he find himself yearning for a new wife before that? Could she do anything to hurry him along, other than pray? Had he meant her to hear that conversation? Had it been rehearsed to warn her against him? Had she been too forward, touching his arm like that at the bookstore and offering him advice? Had she frightened him away? Faith's face burned, and energy drained from every muscle. She glanced up the grand staircase and wondered how she would manage climbing it to get to her cell and bed. She wished she were already there.

Lord Partington offered Faith his arm. "You must be fatigued from your journey."

"Where are my manners?" Jeremy announced. "Please allow John and Martha to show you all to your appointed rooms where you may rest if you like until we dine."

******

The first evening at Deerdon Abbey, Diana couldn't wait to talk with Daniel. They would be under the same roof. Surely, she could find time alone with him here. At their last meeting, he'd accused her of being pushing. It hurt to think he might see her in the same light that she saw Hope or her Aunt Chadwick. She wrote down some things to speak of so he'd see she was not unrelenting. She'd ask him about his trip to Italy. He must have some stimulating observations on the customs and attitudes of the people. As she considered what to say, she thought of his painting. It really was superior. It had made such an immediate impact on her. Could he use his talent to sway the opinions of the masses with a stroke of his brush rather than the political pen? Why not do both? She wanted to encourage him about his calling. His birthright gave him every advantage and power. How could she be a queen of the political scene if her husband was a recluse? She must consider a natural opening that didn't sound forced, didn't sound as if it was all she thought of.

Daniel arrived for dinner but was not seated near her. When they gathered for coffee afterwards, he stood in the doorway, listening to his sister and then Faith as they played the piano. By giving him her profile, and casting a glance his way intermittently, Diana caught him gazing directly at her. What was he thinking? Did he find her so greatly altered? Had he lost his fascination for her? There was no smile on his face, but that was no matter. His face always assumed a solemn expression when at rest. She turned to Jeremy, seated next to her. "Call upon Colin to play," she said *sotto voce.* Daniel could promptly fill Jeremy's vacated seat. Surely, he looked for such an opening. As Faith finished her performance, Jeremy jumped from his seat to entice Colin to play the pianoforte. Diana collected her wits and waited for Daniel to approach. No one came. Perhaps he needed encouragement. She turned to smile at him and lifted her fan to embolden him with a message. He was gone. She looked about the room. He was nowhere. *Does he want me to follow him? That would cause comment. And I have no idea where he went.* When Lady Chadwick made a remark to her, she was forced to re-enter the world. "I regret, Aunt, I was not attending. What did you ask?"

With all the maidens gathered about her, Lady Chadwick happily recalled her own long-ago debut. She spoke in glowing terms of the routes and balls and her search for a perfect beau. At one-point, waxing poetic of the young men at her come-out, she remembered the departed Lord Audley as a charismatic young man, so gay and delightfully handsome and tall, such a gentleman in every way. He had all the ingenuous young girls casting their lures at him as their hearts fluttered fast within them. "I believe he was quite taken with your mother for a time, Diana." Aunt Chadwick admitted she'd been inclined the former Lord Audley's way too until she met her future spouse, Lord Chadwick, at a wedding. The old woman's face glowed as she revisited her younger life. Diana could almost see past the great neck folds, blotched pale skin, and the matted false curls her aunt wore sewn to her toque–to the *jeune fille* she had once been.

******

Daniel sat hunched over a desk in his room, drawing Diana's face as fast as he could, erasing and refining until it was close to what he hoped for. He wasn't hungry for breakfast. He was never hungry if he was creating. When his valet distracted him by brushing down a coat, he forced himself to set aside the drawing and allow the man to finish dressing him. He must put on his best houseguest manners and go down to table. At least Diana would be there to study further.

Hearing a knock at his door, Daniel called, "A moment, please." He yanked open the desk drawer, tossed the drawings inside, and slammed it. "*Entre Vous.*"

"It is merely I," Thomas said. "Good, you're dressed. I was afraid you'd forget to eat."

"I'll force myself."

"Excellent. You were missed last night... by more than one. May I ask something?"

"Ask away."

"I'm confused. I thought you had a *tendre* for a certain lady in the present gathering. Is disappearing after dinner an artifice to inflame her regard?"

"You know it isn't."

"Then, why?"

"I had something to do, and I'm reconsidering my relationship with her."

Thomas' eyes widened. "Truly?"

"She's grown so beautiful and captivating; her esteem would be wasted on one such as I. It would be beauty and the beast all over again. She's destined for better things."

"But the beast was a prince in the end."

"Sadly, I am not. Or I can only play the prince by withdrawing."

"You're mistaken about yourself, Daniel. You must let her know your thoughts. Diana was hurt when you left the group early."

"How could she have missed me? She never gazed my way while I was there."

"Everyone knows a young lady cannot look at one she is fascinated by without causing speculation in the company. Diana is merely being prudent. I'm starving. Let's go."

"You vanished last night," Diana said as Daniel approached with his plate of kippers.

A one-sided grin stole over his face. "You missed me?"

"The conversation was flat without you."

He snorted. "It would've been flatter still with me. I never know what to say in exalted company."

"There are few more exalted than a future marquis, and you are always in your father's company, it seems."

"And I'm always tongue-tied there, so it proves my point."

"Thomas is to set up a bow and arrow trials course, and Jeremy prepared a scavenger hunt to end in the maze. Will you join us when all is ready?"

"If you wish, Diana."

"I do wish."

Though he sat next to her, all his attention seemed on his food.

******

Gathered in the courtyard, the younger set of the house party dared each other to take a spin on Jeremy's velocipede. Faith, Hope, Diana, Daniel, Thomas, Lady Serena, Mr. Dawson, and Lord Fildes were all there to goad each other on. Thomas tried it first. Though he wobbled a bit, he blamed his unsteadiness on the cobblestones and the fact it was made taller to fit Mr. Blake's height. "It's easy. Try it!"

Lord Fildes bravely took the handlebars.

The older participants of the house party remained inside, where it was comfortable. By the French casement doors on the first floor, Lord Partington and Jeremy Blake spoke of books, botany, and biology as they watched the guests in the courtyard below. Then Jeremy praised the virtues of Miss Faith Barrett to his younger friend and ordered him to join those gathered outside and approach her forthwith. Partington shrugged, bowed, and left the room.

Jeremy turned back to his position to gaze out at Faith examining his velocipede. Colin's voice beside him made him flinch.

"I'm surprised to see you watching instead of leading the merriment as usual. What holds you back, Jeremy?"

"I could ask you the same."

"My wife's interesting condition causes me to tarry. But the device your guests are trying out is yours, and I asked first."

"I've become cautious in my maturity. I've decided to leave the young maidens to their *beaux* and not confuse the issue."

"Care to expand?"

"Lately, I've become aware my customary habit of enjoying pleasant teasing banter with pretty young ladies may have inadvertently ignited an unwelcome spark of regard in a green girl."

"Anyone I know?" Repressed mirth gleamed in Colin's eyes.

Sliding his glance to take in Colin's aspect, Jeremy scowled. "It's not an item for jest. I've put in place a plan to rectify the situation, and I intend to be more guarded in the future."

"Then all of Jeremy shall dwindle. You must admit, you've not been your genial self in an age. I miss the old, reckless Jeremy."

In answer, Jeremy shrugged and breathed an extended sigh. "At times, I miss him, too."

******

At dawn's first light, Jeremy and his footmen had spent several hours setting up a scavenger hunt. It was to be ready before the guests came down to breakfast, so no one would see where things were being hidden. The host had placed tokens in the ground cover around the courtyard lamp, scattered them on the seat of a swing by the lake, propped them on a window ledge hidden behind wisteria, and tossed them in a small beached boat. Then Jeremy hung tokens among the clipped yew in the maze and thrust them between the fins of a metal carp spurting water in the pond in the center of the rose garden. Finally, he placed them in the upturned hand of a marble Greek goddess who guarded the folly on the rise. Along with each group of tokens was placed a biscuit jar holding the clues to the next set of tokens. The last group of tokens was to be found in the maze. He'd spent an age writing the clues.

Jeremy called the participants to gather around him and handed them slips of paper to write their names upon. As each person handed him their name, the host grandly placed the slip in the appropriate hat for the gents or bonnet for the ladies. He deftly used his magician's trickery to hide two sets of the paper slips in his sleeves, secretly depositing them at the end in such a way that Lady Chadwick, who picked the names out of the hats, was unaware the game was rigged. Jeremy easily maneuvered her ladyship to choose Diana and Daniel to partner each other in the hunt. He did the same for Faith and Lord Partington. As Faith and her partner eagerly considered the first riddle and hurried to the place they hoped it indicated, Jeremy gazed after them. He'd chosen this friend specifically for Faith. They were made for each other. He cared deeply about both. They were both shy, warm, intelligent and circumspect to a fault. Jeremy had become uncomfortable to be around Faith. Her gentleness astonished him. His desire to protect arrested him each time he saw her. He couldn't tell why. She appeared to need protection more than the others. She seemed to have preserved her innocence and wonder more than others had, and that was always a good thing to protect. Surely these were blameless, fatherly feelings in him. Why did they not feel fatherly? Faith was not a child. She was old enough to be Sandra's mother.

Jeremy cleared his throat and announced he would watch the proceedings from the window above to determine which couple arrived at the final spot first. He wandered inside and up the stairs, taking up his position at the window and watching the progression of the game. His eyes were following Faith's graceful form when Colin came over to him.

Colin raised a brow and inclined his head close to Jeremy. "Your face, old man. Could you be blushing?"

Jeremy briefly glanced skyward. "I admit to having just played a bit of the matchmaker, and it's embarrassing to recognize my willingness to interfere in two lives in such a way."

"Sometimes, the way of love can use a little boost," Colin encouraged.

******

Lord Partington opened the biscuit jar and retrieved a slip of paper. Resealing the jar, he placed it back in its hiding place in the tulips beneath the courtyard lamp. Faith took a single round *papier mache* token with the date and event stamped on it and slipped it into her reticule. Partington glanced at the message on the note and frowned. "What think you, Miss Barrett? I cannot make heads or tails of it."

Faith took the note in her lace-gloved hand. "The secret lies in 'Good Will.' Oh, this is too simple for some and too hard for others." Faith looked about her to see if there were any other guests close by. " 'Good Will' is the name of the little boat Mr. Blake keeps for fishing on his lake. He says only men of 'Good Will' can fit in it with any peace."

As Faith turned to walk toward the spot on the lake that lodged the craft, Partington touched her forearm to stay her. "We're being watched by certain other contestants–your younger sister and Dawson. Perhaps a circuitous route to put them off track?"

"You're devious, Partington."

His expression fell. "I hope you do not, in fact, think so."

Faith laughed. The laugh animated her mild expression delightfully. Partington breathed a sigh. As they purposely hurried in the wrong direction, he attempted conversation. "I savored your performance at the pianoforte last evening, Miss Barrett. You're most accomplished. I enjoyed the choice of composition, as well."

"Thank you. And thank God, a neighbor taught me to play. Music transports me to an even more beautiful place than here. I can get lost in it. Time no longer exists. Friction is washed away. I suppose, for me, it's as close as I can get to heaven on Earth."

"What think you of the beauty of a garden? I dabble in botany. There's such a riot of color and exquisite delicacy in the variety of flowers and even leaves in God's creation. Heaven must be an endless field of trees and streams and flowers the like we have never seen before. Plants in all their perfection. Not a bug in sight."

"No beetles?" Faith chuckled. "We have a shadow box at home filled with beetles and moths and butterflies. Some beetles look frightening, I know, but some have such an iridescent sheen to their wing cases, one wonders if God rather favors them. The Garden of Eden is supposed to be somewhere here on Earth, well-guarded, I understand."

Partington's head drew back. He darted a glance at his partner's face. "Do you jest about the beetles? Oh, I'll give you butterflies. On second thought, I shan't. To become those fluttering flamboyant fairies of the sunlight, they first are fat caterpillars decimating the leaves of your prized anemones."

"Rather like humans before we too are transformed." Faith turned away and hastened her steps. "If we don't hurry a little more, we'll be the last to arrive home."

"Would that be such a bad thing?"

"Of course, it would cause comment."

"Mr. Blake warned me about you. He told me we might suit. All I have since garnered of you supports Mr. Blake's position."

Faith stopped in her tracks. Her smile faded, and the blood drained from her face. Her stomach clenched.

******

Lord Fredric Dawson was delighted to nab Hope for a partner after sitting next to her at dinner and being diverted by her liveliness. She was young and spirited and pretty and willing to play the coquette even with him. His chest expanded full-width as he bragged of his wealth, eligibility, and willingness to marry soon. At thirty-two, he was still young. He could still hide the thinning hair and pains of gout. "The last clue was easy," Dawson said. "This clue is senseless: 'I go back and forth, up and down, but never have I touched the ground.' "

"Don't waste your time trying to solve it; Lady Diana and Lord Eversley went that way. They're in the lead." Hope lifted her skirts enough to afford running after her sister-in-law while showing an ankle in the bargain.

*****

"Jeremy has hidden clues all over the grounds," Diana said. "Now, I understand why the elder set refused to participate. The exercise would have fatigued them greatly. Quick, we're being followed. I see the tokens on the swing and the jar of clues beneath it. We can still be out of sight as we retrieve them and take the path by the lake to decipher the next riddle."

Daniel took a paper slip and hurried after Diana. The swing was sufficiently hidden in a grove of pears in bloom. He read as they walked. " 'I have a thousand stories but cannot speak of them.' Could be the library, but Jeremy said the tokens were all to be found out of doors."

"There's a little library in the folly. It's all fixed inside with a *chaise longue* for reading away from any disturbance."

"Sounds romantic."

"It is. It's a perfect place for dreaming."

"Do you dream these days, Diana?"

"All sorts of things, mostly of my future."

"Care to divulge?"

"Foolish things. I'd like to travel."

"Italy was quite an experience. Rome is the most beautiful city I've seen so far. Every street leads to a more beautiful fountain or statue or ancient edifice. The Pantheon, the Coliseum, and St. Peter's are overpowering. I should like to return there one day."

"I was thinking of going to see the aurora borealis. Is it real, do you think?"

"I hope so. It does sound fantastic."

"It's something to look forward to. Have you any particular visions for the future, Daniel?"

"I form them yet, Diana. I know we're created for a purpose; I want to fulfill that purpose. I've come to think my time in the hands of the chimney sweep may have been meant to teach me about the unfair practices concerning child labor and even the lack of rights of women and children. I once read that a broken bone mends stronger than it originally was. I think there are broken people who mend stronger in the broken place. They can help others with similar problems because of their shared experience. I want to be involved, as your brother is, in helping the poor, especially children. I simply haven't quite decided how I shall go about it."

"Those are admirable dreams, Daniel. I'm ashamed to admit mine have been more selfish, so don't ask me to disclose them just yet. They're not fully shaped. I must work at widening their scope."

******

Later in the day, Eden sat in bed reading *Lyrical Ballads*. Her door was slightly ajar.

Faith peeked in. "In the mood for society?"

Eden placed her book face down on the counterpane that covered her. "How much and whose?"

"Just me."

The older sister's face brightened. "I'd adore it."

Faith entered and closed the door behind her. Eden shifted to swing her legs off the bed, but Faith said, "Stay. I'll pull this stool close, and we can have a comfy coze."

"I watched the scavenger hunt from the window this afternoon. It looked as if you were enjoying yourself."

"I was."

"The young man who partnered you seemed attentive."

"Lord Partington."

"Ah, yes. We've met. He and Jeremy are good friends. I've heard some particularly good things said about him. How did you two get on?"

"He finds me a suitable companion."

"Sounds promising. He's not made an offer, has he?"

"I think he would if I encouraged him."

"So soon?"

"It seems Mr. Blake has touted my virtues to him and influenced him to be partial to me."

"More important, how do you study Partington?"

"I could consider him. He seems admirable. He's intelligent and has a nice sense of humor. He's even handsome, but I doubt there could ever be a *grande passion*–perhaps a quiet love might someday grow."

"You spent time with him today only, and already you're considering him? Are you so lonely you're ready for a 'quiet love that may someday grow?' Ready to compromise? Yet, a *grande passion* may not be all it's reputed to be. In fact, some may be exaggerations in the mind of one of the participants. A growing quiet love may be the truer emotion."

Faith shrugged. "That's why I seek counsel. I don't know. If I discourage him, I may be casting off the very one who is my soul's partner."

"It's early days. Delay decision. Get to know him more without giving encouragement. Make a friend of him. Find out who he is inside. It takes time. Talk it over with Our Lord in prayer. Let him be your guide. Ask him to help you stay in his will. If you still feel no attraction building toward the young man, let him know without hurting him. That's what courting is all about. The good Lord knows, Colin and I thought we were at opposite ends of the poles when we met."

"And yours is such an excellent marriage."
"I think so."

# CHAPTER SEVENTEEN

Matthew lumbered clumsily and carefully down the steps as he exited the Horse Guards. The noon light caused his eyes to squint. The odor of horse droppings in the street mixed with the frying onion aroma of chophouse curled his nostrils. The din of jangling chains on carriages and of wares being called by street vendors assailed his brain. The over-friendly and overloud voice of Major Bradley greeted him, catching him off guard. "Hail fellow, well met. Leg giving you pain today, I see."

"Mm. At such times, I think I should have fared better had I had the deuced thing lopped off completely."

"I, on the other hand, had no choice. They neglected to ask what I preferred. I'm convinced those quacks relished wielding the saw and watching me squirm. You may think me mad, but I swear there are times when my lost leg throbs. I've excruciating pain from a limb that is not there."

Matthew's brow crinkled. "You're not the first man who has told me that."

"I mention it not for pity, but to show off my newest pair of goers. May I offer you a ride?" Bradley extended his hand to indicate two perfectly matched bay geldings hitched to a glowing yellow high-perch phaeton tricked out in the finest leather cushioning. A slender boy in maroon livery held the ribbons. "They're in the line of the Byerly Turk."

Matthew reluctantly gave the horses a quick going over. "They're remarkable, though I don't care for cropping the tails. The poor beasts cannot rid themselves of insects."

"But the tail does not get caught in the tracings that way."

"I know the arguments. I'd not have one of those high-perched carriages. Too dangerous by far if you attempt to turn at any speed."

"Lord, I shouldn't have thought you so skittish."

"You've had a step for your servant welded to the back. I've never seen that on a phaeton. It's a racing vehicle; doesn't a tiger slow it?"

"I don't intend to race it. I only use it around town. I merely like the look of it–the lines. I like sitting high and looking down on everyone else."

Bradley chortled at his own joke. "And I don't care to leave it to just any street urchin at hand."

"What amazes me is where you find the blunt to buy such exorbitant trifles. I was there at White's the night you lost your entire subscription compensation, so you've not invested that. Lord Audley mentioned you have no funds from relatives, especially him."

"Why, Captain Barrett, I had no idea you were so anxious about my living."

"I confess to jealousy rather than concern. The constant need to economize can make one feel that way. Half pay is little more than a jest."

"I hardly think, with your connections, you need to rein in."

Matthew glared. "I prefer to be my own man."

Bradley grinned and raised a hand to ward off the anger. "Be serene. I have friends in high places. I see by your mien you would add 'low places' as well, but you're too much the gentleman. No answer? Strong and silent, eh? Well, in reply, I've devised a secret system to make money which is doing extremely well. I could use a partner if you're interested. I'll not bore you with the details, but there exists a surplus of young green blades only too eager to part with their coin for an older, wiser gentleman who can steer them to certain clubs or purveyors of certain difficult-to-find goods."

Matthew scowled at the pavement. "Fools desperate enough to allow you to take them under your leathery wings are to be pitied."

Bradley hooted. "Good one, Barrett. Leathery wings. Haven't seen you around Horse Guards lately. I suppose you're called upon to squire your sisters about. I attempt to sidestep meeting them. Edmunds seems to prefer it that way. Can't understand that. Are there any amusements I should shun this week: routes, balls?"

Matthew eyed him without lifting his head. "I'm not privy to the calendars of my sisters and brother-in-law. I'm not expected to squire the girls about, though I do often enjoy filling that obligation. I make my own appointments with my own friends. Please excuse me. I don't care to be late for one now." Matthew turned and limped away.

Bradley's eyes narrowed as they followed Matthew's progress. *How dare he judge me! A pastor's cub who never tasted a vile life like mine.* Vivid pictures attacked his open eyes. Memories of being gagged and bound by his own father and locked in a closet so his nanny and father could giggle and wrestle on her bed. Being held half out the second-floor window while his father snarled at him that if he said a word about it to anyone, he'd be tossed off the roof to burst his gut open on the bricks. So many other frightening scenes fought to seize his mind. He refused to entertain them longer. He struck his boot hard with the handle of his coachwhip and called his tiger. "Noah."

The curly-haired boy brought the leads over the heads of the pair of high-steppers. As his master took the reins, the boy let down the steps so the man might use them to spring up into the Phaeton. Once Bradley mounted the dangerous carriage, his tiger jumped up onto the little landing on the back. He rode standing on the metal square wherever the major went. When Bradley halted, Noah would jump down and hold the ribbons until his master returned.

Before giving his horses the office, Bradley barked back to his tiger, "Take a tip from me, Noah. If you want to get on in life, never tell 'em the truth. Always tell 'em what they want to hear."

******

Diana had arranged with Daniel's family and her own that they would attend a musical evening. Yet when all arrived without Daniel, Diana panicked. He was snubbing her. How could he forget if he genuinely cared about her? She thought of no one else. As the guests took their seats to enjoy the soprano's offerings, Diana maneuvered a chair next to Thomas. She promptly quizzed him before the music began. "Is Daniel unwell?"

"He should be here soon. He forgot to get ready. I reminded him before we left." Thomas turned to Diana. "He puzzles me as well these days. I know he hides something before I enter his room. I hear him close his dressing room door each time I knock. Then he stands in front of it and bids me enter."

"Have you considered sneaking in when he's not at home?"

Thomas shook his head vigorously.

Diana sighed. "I wish he made his intentions toward me clearer. I know you can keep this between us. Should I entertain the attentions of other suitors? He forgets assignations, and when we do meet, he speaks of anything but us, and he neglects to pay me the addresses a girl needs to hear. He complimented me prettily at Almack's, so he knows how."

"I must own, it was I who coached him," Thomas said, looking shamefaced. "Daniel doubts himself, and he's mostly unschooled in conversation. He asked me for tips. He knows I study closely the way people speak. I seek to comport myself well in the eyes of my adoptive family. Our life sweeping chimneys was mostly silent, except when Daniel read penny novels to our master, Mr. Crane, and I. The sweep rarely had anything good to say to us. Paying tributes is a learned habit, Diana. I know we've enjoyed five years in the Marquis' home, but there's little praise going on there either. Perhaps you might encourage Daniel to pay you compliments by praising someone who does it well in his presence."

It made sense. How best could she arrange for Daniel to hear her being admired? Partington was good at showing appreciation, but it appeared he'd fastened his interest on Faith. She mustn't muddy that situation. Who of her other suitors could serve as the example? Major Bradley had a knack for flattering, though at times, he was effusive. No, his attentions must definitely be discouraged. Though she'd enjoyed imagining herself as a sort of advisor to him, too many had warned her away. It was too bad. He used to be a friend she looked forward to seeing.

Daniel arrived just before the soloist hit her first note. He smiled at Diana and shrugged. The seats were all taken, so he stood close by. Diana looked about her for a prospect. Baron Tattershall was known to her. He was tall and handsome and could be diverting. He was also snobbish and insincere, so she'd previously avoided him. However, he could be counted upon to pour tributes over her if she came near. A plot formed in her mind. At the end of the final aria, Diana rose with the applause and began to put her plan into action.

Daniel was deep in discussion with several acquaintances as Diana approached with Thomas and Serena at her side. He turned his eyes from his friends and looked about to speak to her, when Diana smiled brightly past Eversley at Tattershall, regaling a bevy of female hopefuls.

The baron took the bait and stepped toward Diana. He reached for her gloved hand and bowed over it. "Lady Diana, allow me to tell you how much I approve your ensemble tonight. The cut and drape of the crème silk you've chosen complements the translucent hue of your too perfect face and shows your figure to advantage. The vine tendril design worked down the center of your dress, is that silk thread?"

*Gad, he spreads it on with a trowel.* Diana fought back a horselaugh. "It is."

"Your hairstyle is refreshing; it looks so natural. A la Grecque?"

"A variation. You are certainly well-versed in fashion, Tattershall."

"It amuses me to be."

"Your knowledge must undoubtedly please the ladies."

Those gathered about the baron giggled and nodded. One perturbed female laid a possessive hand on his forearm and leaned in to whisper something to him.

Diana took the moment to turn sharply and move to Daniel's side. She smiled at his friends and commented, "Tattershall certainly knows how to turn a lady's head with tributes."

Daniel's eyes were slits. "If you so admire the fellow, you may have him. He can easily be bought since he bows only over the hands of the richest girls assembled."

Diana blinked. It was all that gave evidence to her reaction to his words. *Breathe or faint.* The company must not see the chill that crept along her shoulders. She shifted her mother's scarf up to hide the gooseflesh and backed away from the group.

Thomas moved close to Diana and whispered, "I'm so sorry. It's my fault. I forgot to heed the line in the Robert Burns poem: 'The best-laid schemes o' Mice an' Men, Gang aft agley.' "

"Don't accuse yourself, Thomas. You meant well. I meant well. I was clumsy. It's nothing. I must discover a different tactic. I've no wish to force the situation."

Thomas's eyes held hers, his brows drew together, and he frowned. "I'll explain to him it was my fault."

"Don't bother, Thomas. It's nothing."

"Perhaps it's best we don't try to improve him."

Diana looked at Thomas with love. "Probably wisest. People are always trying to improve me, and I too often resent it."

Out of the crowd, Major Bradley approached with two younger men in tow. "Lady Diana, may I tell you how lovely you look? You grow more elegant each time we meet."

Diana smiled at him. Surely, he was a changed man.

"I honestly believe you could redeem this maimed soldier's soul, teaching me to appreciate life again from your fresh viewpoint. May I present to you...." Bradley's introduction to his associates was sliced off mid-sentence. Nervously smiling, he managed to stammer, "Forgive me. I'm beckoned away directly. Come, gentlemen. Another time..." He slithered swiftly out of sight with his entourage in tow.

Eden and Colin appeared at Diana's side. She nodded to them, then turned and gazed in the departing Bradley's direction, puzzled. Redeem him. He'd mentioned something like that before. Could she sculpt him like a female Pygmalion with a male Galatea? Could she teach him to care about himself, to care for others? It was a role that appealed to her. Briefly imagining herself as rescuer, Diana shook her head. She was having a difficult enough time molding herself.

# CHAPTER EIGHTEEN

Against his better judgment, Colin gave his permission to Diana and the girls to appear at a Sunday soiree on the edge of town in a large estate. It was to be attended in Costume de Rigueur even though in the heat of early summer in the sunshine of mid-day outdoors. He prayed the day would be overcast like last year. The *fete champêtre* was to be held as a charity event for a society the Edmunds family supported. Colin rode his favorite horse, Galahad. Eden, the girls, and Judith came in the chaise. Matthew also attended, arriving in his curricle.

Though the soiree was held in the vast gardens of the Harrington estate, it proved a crush. There was something for everyone. Tea and lemonade were served in the Chinese temple by servants dressed as geisha girls. The pavilion held a full spread of foods to delight any age. Footmen stood by to serve the guests their choices on fine Spode China hand-painted with English flowers and set with a gilded Imari border. By the man-made lake sat a folly made to look like a cave-dwelling for Poseidon. It was decorated with thousands of iridescent offerings from the sea. Inside it, a full orchestra played selections throughout the day. A band of Hindu performers were juggling brass balls with great dexterity and threading beads with their tongues.

Diana didn't bother to look for Daniel. There were too many diverting amusements taking place. She avoided a rousing game of battledore for fear of sweating in her sky-blue silk gauze dress or displacing the heavily pinned curls beneath the matching capote bonnet. Hope, who thought the exercise showed off her womanly attributes, participated as Faith and Diana watched.

Partington promptly spied them there as a bee finds nectar. He persuaded the three sisters to play the more sedate game of skittles and to walk the lavender labyrinth. They stopped to watch a group of children playing hide and seek when a slender boy in maroon livery walked up to Diana and handed her a folded note.

She opened the note and scanned the words. "Lady Diana, forgive my intrusion into your delightful afternoon. I have something urgent to tell you which must not be written down. Unfortunately, I remain here on the fringes of the lawn, for my leg impedes my descent from my carriage. I'm on my way to the physician now. My tiger, Noah, will show you where I am. Your devoted servant, B."

Nodding to Noah, Judith closed ranks. She clutched her arms and glanced over the grounds. She'd met Noah on the street the day before as she stood waiting while Diana sat with her family in a coffee shop. He'd been sent to warn Judith to get news of her ladyship's next venue to his master, or her allegiance to him would be questioned, and she would suffer penalties. She told Noah about this party. She moved closer to Diana and cleared her throat. "Milady..."

Diana was focused on the note. The tiger ran back to Bradley's phaeton. She twisted her neck to look for Colin. What could cause Major Bradley to send her a missive? He never had before. Hope reached for the note, and Diana jerked it away, shoving it in her little shell-shaped bag.

"Oh my, what have we? A message from a devotee?" Hope said.

Diana scowled at her.

"If you want to see him, I can accompany you so all will be correct," Hope tempted. Faith and Partington were a few steps away, teaching an urchin how to use the Jacob's ladders the host had given the children. Diana sprinted to follow the path Bradley's servant had made through the crowd as he ran back to his master. Several friends tried to hail her, but she ignored them. Hope and Judith struggled to keep up.

Diana considered the pair of females trailing her. *I need them as witnesses and protection from unwanted advances, but they'll be a hindrance from plain-speaking if they stick too near. Bradley must be given his marching orders out of their hearing. No need to embarrass the poor man.*

Reaching Bradley's phaeton, Diana applied her fan vigorously to her face and blew an errant wisp of hair out of her eyes. "Why do you park your carriage in this manner, Major? Surely you cannot watch the proceedings turned away from them."

"Not here to watch. Not up for frivolity today, but I need to see you." His usual smirk seemed a pain-filled grimace. "I've something particular to tell you." Bradley glanced toward Hope and back at Diana to indicate the problem. His tone reversed. "What a delicious fan you display. I've seen no other to match it. What might the stone in the rivet be? The color is amazing."

Understanding this non-sequitur as a ruse to bring her close to the carriage so he could whisper, Diana stepped up to it, closed her fan and turned it in her hand, so the sparkling blue gem in the rivet was best displayed. "Tourmaline is the crystal."

"Are you quite certain? It seems a tad too brilliant for tourmaline. I fancy myself rather a good gemologist." Lifting a monocle on a chain attached to his vest pocket, he asked, "May I see it closer?" He put out his hand for the fan.

Diana turned to Judith and Hope and glared at them to wait where they were. She stretched up to the high perch Phaeton, placing a gloved hand on the leather squabs.

Bradley snatched the fan from her and brought it close to his eyes. "Someone has deceived you, Lady Diana. This is merely glass."

Surely, he was teasing, but it annoyed her anyway. "I doubt that. My brother gave it to me."

"I'll take it home where I have my loupe." He thrust the folded fan into an inside pocket.

"Major Bradley, will you not get down and stroll with me toward the party so none of the guests should be alarmed at my continued absence?"

Bradley's eyes flashed fire as he growled. "I should love nothing better than to promenade with you, my dear, but as I say, this leg is torture today. I didn't wish to mention it and distress you, but it's why I leave post-haste."

"I apologize. You seemed so gay; I had no hint you were unwell."

He glowered. "An insensitive miss cannot possibly comprehend how greatly I exert myself to ignore the pain so it won't cause another's dismay."

Diana bristled at being called insensitive; he must be in agony. She'd never seen him angry.

Bradley softened his tone and relaxed his shoulders. "My regrets, the pain speaks. If you simply mount the steps with my tiger's help and join me here in the carriage, we can talk in discreet tones. My news is imperative, I assure you."

Diana cast a glance at Hope and Judith. Judith look horrified; Hope, encouraging. Noah let the steps down, put out a hand to help Diana up, then went to the back of the phaeton to mount his post. As the boy stepped up, it caused the carriage to bounce. Bradley turned to him and commanded, "Get down. We remain here."

The major brought the folded fan out of its hiding place and presented it to Diana. "Your reward for understanding my motives so well."

Diana grabbed her favored accessory and spoke first for fear she'd lose her nerve. "I, too, have something to say."

Bradley used his left hand, which held a coachwhip, on the side of the phaeton to assist him in turning his body toward her. Judith flew onto the tiger's step. The carriage rolled from side to side. Bradley twisted backward to slash the whip's handle hard across Judith. Diana grabbed his arm, shrieking, "How dare you!?" He thrust his elbow in her face as he stood and shouted at the horses, cracking the tip of the whip above their heads. Diana fell back against the squabs with the force of Bradley's elbow and the carriage's sudden forward movement. Judith fell to the ground.

## CHAPTER NINETEEN

Noah ran after the carriage but stopped when he couldn't catch it. He picked up a rock and chucked it at a boy helping a man at a refreshment stand make ices. The boy turned, saw Noah signaling with his arms, and ran in the opposite direction to Colin. He ran so hard, he tripped as he reached the earl and fell at his feet. Colin bent to help him up.

"What is it, Turtle?"

"Bradley's tiger, milord!"

"Good God!" Colin looked in the direction the boy was pointing to see Noah and Judith running toward him from the peripheries of the lawn. He put two fingers in his teeth and whistled loudly for Galahad. The steed pulled his head up and searched the field of partying humans for his master. Colin whistled again. The horse pushed through the crowd, effectively separating the guests in waves until it stood in front of Colin. Colin sprang into the saddle and urged the stallion toward the two young servants.

"Bradley, milord!" Judith screamed. "Your sister's in his carriage. They went up that road! She didn't want to."

Lord Edmunds reined Galahad in the direction Judith had pointed and urged the animal's ribs hard. The horse bolted.

Turtle, Judith, and Noah stood bewildered. Then, as one, they raced to alert the rest of the family.

In the phaeton, Diana and Bradley fumed. Bradley tried to defuse her anger and disguise his intent. "You must know, Diana, I didn't intend this: surely not to harm anyone. Your maid and my tiger angered me. What right had they to mount the carriage? I must speak something of a delicate nature to you alone. It's none of their business. They would carry tales."

"You hurt me with your elbow! Do you think I care to listen to anything you have to say now?" Diana watched the road blur by. To jump from this high position at this great speed meant certain death. She'd wait until he slowed.

"Forgive me, Diana, please. I raised my arm to crack the whip. I had no idea it was so close to your face until I felt the resistance!"

"You whipped my maid! That was no accident."

"She wouldn't get down. I had no other chance to get you alone."

"Why are you racing now?" Bradley turned the horses' heads toward an intersecting road, and Diana swiftly let her hand dangle along the outside, tossing her shell purse out onto a bush. She hoped he didn't notice. It would be better than breadcrumbs for following her. To mask her action, she screeched, "You took that turn at full speed! Only a dunderhead would do that in this contraption! Give me those ribbons." Diana grabbed for the reins, but he shoved his shoulder in her way and held them away from her.

"Where are you taking me?"

"Away from prying eyes," he answered. Fury crept into his tone. "It's moments from here. You'll be back before you're missed. I must have my say." Bradley tugged on the left ribbon.

"You've gone far enough. Slow down. What is this lane?" Hardly a path, it was overgrown, rutted, and rock-strewn. Diana swiftly spread the sticks of her fan wide open and let it fly behind her on to the road. She allowed her beloved shawl to slide from her shoulders. It would be the last thing she could toss out.

"A pretty little clearing lies at the end of it. Silence! Sit back. I need my wits about me. The horses are new to the traces. Highfliers but startled. They've taken their bits in their teeth and insist on their own heads."

Diana glanced at Bradley's hands as they clutched the ribbons. He was not pulling back but encouraging their speed. She looked behind her to see if anyone followed: no one did. She searched up the path for limbs, which might hang low enough for her to jump up to catch. *I'll climb trees, if I must, to be out of this rig.* She poised herself on the edge of the squabs to facilitate leaping.

Then she heard the far-off voice. "Diana!"

Diana half stood and twisted to see her brother fast approaching on Galahad. "Colin!" she shouted. She turned forward and grasped at the ribbons in Bradley's hands. "Slow down, you fool!"

Bradley stood and shoved her with his shoulder. He shifted the reins to one hand and cracked the whip over the animal's heads. The phaeton swayed as the horses hurtled at break-neck speed over a trail too narrow for a team. A crumbling, stacked-stone wall came in view on the right.

"I thought your leg ached," Diana snapped.

"It does! Blazes!"

Diana spied a likely bough and prepared to spring. Bradley guessed her intention. He attempted to grab her with his right arm as he tossed the whip out of his left hand and shifted the reins from right hand to left. The wheels on the right slid into a deep rut and the carriage tipped. The horses reared and screamed at the sudden twisting of their traces. Diana leapt for the branch, and Bradley leapt for her. Both were flung from the phaeton. Diana slammed into the trunk of the tree. Bradley landed on his head beside her. The team of frightened horses ran on with the now-righted carriage.

Worse pain than she'd ever known radiated from the small of Diana's back and stabbed down her legs. She panted. Could she stand it? She looked to her right. A mass of blood and tissue flowed from the back of Bradley's head over the flat stone it lay upon. His eyes were open, though staring skyward. "My sister. You're my sister," he breathed. Then his lids fluttered, and he relaxed. Diana lost consciousness.

Colin was off his horse, knelt beside his sister, listened to her heart, and determined she was alive. He was gathering her in his arms as the Edmunds' carriage pulled up beside the scene. Matthew followed closely in his curricle. Noah, Turtle, and John Coachman scrambled down off the bench seat. Bradley's tiger opened the door and helped Judith, Faith, and Eden down the steps.

"Dear God!" Eden cried.

"She lives," Colin shouted. He had no idea how Bradley faired and could care less. From his kneeling position, Colin began barking orders. "Judith, use the carriage rug to make a soft place to lay Diana down on the chaise floor. John, drive us home by way of Mr. Long's house. Stop there and let Turtle off to fetch the physician. Matthew, oblige me and tell Lord Audley what has taken place and where Bradley is to be found."

Matthew nodded and searched for a suitable place to turn his curricle around.

Bradley's tiger volunteered to catch the major's coach horses and bring the phaeton and pair to Audley's residence. Colin asked Noah to stop at the two last turns in the road to retrieve Lady Diana's blue fan and her purse. "She treasures them and will ask after them when she wakes. When we see you, you will be greatly rewarded for your efforts today. I thank you."

Diana stirred. "Colin, it hurts."

"I'm so sorry, Diana. We must move you to the carriage. We'll be as gentle as possible. John will drive softly, too. Can you put your arms around my neck, sweetheart?"

Diana reached upwards as Colin shifted to rise with her. Her eyes closed, and her arms went limp. Colin's heart and gut clenched until bile rose in his throat. He shuddered.

John Coachman helped them up and into the coach, helped Lady Edmunds and Miss Barrett in, then helped Judith up onto the box. At last, he walked round to his side of the box, mounted at lightning speed, and drove swiftly toward town.

# CHAPTER TWENTY

Diana groaned. Eden, Faith, and Hope sat in Chippendale side-chairs drawn close to her bed on her left. Judith stood with her back pressed hard against the bedroom wall by the door, eyes wide with fear. Beads of sweat glistened across the abigail's face and discolored her dress.

Next to the physician on Diana's right, stood Lord Edmunds. His face, drained of color, shouted panic.

Mr. Long bent over Diana. When he saw her eyes flutter, he spoke. "You're on your side because you bruised your back, your ladyship. Please try not to move much. It will intensify the injury. We have built a wall of pillows to keep you immobile. How do you feel? Is there very much pain?"

Diana whimpered and took a few panting breaths.

"I'll give you something to ease the soreness now that you're conscious. Your body has been protecting and healing you by keeping you asleep."

Diana's lips moved. Her tongue touched the edges of her mouth. Long stooped closer to her face. "Say it again, your ladyship. I didn't quite catch it."

"My feet, my legs... can't feel them."

The slow downward movement of the doctor's eyelids as he attempted to hide his thoughts was almost imperceptible. Eden and Colin saw it and went ramrod straight.

"You've endured a shock to your spine. There's a contusion and much inflammation there at present." The doctor hesitated and expelled a puff of breath. His tenor was warm. "You may suffer a form of paralysis in the lower limbs until the swelling has subsided. I don't wish to alarm you, but to arm you with information. You may feel the pain of that bruise for quite some time even though you regain the ability to walk. The soreness will eventually subside completely, but we must not rush things. Don't be anxious to be up again and going and doing. You must change your entire attitude toward time. Spend it thanking the Good Lord for all he's given you with family to love you. Rest until you heal utterly."

The doctor caught Lord Edmunds' glance and faintly jerked his head to indicate he'd like to speak to him out of Diana's hearing.

"Close your eyes and rest, Diana," Colin said. "Doctor Long wants to mix something in the kitchen for you for the pain. I'll take him there now." He led the way out. Eden stood and held up one finger to let her sisters know she would just be a moment. They nodded.

******

In the library, Mr. Long tried to tell the terrified couple what to expect and what to do. "She'll need constant nursing. She'll not be able to care for her voiding needs for a time. I suggest oiled canvas or tarpaulin under the sheets for the accidents, which will undoubtedly happen. Insist she move as little as possible until I return. She may be able to avoid needing greater amounts of the medication by not aggravating the intramuscular collection of clotted blood. The body will gradually take it away if the humours are in align.

"I would there was a better preparation for this type of pain. Ether has been used, but it is too technical, difficult to administer, and unpredictable. The poppy extract I'm prescribing is excellent for a brief time, but the blood soon gets accustomed to it, demanding more and more of the philter to bring about the same relief. It has side effects as well: night terrors and torpor."

The doctor cleared his throat. "Do not misunderstand me–to attempt to take nothing and bear the pain would be as bad for her health as to rely too greatly upon the drug. I'll come back this evening to look in on her unless you feel a need to send for me sooner. I can recommend a service to provide a qualified nurse if you need one."

Colin nodded, "I'll direct my butler to the service you speak of. I want someone sent round immediately for night duty. Eden needs her rest, too. Her sisters can help out today, but they're not trained for this ..."

The surgeon's demeanor changed from serious to fatherly. He took Eden's hand and patted it. "Yes, I was about to suggest, Lady Edmunds, that you take a nice long nap–and soon. Lady Diana is in no further danger at this time."

"Don't be concerned for me," Eden said, patting her pregnant belly. "I've curtailed my engagements to give this expected one all the attention needed. I'm afraid I've put on even more weight than the last time, though I am careful. Are there any signs we should look for in Diana?"

"I'll instruct the nurses myself to pay close attention if she describes any pain in the lower extremities. They should alert you and me if that occurs, for it can be a sign of healing."

"Colin, I'll take Dr. Long to the kitchens to mix the draught. I'll nap in a few minutes, but I need to take a turn before I do. I sat much too long today."

Colin's glance was questioning, but her mild countenance reassured him. He took her hand from the Doctor and raised it to his lips. "I'll come around to your rooms in fifteen minutes, and if you're not there and halfway to slumber, the servants will be looking for you," he warned, then winked at her.

Eden approached the stairs. "You will, of course, take supper with us, Mr. Long?"

Taking the doctor's arm and grasping the rail, she descended slowly. Colin walked toward Diana's room. Before entering, though, he turned back to make sure his expectant wife reached the ground floor without incident. He had noticed her being a bit wobbly several times this week. As Eden neared the bottom of the staircase, she turned to the doctor and spoke in muted tones. Colin listened acutely. "Mr. Long, are you softening the blow? Will she ever walk? Is it possible her back was broken? The sooner we know the truth, the better. I must study how best to prepare her for that possibility."

"Lady Diana may never walk again. However, it's not possible to know for certain for a while. The spine is extremely fragile. If she complains of pain in her lower limbs, it means feeling is returning there because the spinal cord has not been broken." The doctor lowered his voice, yet it carried upward like the resonance of a boys' choir in an empty church. "The lad who fetched me told me his lordship lifted Lady Diana up without stabilizing her back. That may have made things worse. The cord may have transected completely at that time."

Eden's jaw dropped. Resting on the doctor's forearm, her fingers clenched into his flesh.

Placing a soft, hoary hand over hers, the doctor added, "Say nothing to his lordship. We'll know more positively in a months' time."

"Should we move her to our estate in the country?"

"Wait a few weeks until I can determine if it would cause more harm than good."

At the top of the stairs, Colin slunk away. He crept past Diana's door and on to his chambers. He fell upon his bed but promptly rose to run to his ewer to retch.

## CHAPTER TWENTY-ONE

Hope sat gazing out Diana's bedroom window at the darkness. It fit her morose mood. The scope of change to her situation enclosed her and compressed her. All the glamorous plans for a season would now be cast aside. Their debutante ball would be canceled. To be merry at such a time would be insupportable to the family. If she wished to secure a spouse this season, she'd have to choose from the connections they'd already made. Her society would now be shrunk to those visiting the townhouse. In her interesting condition, Eden had curtailed her excursions. She wouldn't wish to go making calls often. Matthew might be persuaded to accompany Faith and her on a jaunt or two, but he obviously didn't approve her flirting ways. He hadn't done the brotherly thing and introduced her to his many acquaintances, though he had done so for Faith in her first season. Diana's aunt seemed to enjoy society, and she was ton, though she was also a quiz. Could the elderly relative be persuaded to accompany Hope and Faith to outings? If she were treacle-sweet and flattering to Lady Chadwick at her next visit, Hope might put the idea into the old crone's bewigged head. *Diana destroyed my prospects with this stupid accident. Faith might as well don the spinster cap now.*

*I'll elope, if I must, to get out from under all the disapproving eyes in this family. But I'd rather not elope.* Even now, she'd chosen the bridal gown she would order. She envisioned being princess for a day as her family was forced to attend the ceremony at St. George's. Wouldn't that shock her mother? Her youngest daughter married better than all the others–her wild daughter, the greatest success!

*****

Stirring from slumber, Diana whimpered. In the silence, the sound magnified. Faith, sitting near the head of the bed reading her bible, immediately closed the book and fussed over the invalid. "I'm right here, Diana. May I get you anything?"

Eyelids closed, Diana croaked, "Water, please. The medicine tastes like metal in my mouth."

The nurse, sitting silently beside the bed, jumped up and raced to the pitcher, poured a cup of water, and brought it to Diana.

Diana slowly opened one eye. Finding her head and chest ensconced in pillows to keep them angled in a half-sitting position, she sipped at the cup offered. It hurt to swallow. It hurt to think. A strange woman waited on her. "Who are you?"

"Your brother has hired you a night nurse," Faith explained in her soothing voice. "Her name is Cora."

Diana glanced at the thin, neatly attired, middle-aged woman who beamed at her. There was something insincere about the nurse's smile, but who could blame her? A life of ministering to the intimate needs of ill people must surely be taxing. Diana waved the water away and thanked her. Now she was stuck with three full-time servants to hover over her. "Where's Judith?"

"I'm not certain," Faith said. "She was here in the room a long time. Your brother dismissed her when Cora arrived. He told her to get some rest. She looked unwell."

"How is her arm?"

"Her arm?" Faith asked.

"She had a nasty welt on it, but she didn't complain," Hope interjected, entering the room. "Lord Edmunds was concerned with you and with Eden. Judith hid her injuries as she stood in that corner there."

With a blank frown, Faith turned to Hope, "Injuries? What is this about?"

"Later."

"The water doesn't help," Diana said. "Is there something sweet to drink downstairs? No tea or lemonade, please. My stomach feels unsettled. I fear anything acid would be too much."

"Perhaps an infusion of chamomile. I'll fetch it for you." Hope ran out the door before the nurse could stop her.

*****

"Ah, you're awake. I bring you two friends who've been badgering me to see you," Colin announced heartily as he entered with Aaron and his old setter, Sean. Eden and Hope followed him in. Hope approached Diana and held out the herb tea to her. "I had cook add a large dollop of honey."

Diana sipped and thanked Hope, telling her it was the perfect warmth and sweetness. Eden told Diana she would return later but wished to take her sisters away for a while. "The physician said you should have few visitors at a time."

Diana could hear Hope in the hall telling Eden she was glad to have an excuse to leave. "Sickrooms are so dismal."

Aaron attempted to climb onto the bed, but Colin picked him up. The child spoke from his father's arms. "You didn't come to see me at the children's hour. I missed you."

"Did you, Aaron? I would have come, but I should stay in bed for a while. I got hurt when a carriage turned over."

"Daddy told me that. That makes me sad."

"It makes me sad, too. But if I'm a good girl and obey the doctor, I'll get better. Then we can play." Diana held her teacup up to the maid, who swiftly took it.

"Good. I made up a new game to play. It's called hunt the tigers. You play it at night with lanterns."

"That sounds exciting, Aaron. I cannot wait to have you tell me the rules."

Sean took this opportunity to position his tall, lean setter chest against Diana's bed and place his furry face on her coverlet. Enormous, glistening brown eyes communicated his adoration of this long-standing partner in the exploration of woods, barns, and attics. Diana smiled, gazed into Sean's eyes, and limply stroked his silky ears with her closest fingers. The dog's hackles pulled back and up into a great doggy grin. He was in ecstasy.

"Is Judith well? Has she been seen to?"

Colin's countenance darkened. "I told her to take the day off and rest. She seemed distressed."

"She tried to stop me from boarding the phaeton, and him from driving off. He slashed her with his carriage whip when she jumped on the tiger's mount. She fell off when the carriage lurched forward. Hope said her arm had a welt."

"Good Heavens! I didn't notice. I was... Her injuries will be cared for, I promise. I'll take Aaron upstairs and see Judith right now." Colin walked to the door and turned. His faithful friend didn't follow behind him as usual.

"Sean?"

The dog cocked his head at him but didn't budge.

"Let him stay with me, Colin."

"How shall I write at my desk without him keeping my feet warm?"

"You'll manage. I have faith in you."

"Very well."

Moments after Colin left the room, Cora opened her pursed lips. "It's unwise to have a dog in a sick room."

Diana painfully turned her head to look at the nurse. Her first impulse was to insult the woman. She closed her lips. She'd been raised to give the benefit of the doubt, especially to those beneath her station. Besides, this woman must like her if they were to get on. She fought to keep the sarcasm from her reply. "Truly? Pray, tell, why not?"

"They harbor insects and dirt. They slobber on things, shed their hair, and dirty the rugs."

"Sean is well trained. He'd rather die than soil anything in the house. He enjoys a warm bath at least once a month–much more than some people. And, he's not the slobbering kind. Are you, Sean?"

The dog answered by yawning, effectively displaying his many large, sharp teeth.

A thought occurred to Diana. "Are you afraid of dogs, Cora?"

"It's rather a big brute."

"Merely refrain from making sudden moves. Sean may interpret them incorrectly." Diana impishly raised a single brow. The setter would never so much as growl at a human.

*****

Eden, Hope, and Faith arranged themselves in the drawing-room to receive callers. Since many visitors today would be eager to hear details of Diana's escapade, Eden had rehearsed an acceptable story to quell any suspicions already flying. Captain Barrett and Lord Edmunds presented themselves to support the ladies. The first admirer to arrive was Lord Fredrick Dawson. He made his bows, asked after Lady Diana's health, expressed his concerns, and took a seat next to Hope.

Hope froze. Dawson appeared to consider her his territory. She began to plan how to escape this prig's side before Lord Partington arrived. She must be pleasant to him because he had money and a title, though the lowest. He must be kept on a string just in case. She decided to adopt a cool demeanor toward him.

Dawson inclined his head close enough to Hope's ear to whisper. "I admire that you choose to act so restrained, considering the seriousness of the present circumstances."

Hope turned her head aside, crossed her eyes, and blew her bangs off her face. At the sound of footsteps in the hall, her expression instantly rearranged to demure-miss-mask.

Lord Darrow's troupe arrived *en masse*. Daniel, Thomas, and Serena seized every word about Diana's health. They were loudly disappointed when told they could not see her. Daniel asked that word be sent the very moment the doctor allowed her visitors. "I was desperate when I arrived at the fete to be told the entire Edmunds clan had just left in haste."

Aunt Chadwick came and listened intently to comments about the odd happenings of the previous day with a tight mouth and wrinkled nose. "It's a mercy the invitations for Diana's ball were not yet sent to the printers. She may need more than two weeks to fully recover. I've conferred with my gardener about flowers since it will be held at my estate. You'll be happy to know, Lady Edmunds, my town menagerie does not reside there as I'm rarely there myself. Thus, the guests for the planned party will not be eaten by fleas."

Eden smiled wistfully and nodded. "It was gracious of you to offer your home, Lady Chadwick. I pray it doesn't put you to too much trouble."

"Nonsense! It will be amusing."

Hope turned to Aunt Chadwick and parted her lips to speak but jumped up to help Eden pour the tea when she heard the voice of her long-anticipated Lord Partington in the hall. He arrived at the same time as Lord Montcrief. How was she to encourage both without inciting jealousy?

Partington, Jeremy, and Montcrief were announced. Sandra and Sandra's middle-aged nanny followed the gentlemen. Faith put her tea down. The cup and saucer had begun rattling.

Partington stood waiting for an opportunity until fortune presented a vacated seat by Faith. He promptly claimed the space. As Eden poured for him, Partington complimented her home, the flower arrangements, and her china. After inquiring after Lady Diana, Partington asked if he might bring his sister with him on the next call. "It is her first visit to London, and there seems a surplus of feminine contacts here for her to befriend." He turned then to Faith and smiled. "Would you be so good as to set my cup on that table beside you?" he said. Faith reached to take the cup. A finger of his gloved hand slid along hers as she removed his tea. She flinched. Her eyes widened.

Quietly he told her, "My sister says she cannot wait to meet you. I've told her all about you." He sat as close to Faith as he decently could for the entire fifteen minutes of a formal call.

When Partington rose to leave, Jeremy said he intended to stay since he'd brought little Sandra to visit Aaron. He picked his daughter up from the sofa and walked Partington to the door of the salon, took leave of him there, and continued to the staircase. Sandra's nanny followed Jeremy up the stairs to the playroom. Setting Sandra down, he left her with her nanny and Aaron's nanny. The two ladies immediately began to compare their charges' health and precociousness. Jeremy descended to the first floor and proceeded to find Diana's room by peeking through several open doorways. After being granted entry, he came to sit beside her bed. Sean placed his silky face on Jeremy's knees and received his expected caresses.

Alone with her nurse and Jeremy, Diana said, “My oldest, dearest friend, no one has yet dared speak to me of Major Bradley. He looked... Is he dead?”

Jeremy nodded.

“I thought he might be.”

Silence reigned a time as Diana absorbed the news, and Jeremy searched his mind to know how to begin gently. She spoke first. “At least he’ll know some peace and no more agony. He was unhappy in this world, and his leg pained him a great deal.”

Jeremy remained silent. He didn’t care to listen to the blackguard sanctified, but it was early days yet. Contention was not conducive to Diana’s recuperation.

“I hate that I was involved in his death,” Diana said. “I thought I could help him.” Jeremy shifted and opened his mouth to answer, but Diana continued, “He saw Cassandra at the last. She came to meet him, to guide him to the next world, I think. He once told me he’d seen her ghost, but she scolded him, and he dreaded seeing her again.”

Jeremy sat straighter. “He saw Cassy at the mishap? I heard none of this.”

“I just now remembered it myself. When we were thrown together there on the ground, while Colin was riding toward us, Major Bradley said, ‘My sister–you are my sister.’ His eyes were glazed, staring straight into the sun. He breathed a long, tortured breath, and I knew he was dying.”

Jeremy’s Adam’s apple dipped and climbed as if attempting to escape its chamber. “I’m ashamed to admit I’m jealous of him. Would that my wife would appear to me. I must know she’s at peace. It’s my dearest wish I could speak to Cassandra just once more.”

“Hope told me you felt that way. I think she will come, Jeremy, when the time’s right. But you can speak to her now anytime you wish. She hears you. I believe she’s not far from those she loves. The spirit travels more freely and swiftly than the body.”

Jeremy gripped his knees. He swallowed hard. “To tell Cassy the things I ache to tell her, I need to read her eyes.”

## CHAPTER TWENTY-TWO

Judith's gut wrenched. She might as well run away. The housekeeper had said Lord Edmunds wished to see her immediately in the yellow salon. Facing his disapproving eye was more than she could bear. He'd been so kind to her, yet she'd failed him. She was supposed to protect her ladyship. She'd botched it wretchedly. Her father would tell her to be brave–to tell the truth. How could she tell his lordship she'd been working for the man she was supposed to protect his sister from? And now that man was dead. Her father would get no more extra coin from him. She'd be dismissed. What would become of her family? If she hadn't given Noah the message about where Diana would be, none of this would have happened. It was all her fault. If it were possible in any way that Lord Edmunds would retain her, she must do all in her power to keep this position until the family returned to their seat. She must not volunteer information. Only if he asked, would she tell her connection with Major Bradley. Judith trudged down to her doom.

In the salon, Lord Edmunds and the physician awaited her. His lordship spoke as Judith crept in. "You must know, Judith, you were quite brave to attempt to stop what happened today. I've brought Mr. Long to have a look at your arm. Diana tells me you fell from the carriage. If you sustained any other injuries, please inform the doctor so he can care for you properly.

"Be assured I do not blame you for being unable to stop Diana from answering the note or boarding the phaeton. I know how headstrong she can be. You're needed now more than ever since I want you to learn from the night nurse, Cora, how to care for my sister during the day. Her ladies' maid is petite and will be unable to effectively move Diana to see to all her needs. If you keep an ear out and report to me anything you think I need to know, it will serve to keep Cora honest as well. I'll leave you with Mr. Long now. Rest until tomorrow."

Lord Edmunds left the room. Judith collapsed.

******

"It's easier to roll her on and off the chamber pot than the bourdaloue. Two nurses is best." The new night nurse, Cora, leaned over Diana's prostrate form to grasp the linen on the other side. "When she's on it, we roll the old sheet up like this close to her body. Then place the rolled part of this clean sheet right next to it. Now that her ladyship is done making water, we can lift her over onto the clean sheet. Keep her on her side until this old sheet is pulled away and the new one unrolled. Let me set the pillows on the clean sheet. Now, slowly roll her back into them."

Diana felt blood drain from her face. She couldn't control the rigid tremor. She must endure her pain stoically. She knew Judith had tried hard not to jostle her charge's back. The girl looked terrified.

"It's been a while since I had a parapleptic like this," the night nurse continued. "It's hard on a body's back. I'm glad you got the daylight hours. More movin' then. You're a strappin' girl, you are. We'll have to cut her hair short like Caroline Lamb's. Lucky it's the rage now. Cleanin' it long like that is too much trouble."

"I don't mind applyin' the starch powder to it to get the grease out," Judith said. "Martha showed me how to do that yesterday, with the towels over her like a smock and the cone to protect her eyes and nose and mouth."

Tears brightened Diana's swollen eyes. "I had it trimmed the first time in my life only a month ago. But I see what a problem it is. It will be an act of humility for me. Judith, have the housekeeper send for my hairdresser for tomorrow." Diana's glance lingered on Judith. "Don't worry. It's just hair. It grows. I'm in so much pain right now, I'm afraid to move. I suppose I must have more of the laudanum, Cora, but not too much. At least it removes my appetite." Her smile of reassurance was forced. "The less I eat or drink, the less I'll need that nasty chamber pot and all it entails."

Feeling more the thing a few days later, Diana allowed Daniel's family to visit her after being beautified and properly dressed in a bed jacket and propped up for receiving. A lacy cap hid her cropped hair. Daniel had decided to impress Diana with items he'd heard at the Lord's. She would see that he'd taken her strictures to heart. As he sat by her bedside, though, he slowly realized he could be talking to a rocking horse for all Diana seemed to care. She didn't press Daniel about anything but agreed with everything he said. Lost in her thoughts, she was not attending.

"I wonder how long it will be before I can ride in the park again," Diana said, looking longingly toward the window. "Are the orchards blooming yet at Chadilaine? Daniel, recall the ancient pear tree we once climbed in to hide from Thomas. When it blossoms, it's the most beautiful thing in the world."

Daniel wondered about her subdued manner. For a moment, the thought presented itself that she thought of Major Bradley. He slew the idea as quickly as it came. It must be embarrassment of her situation or the pain she endured or perhaps her restricted environment that sapped her usual animated society. Diana was most alive out of doors. Sitting at her side, he allowed his family to carry on the visit for him as he slid into a reverie of invention of a low-to-the-ground carriage that would be comfortable for an invalid. It should be a sort of traveling chariot with a dormouse boot rigged so a passenger might ride in a half-sitting position with legs extended. Something like a chaise longue Bath chair. The walls must be thickly padded with soft batting. This was something concrete he could do for Diana. He couldn't wait until the fifteen minutes were up. He would start drawing his ideas for the carriage immediately.

Once the call ended, Eversley took leave of his family also. Thomas chose to walk along with him. His father mentioned meaningfully that the family was invited to dine at Carleton House at eight. Thomas promised to get his brother home in time to dress. Daniel discussed his designs with Thomas as they walked to the warehouse of Rudolph Ackerman. Once the proprietor met him, Daniel described his idea for a traveling carriage for an invalid, sketching for him the concepts he'd refined in his mind as he walked. Ackerman agreed to meet him at Thomas Coutts on the Strand the next morning to arrange the funds to cover the costs.

As he entered the Ashton townhouse to visit, Jeremy encountered Mr. Rhodes on his way out. He greeted him, asked how he read the mood of the situation within, then handed Sandra to her nurse, and bid him step away from the group a moment. Rhodes did so with a look of unease. Jeremy promptly allayed his fears, saying he merely had a scientific request. "I wonder if you might have come in contact at the Academy of Science with anyone who practices Mesmerism or its newer versions. Lady Diana asked me about it once in the bookstore. I like to have her think I know everything, so I made a little study of it. The French commission of scientists judged any good effects of Mesmer's treatments were due only to the imagination of his subjects. Diana has a superb imagination. The Marquis de Puysegur feels he has taken Mesmer's magnetic experiments to a more efficacious plane. He rejects the magnetic fluid theory altogether and concentrates on a gentler "crisis." There's an Abbe Faria in Portugal as well who experiments with inducing a "Lucid Sleep" and suggesting things to the mind to cure one. So far, the doctors who've seen Lady Diana can only offer pain killers and tell her not to move. With my dabbling in the arts of illusion, I'm most aware the mind can play tricks and mislead people, causing them to think something happened that did not. I'd like to be present at one of these ‘experiments.’ ”

Rhodes shook his head. “There’s only one person I’ve witnessed who’s been at all scientific about it. He gave a demonstration at the academy. The patient was suffering from a dropped foot, and it healed before our eyes. He used the music of a glass armonica to induce a peaceful rest, along with a soothing voice and word pictures. Three-quarters of the class were asleep by the time he got around to suggesting to the patient his foot was feeling stronger and stronger, that it was healing itself. The subject’s foot lifted back into place, and he walked away without the limp he came in with. It could as easily have been a performance. None of us knew the patient or who may have treated him before that day.”

******

In the middle of the night, Diana complained to Cora of shooting pain in her back and a sort of burning in her feet keeping her awake. The nurse scurried to give Diana more of the elixir the doctor had prepared. Diana hesitated to take it. “I fear dependency on this drug. Is there no other treatment?”

Cora shook her head. “It contains a tiny quantity of the preparation you fear. Even a baby can tolerate this amount and show no ill effects.”

“It does help,” Diana said, draining the glass given her.

“Preferring pain to medication is foolish. The greater the pain, the weaker you’ll become,” the night nurse said. “And I fear in your case, the longer the pain continues, the more likely you’ll never recover. It would be best you try not to complain of it to the others. Lord and Lady Edmunds will be burdened even more since the maids will report it. Your family is already anxious and disheartened from your tragic condition. To allow them to know how much pain you experience can only cast their spirits lower. In her ladyship’s condition, she must be kept in the best of health. Distress can cause a baby to come too soon.”

“But how can I endure during the day…” Diana began.

“I’ve thought of a way,” Cora said. She brought the counterpane off Diana’s legs and exposed her feet. Then she took a jar of face cream from Diana’s dresser and opened it. She gently began to massage the cream into Diana’s feet. “The burning, as you call it, is due to the nerves dying. When they’re completely dead, it’ll go away. I’d like to give you extra medicine you could take secretly throughout the day only if you need it. The pill form is easy to acquire and cheap, but I could be turned off were it known I gave it you, so we will say no more.”

“Someone’s bound to find the pills anyway. I’m watched like a thief.”

“You could hide them in something small that you keep about yourself: a scent bottle, a Hartshorne flask?"

"I never use those. It would appear suspicious."

"Your reticule?"

"I only use that if I'm going somewhere. The massaging is helping. Thank you."

"I once knew a lady who kept jewels in her pincushion. She had it made so it opened at the bottom and closed with the pull of a string."

"I'm not good at sewing. What use would I have for a pin cushion?"

"You could ask for the materials to make one, letting on to anyone who might question it that you're secretly sewing it as a gift for the future little stranger to hold the pins for his nappies."

Diana's expression brightened. "The very thing. You have quite the devious mind, Cora. I should be making something for the new baby anyway. And thank you for being so frank with me. Everyone else speaks in euphemisms. You're a true friend."

With the morning's light, a twinge of pain reminded Diana of what the night nurse said. She was utterly helpless. Before now, she could tell herself this was a passing stage. She'd recover and be as active as ever. But the nurse said her nerves were dying. Would gangrene set in? Reality fell over her like darkness in an ancient wood. Her condition could be forever. Forever in bed, forever unable to do the simplest thing for herself, forever dependent on strangers to help her relieve herself and bathe her and change her soiled bedding. Forever an object of pity. "God, is this truly what you have in mind for me? All that happens, happens for a purpose. I believe that. Is this to teach me humility because I've been proud and headstrong? I didn't take the time to ask your will, Father. I know that now. I didn't stop to think. I just did what I thought was right, but... Dear Lord, help me learn my lesson well and learn it swiftly. When I've learned it, Lord, lift the penalty. I cannot bear this constant pain. I cannot think straight. How can I serve you in this situation? Are there not burdens enough in this world, Lord, without me adding to them? I so wanted to be one who lifted troubles from the shoulders of the less fortunate. You know I've wanted to use my money and influence to help society. Was it all for my vanity I wanted these things? Is this why I suffer? Is this why I'm laid low–to force me to take the time to assess my motives? I know it's the consequences of my foolishness, but it was innocent, was it not? I thought I acted with a good heart. I'm confused. Have mercy. All I can do here is pray, Lord. There are so many others who are better at that than I am. I surrender to you, Father, because I must. I do trust you, Lord. You've had much practice running the universe. You know what you're doing. Indeed, I do not. I leave it in your hands, Lord, as I see I must."

The dismal thoughts and lack of sleep gave Diana an agonizing headache. She asked her lady's maid to tell the house steward she was not receiving visitors today. While the maid went down the backstairs, Daniel was bouncing up the hall stairs. He carried a cumbersome canvas wrapped in brown paper, excited to show Diana the completed painting. First, he'd explain how he had envisioned it and how he accomplished it without her knowing. Then, he would tear off the paper to reveal it.

As the excited Daniel burst into the room and began animatedly explaining what he'd done and how he'd done it, Diana realized that was why he kept disappearing at parties. He'd wasted so much time on something she'd no desire for. They could have been together, discovering each other's likes and dislikes, wants, needs, dreams. What a fool she'd been devising all those plans to carve out intimate time for them. Hadn't Daniel's absences caused her to turn to Bradley, giving him the wrong idea?

As Daniel propped the painting in front of him and took a corner of the paper to rip it open, she shouted, "Don't you dare unwrap that! I never want to see it! Leave at once, and take that thing with you!"

Daniel stiffened, mouth agape. He stood staring at her several moments before he came to life again. His jaw snapped shut, he spun on his heel, hefted the wrapped painting under an arm, and left the room, almost colliding with Faith in the hall.

Faith stepped into Diana's room and pleaded. "How can you treat Daniel so callously? It was Colin who asked Daniel to do the portrait, and they conspired to keep it secret, thinking you would enjoy the big surprise. Daniel put time, talent, and love into that painting. It was all to please you. You're usually so circumspect. What made you fly at him that way?"

Diana's head was in her hands throughout the gentle scold. She lifted her face, fighting back the pain and tears. "Forgive me, Faith. I'd just sent Martha to tell Perrin I'd receive no visitors today. I got no sleep last night, and I have a beastly headache. Please, for my sake, run downstairs. If Daniel's still there, apologize for me. Tell him to come again another time. Then come back here with your sewing kit. I've thought of a gift to make for the new baby, and I need you to help me."

Faith's brows scrunched together. "A gift for the baby?"

"Yes. Go."

# CHAPTER TWENTY-THREE

As Faith descended the stairs, Lord Edmunds' deep voice greeted her. He stood in the hall with a hand on Daniel's shoulder. "Forgive her, Daniel. The constraints of her confinement weigh heavily upon her. She's restless to be up and active. She was never one for sitting still–except upon a horse. She's in constant pain. She puts off taking her medicine until she can bear the pain no more for fear of succumbing to dependency on the drug. Entertaining callers takes its toll on her. She strives to appear all sweetness and hope and health for guests. That leaves family to bear the impact of her exasperated outbursts. You're family to her. She's not herself and will not be for quite a while. Give her time to cool down. Return in a few days. I'll keep the painting to show her when she's feeling better. If she doesn't drench your head with a generous apology then, I shall be astonished."

Faith relayed Diana's message to Daniel and left to carry out Diana's second commission.

The young man nodded and turned to leave, shaking his head in confusion.

After Daniel left, Colin asked a footman to remove the paper from the painting and lean it against the wall. He scrutinized it. Daniel had caught her every good feature: the warmth and playfulness in Diana's eyes, the noble tilt of her chin. Her intelligence and openness were there for all to see. She was alive and approachable–a person one longed to know better, a person whose very presence made life worthwhile. Life burst with promise to the innocent in this portrait.

Colin's chest expanded with a heavy sigh. There had only been hints of this in Diana since the accident. She'd changed radically. Would she ever be happy again? Had he been the cause of her paralysis? How could he live with himself if he had? What if she never recovered?

Colin tore himself from his morbid reverie and sent for the head butler. When he arrived, Colin showed him where and at what height he wanted the portrait hung in the entrance hall so all visitors could not help but notice it. He summoned the staff and asked them not to disclose the name of the artist if they knew it. Then he plodded up the stairs to see the invalid. He hesitated outside Diana's door, gathering his thoughts. He was determined to discuss her reaction to Daniel without provoking annoyance or guilt. He'd tell her what he'd done with the painting as well, and why, and ask her to remain silent on the artist if anyone should ask. He was certain visitors would mention it. It was that striking.

Faith and Eden were the first visitors to see the portrait and visit Diana to tell her their reactions. Diana believed them prejudiced in her favor. When others praised the painting, Diana supposed them to be insincere about its beauty through good manners. Or their fulsome comments could be the result of Daniel romanticizing her portrait when he painted it, making her prettier than she was. He had not painted her "warts and all." Eventually, she craved to see it, to see what every visitor raved about, to form her own opinion, but pride wouldn't let her admit it. It would now be best for Daniel's sake to discourage him from considering her anything more than a friend. She was not improving. The pain in her back and shoulders was still there, though not as intense. She had tried to move a leg, but the shock that ran up her hip made her catch her breath and bite her lip hard to keep from screaming. Luckily, she'd tried it at night when Cora was there. Cora gave her an extra amount of the black drop, and she fell asleep. She'd not try moving her limbs again until the physician said she should. She feared the nightmares the medicine gave her.

Diana glared at the ceiling. She despised self-pity, but the possibility of remaining crippled the rest of her life had put a nail in her hot air balloon and sent it careening out of sight. Diana's dreams of a life of use to a future husband and to her country, of travel and of children, would never be fulfilled. A future marquis would need at least one son to inherit his estate and seat in the Lords. Several sons were preferred, in case the firstborn did not make it to maturity. The thought teased Diana that she should be grateful her state would relieve her of the dreaded duties of childbearing. Yet she'd looked forward to rearing children. She loved little ones. She'd meant to encourage Daniel to adopt a brood. With his soft heart, it would be easy, and there were so many in the foundling homes. But chained to a bed like this, she'd be a poor parent. She'd grown irritable and cruel–bad mothering material. No one would want her like this–no one admirable. Pain and powerlessness made her quarrelsome. She refused to chain her tender Daniel to the shrew she was becoming. He deserved much more.

She glanced at the little cushion for nappy pins that Faith helped her make. She was painstakingly embroidering a welcome to the little stranger on the top as an excuse for keeping it by her. In the middle of the night, Cora helped her remove a few stitches from the bottom of the gift, and she added the pills she promised. Then she threaded a drawstring through it.

When Cora admired aloud a pretty bonnet of her charge's, Diana told the nurse to keep it as a reward for all her help. She'd not have a chance to wear it anyway. It would be out of fashion before she ever went outside again. And the nurse might as well take the pelisse that matched it as well.

A knock at the door caused Diana to snatch the pincushion and remove the embroidery needle stuck in it. Matthew poked his head around the frame of the door and smiled brightly.

Diana laughed. "If you knew how comical you look doing that, you'd not do it."

He straightened up and brought his entire form into view. "If I could hear your laugh every time I did it, I'd never stop. Such a delightful laugh, it reminds me of someone, but I cannot recall who."

"I used to try to imitate Cassandra's laugh; it was so musical."

"Possibly. May I stay a moment?"

"Please do, but no frowns allowed."

Matthew pulled the new stuffed wingchair away from the wall and positioned it close to her bedside. The chair had been added because it had little wheels for rolling it about and was comfortable for extended visits. He watched the way Diana clasped the ball of material she was poking at with a needle. "What will it say when finished?" he asked.

"I started out with, 'Welcome to the world new arrival.' Halfway through, I thought that was too mundane, so I pulled it all out again. I have an idea which I had just as soon keep secret lest I look foolish if I change it, too."

Matthew seated himself and placed a hand on her bed. "And we must never look foolish. We can be foolish, but we must never look foolish." He grinned in self-deprecation. "I say that aloud to appear clever, but inside I believe the opposite. What's wrong with looking foolish, or tired, or upset, or frightened?" He'd seen signs he didn't like in her actions, especially with that "gift" she kept poking at with the needle. He knew first-hand about treasuring little accoutrements that could be depended upon to hide pills. She was not as strong as she wanted everyone to believe with her bravado performances. The pucker at her brow was a constant furrow now, ploughed by pain. She needed a friend who would help her avoid the same mistakes he'd made. He reached toward the cushion to tug at its tassel. She stuck the needle into the "gift" and placed it close to her other side on the counterpane.

"It tends to frighten the visitors away," she said.

"They were not friends if they frightened so easily."

"I know. I frighten some on purpose."

Matthew chuckled. "When I was active as a major, I had young soldiers under my command that put on a great show of bluster, but it was merely to mask the fears and doubts that beset them. They felt they had to appear as certain and valiant as their brother soldiers. If only they knew the rest were as frightened as they. We're all of us unsure of our worth, our abilities, our reception, our charm in this world. All reach out, all wonder what will be and what if. We all fear something."

"What are you afraid of, Matthew?"

Matthew drew back in his chair. He hadn't expected that question. He'd been setting the stage to elicit disclosures from her. But if she were to trust him enough to take direction from him, he must be honest with her. "Let me think a moment. I do believe I've not truly asked myself that question before."

"I ask myself all the time. But you must go first."

"For one thing, I fear spending my life a slave to the black drop. It commandeers your mind and your time. You care about nothing but taking more of it. It distorts your thoughts and dreams until you're not certain whether you're awake or asleep in a nightmarish world. You think of doing things beneath you to attain it. When I'm lucid, I want to matter... to be useful.

"But it calls me, and I cannot stop my ears and eyes from its haunting. I ache for it. I..." Matthew stopped speaking from frustration. How could he explain? He sighed heavily. "May you never understand."

"And what do you do to fight your fear?"

Matthew shifted in his chair and cleared his throat. "I've made enquiries about a certain scientist who claims to have slowly made his way back from the same situation. I hope to be able to contact him and ask him how he achieved freedom."

"Have you asked God to help you?"

Matthew straightened his back further and drew his hands together in front of his chin. "You sound more like Eden every day."

"I wish I'd listened more closely to her. I might not be here. You avoid the question."

"I asked him for help too many times."

"Is there such a thing as too many times?"

"I suppose not. I lead you astray. Prisoners of opium rarely think as incisively as before their introduction to it. Father used to say to discern the spirit that prods you. The spirit that goads me is too often a bad spirit."

"How does one know?"

"My father taught us that if you're tempted to do something that would affect yourself or others in any negative way, it was a bad spirit prompting you, and you must call upon Our Lord for help, for you cannot fight demons on your own.

"And when you called upon the Lord?"

"He helped me each time, and I fell again each time. Disappointing God so often takes a toll on a man."

"He only asks you to try with his help and not give up."

Matthew stood. "I can see you're tired. May I come again?"

"Don't be a stranger."

Matthew left without asking her about her fears. Merely by prodding him, she'd opened her mind to the questions he wanted to ask. Best to let her mull them over for a while.

******

Daniel arrived at the townhouse on St. James Square, excited about the carriage he designed for Diana so she could recline comfortably while being driven through the park. Lord Edmunds had told him to give her a week before visiting again. He couldn't have stood the wait if he hadn't his newest painting to distract him. He busied himself completing the second portrait of Diana, the one he was sure she would love. He spent time sketching her favorite horse and refining its face on the canvas. To that end, he'd studied all the George Stubbs' paintings he could find.

Diana decided to tout up Faith's graces to Daniel. It wasn't what she wanted, but it was the kind thing to do for them both. She was not improving. She'd be useless to him. She saw Partington's preference for Faith, but her sister-in-law seemed indifferent to him. Faith's thoughts were easily read in her expressions, but her look was mild at the mention of Partington's name. She didn't fluster or color. In fact, if anything, she looked annoyed when he was there. Faith would be a perfect, biddable wife for Daniel. Diana felt drained when he was announced, but she did want to apologize for her outburst the last time they met and to drop a few hints about Faith before he left.

Daniel again entered in an unforgivably exuberant humor. Then Diana saw the shock in his eyes when he regarded her face. He suspended motion, his gaze resting on her eyes and softening. Earlier, she'd asked to see the looking glass after her hair was done. The gloss had been powdered out of her shortened curls, and the honey color was now chalk-grey. She'd lost weight, and the flesh beneath her eyes had taken on a blue hue. She recalled the street boy in Daniel's painting when she looked at her image. Poor Daniel didn't expect her to look so ill.

She watched his expression cloud, then clear, then resolve, then brighten.

He was steeling himself to not distress her by mentioning the change in her appearance. He came to bring hope. She would prepare him to detach from her. It would only be kindness to do so.

Daniel revived, drew out his folded plans from an inside coat pocket, and spread them on the bed before her. He glanced right and left and sat carefully on the bed. "Is she not up to the nines? It's a traveling chariot, and this moment it's being fitted out to my specifications as a gift for you."

Embarrassed by the expense of the gift, though pleased by his obvious consideration for her comfort, Diana feebly attempted to decline it while praising his thoughtfulness.

In his excitement at the perceived encouragement, Daniel ignored her refusal to accept it and continued extolling the new carriage. "The dormouse boot will be upholstered extra plush with goose down, so you'll think you are stretched out upon a cloud. I thought a robin's egg blue for the fabric, with gold trim; silk or velvet, what think you?" Before she could answer, he continued, "Look, I've asked for iron-shod wheels, so there are no breakdowns on the road."

"Daniel." Her voice was weak. He closed his mouth and regarded her. She began, "It's a marvelous idea, but it's not proper for me to receive a gift of such magnitude from you..."

"I will gift it to the family then. It's ordered and paid for."

"It's a deal of money."

"I spend next to nothing. My money wonders if I'm a miser. Having experienced pennilessness, I cannot abide betting on dogs, horses, or fisticuffs, and diamond-encrusted snuff boxes and toothpicks make me cringe with the thought of all who could be fed and clothed with the money spent on such trinkets. Let me splurge on this. The carriage is a good investment because it shall be in the family when we..."

"Think, Daniel," Diana whimpered. "I've been ordered not to move at all. It may nullify all possibility of healing, of walking again. Why do you think they do not wash my hair? I can barely..." She stopped herself before revealing the unmentionable part of her life, but she couldn't stop herself from blushing. She'd lost the control over him she once had. She must put up defenses.

"You're always beautiful to me, Diana. You *will* get better. I have faith in you and in God. You're valiant; you will fight this struggle until you win..."

"How can I fight when I cannot move?"

"Not all battles are physical. Your mind is your strength. With God's help..."

"I'm useless this way."

Daniel jumped up from the bed and strode back and forth. "Never say such things, Diana. You're needed, wanted by me!"

"I'm too tired to argue, Daniel. Please have a servant ask Faith to see me as you leave. She's such a comfort to me in my illness..."

"And I am not?"

"I truly didn't intend to give that impression. It's merely that I can rest with my eyes closed and not feel the necessity to respond as she reads. I often fall asleep. She has a lovely, soothing voice, do you not think?"

"Diana, why are we speaking of Faith when I need to speak of us?" He seated himself on the wing chair and leaned in toward her. "You mean so much to me..."

"No."

"No?"

"Do not say it. There was a time when I should have loved nothing more than that you say the words you insinuate, but that time is bygone. I'm not improving, Daniel. If I live, I'll be an invalid all my life. I wouldn't burden any man with that. I've decided never to marry."

"Nonsense. It's early days yet for giving up. You need time to heal..."

Feeling the call of nature and disgusted with him because he refused to take her hints or do her bidding, Diana growled, "You're living in a dream world, Daniel. Judith, I need you. Daniel, leave now, close the door behind you. Please. I need to have you leave."

Bewildered, Daniel stood as Judith approached, but lingered.

Feeling she would have an accident with him present, Diana panicked, screaming at him, "Get out! Go! You're not wanted! Can't you tell that?"

Daniel, plans clutched tightly in his hand, passed Thomas outside the door without a word. He left the door ajar, and Thomas delayed there, thinking to allow Diana time to cool down before going in to find out what disturbed her. He heard her tell the nurse, "Oh God, I am in such pain! Hurry, bring the chamber pot and the rags, I'm about to soil myself. Judith, shut the door!" Thomas turned sharply and left.

******

"I believed she returned my regard," Daniel told Thomas as he opened the door of his flat. When his brother entered, Daniel poured his frustration out. "Until the accident, she always received me with the most sunrise of smiles. She seemed sincere in her interest in my career and in my paintings, offering to help in both. Now, she's ice. She refused to see the portrait I was so proud of. Lord Edmunds told me to give her a few days. I did. I thought she'd be pleased by my inventing a carriage just for her. She ordered me out a second time. This is too humiliating to bear. She was insulted. I knew she was dramatic, but that was not acting. Those were her true feelings.

"I never thought myself deserving of her, Thomas, but when she was injured, I thought it was a sign we were destined to be together. We're now two invalids who can lean upon each other. I was willing to work hard to better myself, to become someone she could admire, to justify her faith in me. Now..."

Thomas held a finger to his brother's lips to stop the flow of words, then proceeded to tell him delicately what he heard Diana tell her nurse and maid after Daniel left. "She loves you, Daniel, but of course she's changed. This tragedy completely altered her life. She needs time to sort it out. She's always been so independent. It must be humiliating for her to be subject to others waiting upon her most intimate needs. Just think what an invasion on her life this is. And the pain she's in must surely muddle her thinking."

Daniel stared at his little brother, then drew in a deep breath and expelled it rapidly. "You're too wise, Thomas. I was thinking of her boredom, her need for a change of scenery. There's so much more that goes on I'd not considered."

******

As the interminable days approached two months, Diana became certain she'd never walk again. She'd been hoarding the opium pills. The pain in her back subsided little by little each day, but the pain in her feet and now down her leg if she moved had increased. The servants were all as gentle as could be, but elimination and bathing required movement and, at times, movement caused excruciating cramping in her left leg. It was impossible at times not to scream out. Cora said the pain meant her nerves were dying. She wished they would die already. She wished the surgeon would cut her limbs off.

Sleep was the only time she felt no pain, and the only time she could sleep was when she had taken the poppy's draught. Diana considered the idea that if she "accidentally" took too much opium, she might never wake again. The thought frightened her. It frightened her because it appealed to her. She had the power to end it all right now. Cora was sound asleep in the wing chair. There was a full glass of water on the nightstand by her bed. If she reached for it, the spasms would surely overtake her. But she could take all the pills in the pincushion, pop them in her mouth, grab the glass and swallow its contents before she allowed herself to scream in pain. No one would know.

She reached carefully for the pincushion and drew it to her. She maneuvered the drawstring and opened the bottom. Thirty pills spilled onto the sheet. They could remove all her problems in a few minutes. She picked each one up and held them all in one hand, looking longingly at them. There sat her wretched life in her hand. It would be so easy, so quick and painless. The pills would dull the agony and her mind, and she would fall asleep and enter the next life.

That was what stopped her. The thought of a next life. Her soul fought against the thought of death because it knew life was infinite. In her darkness, she spoke with her beloved confidant. *Dear Lord, I do believe this life is just the beginning. I do believe in Heaven and Hell. It only makes sense. You never force a man to love you; authentic love cannot be forced. You wouldn't force a man who hates the thought of you to dwell with you. You wouldn't force people who strove their whole life to imitate you in love to live forever with people who despise the mention of your name. There must be more than one destination for our souls. Thou shalt not kill. It's quite clear. If I take these pills, I'll be killing myself. It will be a grave sin, a premeditated sin. I have full use of my reason. I have no excuses. I desperately wish to be with you when I leave this world. If I disobey your commandment so blatantly, I'll never see you. Never is too long, Lord. I so want to see you. I'm so tired of hurting. Lord, help me take the pain as you took it on Golgotha for me. Help me persevere. Fight for me the bad spirit who tempts. I am too weak to fight.*

Thinking Daniel would be forced to make new female connections if she was removed from him, Diana sent for Colin the next morning. As he entered her room plagued by parliamentary concerns, Colin momentarily neglected to assume his customary cheerful visitor's face. Diana caught his brief look of aggravation. *He doesn't wish to see me. I'm a nuisance to him. He cannot bear to watch me decline. I look shocking.*

Colin stretched and straightened. "Forgive my mien, Diana, I have much on my mind."

"The uprising in Derbyshire?"

"Yes, and Sidmouth's attempts to prevent greater revolution with his spies and punitive measures that serve only to incite the citizenry further."

"I'm sorry, Colin, that I add to your worries."

"My shoulders are broad enough to carry my family. You had a request?"

"Yes. I want to go home to Chadilaine. There'll be fewer visitors there, and the views of the gardens will give me something beautiful to rest my eyes on. I fancy reclining in the orangery and in the ballroom by the great windows. I just want to go home."

Colin moved further into the room and perched on the edge of the wing chair so his face was more on a level with hers. "You're happiest in the country, are you not?"

"Deliriously."

"What's the happiest moment you can recall, Diana?"

Diana's brow furrowed. "There have been so many."

"I'm glad to hear that. Is there not one moment that stands out?"

"Yes, but I'm not certain I can explain it."

"Try."

Diana rested her chin on a fist and gazed far off into her memory. "One spring day I climbed up to a thick branch in the ancient pear tree in the orchard."

"What made you happy there?"

"I was happy just to be alive, to see the glorious profusion of white blossoms. The air was thick with their sweet scent. Sunlight made the petals glow. Suddenly I felt drawn out of the world and melted into nature at the same time. I felt as if I was alone in a secret hiding place in God's heart–like he created the crook in that tree just for me so we could be happy together there, so I could feel him delight in me. I could breathe in the warmth of him. I could rest in him. I stayed there a long time. I think when the bible speaks of joy, that is what it alludes to."

"That's a beautiful memory. I recall you being happy to visit the tenants who needed comfort or companionship."

"Yes, I like being useful."

"There are times in our lives, Diana, when we can be useful by giving of ourselves. Then there are times when we can be useful by receiving."

Diana's brow crinkled again. "By receiving? What do you mean? How?"

"We serve God by serving our brother, right?"

"Yes."

"For now, the Lord can use you in your situation to provide a way for your family and friends to give of themselves. You must graciously receive their love, their foolishness, their patience, their counsel, their companionship, their little ministrations so they can love God by loving you."

She licked her mouth and blinked her eyes. "A unique concept."

Colin chuckled. "Think on it. I'll ask the doctors to assess you once more. I fear moving you."

"But Colin, they must move me often every day for sanitary needs–forgive me for mentioning it. Doctor Long told me the inflammation has gone down almost completely, and that's why my back gives me only a dull ache most times. We could use the carriage Daniel commissioned for me."

"I'll consider it. I want you to try to eat more. You must build up your strength for the journey."

Diana added, "The time for Eden's lying-in draws near. She looks forward to returning to Chadilaine to give birth. She said she trusted the accoucheur in Edmundston, who had attended her on Aaron's natal day."

"I'm aware. So, both my ladies want to leave me to my own devices to clash with the lords while they fight their more vital battles. I do not care for the prospect. How can I protect and provide for you both so far away?"

"It's a two days' journey at most, Colin, and you've made it in one day with horses stationed along the way."

"I'll speak to Long. Shall we retain him for Chadilaine?"

Diana shook her head. "I like our physician there."

Diana was pronounced fit to move if every precaution was taken, and the journey was slow. It was determined her spirits needed the diversion. Colin sent for Daniel to purchase from him the carriage he'd fitted for Diana, telling him in the note that Diana had suggested it. Daniel penned that he was overjoyed Diana wanted the carriage, but he insisted it be a gift to the family.

As the maids were packing for the journey, Diana asked Colin to convince Judith to come home with them. She didn't wish to start over with different caretakers. She told him that when she mentioned the idea to Judith, the abigail didn't seem pleased. He nodded and sent a footman to request Judith's presence in the library.

"Judith, the family is repairing to our seat in Edmundston. I wish you to remain in my employ and go with us."

As she spoke, the hefty young lady's eyes began to well up. "I'd like nothin' better than to stay on, your lordship. I need the wage to help my father pay his rent. But if I'm so far from my family, I can't watch out for my brother and sister. I fear my brother may die soon from his illness. My little sister will be left alone all the time my pa works, an' that's often at night. The neighborhood ain't the best..."

"I didn't realize your circumstances were so dire." He thought a moment and continued. "Tell me, Judith, is your father any good at gardens?"

Judith's tears stopped their flow as she looked up. She sniffed loudly and wiped her nose with a kerchief from her apron pocket. She said, "He can dig a proper hole all right, big enough for a tree."

"Do you think he would mind moving the family at my expense to...?"

"He'd jump at the chance, milord."

"I'll speak to him. The head gardener at my estate is now of a certain age and would appreciate another to dig the holes for his plantings. He complains of heart flutters when digging. Your family can live in the gardener's hut with him. There are rooms enough. The gardener has told me often that he's lonely since his wife died. Perhaps your brother and sister can help remedy that."

Judith fell on her knees and clasped her hands. Colin was about to tell her she needn't do that when she began sobbing and thanking God loudly for answering all her prayers. He slipped soundlessly away.

******

The journey home to Chadilaine began. Diana resolved to enjoy her last trip anywhere observing all of nature. She tried to be constantly bright and conciliatory with the family. She must behave better from now on. She'd disobeyed Colin's strictures about Major Bradley and look where it got her. She'd disappointed God. It had been ridiculous of her to attempt to blame Daniel for her own actions. She must apologize and get back in God's graces. It was probably not long now before she died. She must clean up her soul if she was to behold the face of the Almighty in heaven. She would send for the parson to confess. Diana asked for a journal and pencil. Between pointing out blooming trees and picturesque mills to Eden and laughing at the amusing antics of hogs and sheep they passed along the way home, she recorded a list of transgressions to accuse herself of.

As they approached the gatehouse to the estate, Diana's mood lifted considerably. She told Eden she didn't want to sleep in her own room, but somewhere on the ground floor where she would have a vista. She committed to memory every stone and tree and tenant house along the five-mile path from the gatehouse to the mansion. When they rounded the corner that brought Chadilaine into view, Diana asked the coachman to stop so she could gaze at the ancient edifice for a while. This could be the last time she'd ever see this prospect of her ancestral home. She would not tell her companions that, of course.

The staff lined up outside as the metal carriage wheels rang on the gravel approach. Lady Edmunds was helped down first, and she greeted the staff. She promptly gave orders that a fainting couch be made up with downy pillows in the music room close to the French casement doors so Diana could look out on the rose garden.

When the footmen shifted Diana onto a blanketed pallet to carry her indoors, she told them she felt like Cleopatra without the peeled grapes. From her pallet, she oversaw the positioning of her couch and the pillows upon it. She felt most comfortable on her right side, she informed them.

Once she was in position, and Judith had arrived in the second carriage, Eden begged to be excused. Diana asked that Sean be brought to her after he was walked. She watched with great interest a bird and several butterflies outside, commenting to Judith it was a good sign of a warm summer. When Sean entered, he padded quietly over to Diana and placed his wet nose opposite her eyes. The setter was the only one she would allow to commiserate with her. As he gazed soulfully into her eyes, she stroked his soft head and long ears until all her tension dissipated, and her muscles and thoughts went soft. Then Diana slept.

## CHAPTER TWENTY-FOUR

Faith watched through a first-floor window as a carriage pulled up at the entrance below. She recognized Colin riding a post horse behind it. Jeremy and his daughter disembarked, and then Lord Partington alit. She said nothing but turned back to the room and seated herself with her sister. The ladies had been reading aloud *The Merchant of Venice,* each taking parts. The visitor's voices could be heard on the stairwell as they came up. Once the greetings were expressed, Lord Partington promptly asked Faith if she would be so kind as to accompany him as guide through the orangery. Glances darted about the room between all gathered there, but no one hinted there was anything amiss in the request, so Faith expressed her delight in the task. She loved the omnipresent aroma of the orchids and other exotic plants.

Two steps into it, Partington allowed it was to get her alone that he asked to see the glass-domed room. "Miss Barrett, I must speak my mind promptly or lose my nerve. In those few instances when we could converse at length, the opinion I formed of you is of one whose values resonate with my own. You aspire to a happy life of use. I've spent my days since last we met comparing your disclosures to me with those of other young ladies of my acquaintance. I judge you so superior that I have no qualms in now telling you I am most willing to declare myself, if you will have me." Partington swallowed hard. "I'm careful with my resources. I'll be able to provide quite handsomely for you and any progeny the Creator may choose to bless us with."

Faith's cheeks burned and her palms sweat. "Though I'm greatly honored by your declaration and appreciate the regard of so worthy a gentleman, you take me by surprise. We've met infrequently. I admit I've not satisfactorily learned your character, though from what I've gleaned, I do admire your hopes and dreams. I've not formed an answer. I need time to consider your offer."

"Only natural, Miss Barrett. Forgive me if I cause you a moment's distress. I do hope you can come to a swift decision and put me out of my misery. Will half an hour's consideration suffice?"

Faith looked at him with wide, puzzled eyes.

"As I accompany Mr. Blake, my time is not my own, or I would not press you so. You may, of course, take all the time you need. But that could raise suspicion among your family by necessitating you post a letter to me. Mr. Blake doesn't mean to stay long." Partington glanced around him at the profusion of greenery. "If I wander in this glass-enclosed jungle anxiously awaiting your response, might you form one?"

"I'll do my best." Faith dipped a curtsy and escaped to the nearest empty salon, closing its door behind her. She leaned against the heavily carved figures in the warm wood of the door a moment. Her body trembled. She ran to the deep blue velvet settee opposite the door and fell upon it.

At first, her thoughts were so wildly unrelated she could make nothing of them. She gave herself up to dwelling in the euphoria of having acquired the genuine regard of a worthy man. In her first half-season, she'd had some puppyish declarations from swain more in love with the idea of being in love than of contracting a sacrament till death. It'd been painful to receive them. She promptly sent them packing. It must be authentic love or nothing. Was this love? On his side, it seemed it was. He was certainly intelligent. He had ideals and morals. He was quite nice to look at. His conversation was delightful. He danced wonderfully. She could easily see having him as a good friend for life. But as a husband? Could she love him in that way? How would he behave after she was secured? He seemed completely biddable now, but so did any suitor wishing to please.

Her eldest sister Mary had been head over heels with her beau when she married him. The last time Faith visited her in Bath, marriage, children, and life had drained the light out of Mary's eyes. Her husband was rarely home. In his favor, it was work that kept him away. When he was home, he seemed interested only in his food, the Morning Chronicle, and sleep–which he often did in front of the newspaper. Yet, Mary was *enceinte* again. Something must be going on behind the bedroom door. Faith's cheeks colored at the thought. How would she be with Partington? The closest thing to physical intimacy in courtship was dancing. Kissing was only for after the engagement. How could she be expected to hunger for more?

Eden had told Faith of the time Colin kissed her against her will by the lake when she was merely a governess to his sister. She said it changed their relationship completely and clouded her judgment, stirring confusion in her and a longing for she knew not what. It had ended well, though. Eden seemed happily fulfilled. The difference in Eden's and Mary's stations must have much to do with that. Most of the burdens that Mary had to shoulder in her day to day struggles caused but a moment's decision in Eden's case. Menial work was merely delegated to the large and efficient staff at Chadilaine Manor. Much of the difference in the two marriages could have to do with Eden's temperament, though. Eden had always been livelier than the rest of the Barrett clan–more forceful, more independent, more sure of her opinions. At least she was always willing to take a chance. *Is that what's missing in my life? Do I over-consider each possibility? I'm afraid to take a step lest it be the wrong one and be my ruin. Dear Lord, direct my thoughts. Make your will mine in this. Give me clear knowledge and understanding. Help me make the choice you wish for me.*

Her parent's marriage had greatly influenced her. They were both good people, but so mismatched they merely tolerated each other. Her father tried valiantly to hide his discontent with their mother, but she constantly carped and criticized about his shortcomings. The only one unaffected by this discord had been Hope, who was yet a baby when their father died. Her mother believed it wrong to speak ill of the dead. Faith reined her thoughts back to considering Partington's proposal. He'd looked so pitiful; she must tell him something. She stood, gathered her courage, and strode for the orangery.

As she opened the glass door, Partington appeared among the plants and approached her forthwith. Faith blurted, "Though it distresses me, I must be frank and confess that at present I prefer we remain merely friends."

"I admit disappointment but am glad of your honesty." His eyes lifted from their downward glance and searched hers. "May I be so bold as to ask if your heart is currently engaged elsewhere?"

"It is, but the sentiment is not requited. I admire you, but do not wish to give false hope."

"Can you see a time when your heart may be your own again?"

"Possibly, but not imminently."

"Then there is hope. I'm yet young enough to wait a while for someone so original as you."

"You flatter me, my lord. I do like you, but please, do not overlook another on my account. It may be an awfully long while before I'm sufficiently ready to move on."

"As you wish."

"We must go in now."

"Must we?" Tilting his head, he held his palms face out. His brows curled up in a question. "I came all this way."

Faith shrugged. It did seem a shame to dash his dreams and send him home so dismissively. He was good conversation and could make a lovely friend. “We could feed the swans.”

He grinned a smile of submission and bowed. “Delightful.”

Jeremy tested the closed door in the library to make certain it was locked. Colin sat at his writing desk. The Member of Parliament approached his friend and spoke quietly. “I notice your wife seems worried when she looks at you, Colin. Your attitude lately is erratic. You left Whitehall at a time when your vote is essential. That’s unlike you. You know suspension of Habeas Corpus must be repealed. And with this Pentrich rising, who knows what else Liverpool will try to get through? Is it Diana? Is there something you hide? I thought her health was improving. Or rather, her manner has or seems to have. Yours has declined. What gnaws at you?”

Elbows on the arms of his chair, Colin rested his forehead on his folded hands and closed his eyes. From that position, he answered his comrade. “Mr. Long said I may have caused Diana’s paralysis by lifting her from the ground. Her back should have been steadied first with a flat board. She did sit up in my arms when I reached her. She moaned and fainted when I moved her. She can no longer...”

“You didn’t know. It was a natural reaction. Lord, I too would have lifted her if I were there.”

Colin brought his head up, his expression bleak with anguish. “I was warned against bringing her out and ignored the warning. I caused the mishap in the first place. Bradley looked back at me as he whipped up the horses. He drove them hard to escape me. I saw that his driving was reckless. I should have kept out of sight until he got where he was going and stopped. Diana was leaving me signs along the trail.”

“Who knows how long that might have taken? Perhaps he was headed for Gretna Green. Diana would have run out of things to drop behind them. This is nonsense, Colin. Next, you will tell me it is your fault the king is mad, and the sky is blue. You were more composed a month ago. What’s changed?”

“At first, the doctor thought she could improve as the swelling went down. Her condition is the same. Don’t allow her wan smiles to fool you. She’s giving up. The light of joy has left her eyes. Her hope disappears.”

“Then it’s up to you to hope for her.”

Colin glared at Jeremy. “What hope? Five surgeons have seen her, and none has anything encouraging to report or to suggest. She’s skin and bone and dark circles under the eyes. Must I say it?”

“I had not intended to bring this up at all, but you’re so obviously in pain." Jeremy walked to the empty fireplace and glanced at the portrait of Colin's mother above it. "Perchance conventional medicine is not the answer."

"You suggest a quack?"

"Possibly, but perhaps not."

"I know you delight in being enigmatic, Jeremy, but not now, please."

"It's something I've been researching. Diana is the one who started my quest. She asked me about Mesmer. I had to admit I knew little of him. Since then, I've made a study of his experiments and, more to the point, of his followers. I've been talking to some of the science fellows at the Academy."

"Rhodes?"

"Among others."

Colin pushed against the little desk until his back was ensconced by his stuffed leather chair. He stretched his arms outward and blinked his eyes hard. "The Paris doctors commissioned to investigate Mesmer's work ruled that any effects of his treatments were due only to his patients' imaginations."

"But that's the thing, Colin, there were results–amazing results, and the imagination can cure. How often have you heard a physician speak of a person's will to live bringing him through?"

"There were unsavory reports of Mesmer's character."

"That was his character–not his science."

"And I don't like the idea of bringing her to a dramatic crisis. How much more can she bear?"

"This is my point. There are followers of Mesmer who've taken it further: Abbe Jose Custodio de Faria and The Marquis de Puysegur, now mayor of Soissons, where his castle and estate were before the Revolution demoted him. Puysegur has successfully used his own form of Mesmerism, which he calls 'artificial somnambulism,' to improve mood and remove pain. He doesn't require a dramatic crisis at all. Neither does Abbe Faria, who terms it inducing a 'lucid sleep': a state where a suggestion may be introduced to the subject to ease the pain. He, too, has had documented miraculous successes, and he is a beloved man of God, above reproach."

Colin stood and moved to a side-table set with a brandy decanter and glasses. He held up a flute to Jeremy, who shook his head. He poured a glass of water for himself and sipped. "You seem set on this, Jeremy–excited about it, actually. It could give Diana something to look forward to. I'm doubtful, but in no humor to refuse a try. Where do we find one of these magnetists?"

"Followers of Puysegur prefer to call themselves 'experimentalists' or 'revisionists.' Let me arrange it when I return to London. I'll write you the particulars when it's set."

"Make certain the man will have no qualms about our being present at the demonstration. I don't want Diana coerced into anything that alarms her."

Jeremy nodded. "All will be perfectly safe, I assure you. We'll both be there to prevent anything which might be objectionable to you or her."

"I'll speak to her now." Colin set his glass down and headed toward the door. His face was eager with anticipation. "The sooner she has reason to hope, the better."

"And I'll gather my little chick from the nursery, hunt up Partington, and return to town to work on it. Is Matthew about the house, perhaps? I've a message for him from a mutual colleague."

"He went down to the dower house after breakfast to visit his mother." A sly grin invaded Colin's mouth as he cut a sideways glance at his friend. "I'm sure the *grande dame* would delight in a visit from you as well. Allow Sandra to stay here with us while you're in London. The surroundings and the company of Little Aaron keep her well entertained."

"No, Colin. I cannot leave her for a day. I've grown to depend upon the glee in her eyes and her fresh interpretations of the simplest things in life for relief from the burdens of my office and for a reason to continue living."

"Children are ever amazed and amazing, are they not?" Colin encouraged. Yet, his brow puckered at his friend's ominous statement.

Colin approached Diana with Jeremy's idea. She feigned excitement about it for Colin's sake. She could see he wanted her to be attracted to the idea. He hoped to provide her with something to anticipate. Mechanically, she forced herself to ask about the arrangements for the healer each day. What was his name? What would take place? Where would they receive him? Would the family be present in the room? She could care less, but Colin must be allowed to think that she was willing and hopeful.

******

Several days later, as Daniel stretched his slender form on the leather squabs of Mr. Blake's excellent carriage, he breathed copious invigorating breaths and grinned. The news he was bringing to Diana was certain to brighten her outlook. It had brightened his. When the Guy's Hospital physician assured Thomas and him that his asthma was not cancer, Daniel was exultant. He'd asked his brother to go with him to the hospital in case the prognosis was negative. The pain in his chest when he coughed had grown more intense in Italy, and the idea of cancer had grown proportionally. After delivering the good news, the doctor advised the use of coffee to control his asthmatic fits. He had prescribed eating more beef and apples and taking a preparation of three grains of vitriolated iron and six grains each of myrrh and kali twice daily. Surely Diana would be surprised to see how the beef and iron had brightened his complexion. He'd been attending the House of Lords' sessions religiously and had become absorbed in the plight of the weavers, especially when he heard of the children being injured by the machines and care not being provided for their injuries by the employers. He'd spent his time gathering more facts about children working in the industries of coal and weaving.

As the carriage came to a stop, Lord Eversley exploded from it and ran up the steps of Chadilaine Manor. He struck the knocker on the massive door three times. Jeremy, Sandra, and the slight figure of a dark-haired stranger straggled behind him. When the door opened, Daniel gave his hat and gloves to a footman and asked if Lady Diana was receiving. He was shown directly to the blue salon in the back of the house. Diana lay slanted in a mass of pillows on a chaise form of bath chair extended to accommodate her stiff legs. A muscle in Daniel's jaw contracted. She'd lost too much flesh. Her bones were visible. Dark hollows had formed beneath her eyes. A skull stared at him.

Once she left her reverie and noticed him, Diana's countenance brightened. "What a lovely surprise. Delighted to see you, Daniel. I hoped you would come soon."

He took the offering as encouragement. But he couldn't be delighted–she looked so ill.

He told her of his doctor's diagnosis of asthma and treatment, and she was genuinely happy. She wagged an accusing finger at him for not having told her his true fears about his health, but the reprimand was mild. "I'm actually feeling better here at Chadilaine. I have a new doctor, Dr. Carter. He's having the nurses move my limbs and massage them. He says being so stiff and still is bad for the muscles and makes them weak. How do you spending your time in London these days?"

Perhaps she'd see him in a better light when he told her of his changing opinions of his role in politics. Daniel spoke to her of several incidents that happened lately which he felt strongly about. He suggested he could see making it his life's work to improve such conditions. Diana smiled weakly but seemed more invested in the afterlife than this one. She encouraged his aspirations wanly and waved away any expression of his esteem for her.

Each time she praised Faith to Daniel, he merely agreed with Diana's estimation. Yet he wondered what her sister-in-law had to do with them. Finally, it occurred to him what Diana attempted to do and why. He was horrified. She was conceding the battle for life and offering him a consolation prize. He felt his muscles strain against his skin as his temper flared. He stood and paced. He must remove himself from her presence until he regained control of his emotions. Daniel yawned. "You must excuse me, Diana. The journey was long. I need to freshen up and nap a bit. I'll return to you soon."

As Daniel left the blue salon, Colin caught up with him in the hall and asked him to assist him. Daniel followed Colin to the library and watched him close and lock the massive doors. He'd never seen those doors closed. The room was as he recalled it five years ago. Enormous mahogany shelves stuffed with leather-bound books, ancient and new, stretched to the ceiling. Dominating the floor was the plush burgundy-wool Turkish carpet he, Diana, and Thomas had imagined could fly them to Constantinople. There was the immense fireplace Thomas had been forced to climb when Lady Edmunds had flown at Mr. Crane in a rage to rescue Thomas and he from the chimney sweep. She was Miss Barrett then. Daniel looked enquiringly towards the earl.

Colin smiled reassuringly. "I'm about to reveal something to you which most of the staff are not even aware exists. I've my reasons for keeping it that way." He led Daniel to the fireplace and pushed on the edge of one of the stones that made up the left side. A serpentine crack appeared in the wainscoting to the left of the stone. Colin pressed the crack gently, and the wall swiveled open easily and soundlessly.

"Those of my staff privy to my little hiding place are too old, too heavy, or too rheumatic to hide in it. If it was included in the building as a priest hole, the man who designed it must have expected any priest in it to be on his knees. I used to hide here from pirates or dragons in my youth. At times, the dragon was my father." Looking into the space, Colin added, "I've heard of a castle with a priest hole located beneath the latrine in the turret. This one is much more sanitary. I apologize for the dust. It's been years since this was opened. I'd no idea so much dirt could collect in a closed and undisturbed space, or I would have had it cleaned."

Colin indicated a tiny hole perforating the wainscoting. "This allows in the only light. One can get a restricted view of the occupants of this room from it. Merely pull on this crossbeam to close the door after you and press gently on the door from inside to open it. The hinge on which it pivots is wonderfully sensitive. Knowing I could hide someone here, I insisted the experimentalist perform his treatments in this room. Otherwise, I'd not inconvenience Diana by moving her."

Colin lifted his chin toward an odd apparatus of glasses set up on the side-table that usually held a pyramid tower of fresh fruit. "As you see, Mr. Swinton begins to set up shop. Music to soothe the savage breast. Jeremy and I insisted we would be present, and the man assured us it would cause no problem. But, after arriving and assembling his instrument today, he hinted there were 'rare incidents of people who disturb the magnetic sphere by an excess of iron in their blood.' I had the unnerving feeling it was a precursor to banning us from the proceedings. I've read that Mesmer himself played some abhorrent tricks on suggestible ladies in his time. Thus, you are to be my sentry in reserve, so to speak–Diana's knight-errant."

## CHAPTER TWENTY-FIVE

Daniel crawled into the hiding space and drew the case wall back into place in front of him. He located the spyhole easily as it sent the only ray of light into the darkness. Almost immediately, he heard footsteps and the muffled sound of Colin's voice directing the footmen.

"Be gentle; take your time. Place her ladyship on this sofa on her side. Don't disturb the pillows as you do. Keep her completely level until she's lowered on to it."

The trapped sensation he remembered from his years as a climbing boy closed in on Daniel. It locked a strap about his chest as effectively as a cooper tightening metal bands around a barrel. He sipped shallow breaths. Daniel eased down on one knee to avoid having to bend his back for too long. A cobweb grasped his face, and he tore it away. His slight movement disturbed the accumulation of dust about him. His throat itched intensely. He clutched it and struggled to clear it soundlessly. He felt for his handkerchief and drew it from his coat. The dust clouded over him. He must not wheeze and give away his location. He quickly folded the silk cloth, positioned it over his nose, and cupped his hands over the kerchief to filter the air. He must not panic for her sake. He wasn't trapped in a chimney. He could escape immediately. Sweat rose on every pore of his flesh. He placed an eye to the tiny opening and stared into the large, well-lit room of the library. It felt more like being in the larger room. Tensed muscles relaxed. The merest push on the panel door would open it. He was fine. Daniel froze. The soft tickle of a spider travelled down his neck...

******

Diana shifted on her elbow on the couch. The experimentalist, Mr. Swinton, was introduced to her. Diana's nostrils flared. At least Colin and Jeremy were staying there with her. "Where's Eden?" she asked her brother.

"She wants to be with you, Diana, but Mr. Worth, her *accoucheur,* demanded she remain abed. Her pains have started, though they are twinges and with a good deal of time between each. Faith is with her. Worth seemed eager about something he said could be a pleasant surprise.

I cannot imagine what. What could be more agreeable than a new little stranger come into the world to meet us? I pressed him, but he refused to answer, saying it might spoil the surprise if it failed to come about."

Mystical sounds arising from the instrument by the sideboard enveloped them and brought Colin's *tête-à-tête* to a halt. Swinton was testing a few notes on his armonica. He dipped a finger in a bowl of water and held it to the rim of one of the many-sized glass bowls threaded sideways on the device. His foot rose and fell on a pedal that turned the bowls. Satisfied his contraption was in order, Swinton dried his hands and turned to the patient.

He approached Diana like a connoisseur approaches a fine wine. In a low, modulated voice, he explained to her everything that would take place. The slender scientist stressed that Diana must work on ridding herself of any tension or negative thoughts. While he played his music, she must breathe in through her nose as slowly as possible, hold the breath as long as possible, then breathe slowly out through the mouth. This would relieve rigidity in her humours. Swinton used a candle snifter to quench several candles on tables about the room. "For a more soothing atmosphere," he said. At last, the man began to play on the glass apparatus. "The melody I play on this instrument can calm and focus the mind," he said.

The resonances reminded her of a mellow, seasoned violin, but the tones remained in the air longer and blended with the next ones to produce a sound both eerie and ethereal. The music transported her. Diana concentrated on the slow breathing. Her bones seemed to melt, and her eyelids fought to close until she yawned and woke. Colin and Jeremy watched her intently. They had been breathing along with her in sympathy, it seemed, for Jeremy sighed too. Swinton stepped away from the instrument. Diana hated to hear the music stop. She opened her eyes. The experimentalist moved to the back of the couch on which Diana was positioned. He opened his large hands wide and began to move the palms in circular motions in the air above her midsection. The dance of the splayed fingers above her was both frightening and fascinating. Diana followed the hands intently. He broke the spell when she heard his low tones. "Do you notice any sort of mild feeling in your body whatsoever–a twitch, a warmth, a movement of the blood toward my hands?"

"No." When she said it, she did notice his mildly irked expression in response.

To Colin, Mr. Swinton explained, "The magnetism in her blood may be very weak from bleedings."

"She's never been bled. I do not hold with it," her brother said. Colin's eyes narrowed.

Swinton lowered his head close to Diana's and whispered, "Perhaps your monthly visits have depleted your iron." The subject he chose to address stunned and humiliated her. The nearness of his face to hers exposed a sickening little smirk. Diana controlled her involuntary gasp to hide her shock, but she glared a challenge at the man.

Straightening up and speaking to the others, he said, "I have a mixture containing the tiniest amount of powdered iron which can fortify the natural magnetism in your sister's blood while strengthening her as well. The intended reactions to my magnetism will then take less time and be more intense and efficacious. I warned you it might be necessary. I may also need to use the iron rod to shift the humours." He wandered to his leather case to retrieve a cork-stoppered bright blue bottle. Picking up a teacup provided for this possibility, the man poured a small amount of his mixture of powdered iron filings and some milky fluid. "It will be best to drink all of this at once. If it is sipped, the throat will tighten in a gag reaction against any more of the liquid. It's metallic tasting. Should you prefer not to do this, that's fine, but I may then need to carry out a series of treatments over several days."

Diana glanced at Colin. He was leaving it up to her. She didn't want this nonsense dragged on. She took the glass tumbler from the oily snake's hand.

Swinton told her to breathe slowly again. "When you feel your throat sufficiently relaxed, drink the medicine–all of it–in one swallow."

Diana sent a wild pleading expression to Jeremy. Did he really want her to drink that stuff? It could be poison or drugged.

Jeremy took the cup from Diana's hand, sniffed it, and held it up to the light. "Iron has been used by magnetists to control the motions of the blood." He wrinkled his brow and shrugged to let her know he was unable to determine if the current potion were harmful or not. "It's your choice, Diana. Would you like your physician to test it first for harmful ingredients? Doctor Carter is staying here a few days to attend you." Jeremy's eyes slid to the figure of Mr. Swinton. They accused and challenged.

"I'll take it," Diana said. Reaching weakly for the draft and bringing it to her lips, she tossed the contents down her throat. The foul stuff fought to come back up, and she fought to keep it down.

"Excellent," Swinton said. "We begin again." Another melody was played on the armonica, and the experimentalist approached Diana and motioned with his hands above her again for a longer period. "Do you feel anything at all?"

"Violently ill in my stomach."

"That will pass. I'll try the iron rod." Swinton walked back to the armonica and picked up a metal wand.

For a second, Diana imagined he intended to strike her with it, but he merely waved it over her. When nothing happened, Swinton turned to Colin and Jeremy. "Gentlemen, I sense that one or both of you harbor a profusion of magnetism in your blood such that your very presence interferes with my ability to bring about a healing. The aura of skepticism I detect in this room further hinders my powers. Therefore, I must ask you to leave the room for a brief time. We did speak of this before."

Diana gasped. Her eyes blazed a message to her brother. *Don't desert me!*

Colin seemed to answer her by darting glances toward the fireplace and winking. He said aloud, "We'll be just outside the door, Diana. It will be left ajar. All is well. Call out if you need us. We'll be listening. Doctor Carter will attend you when Swinton is finished."

Jeremy and Colin left the room abruptly, pulling the door almost closed.

Swinton examined the position of the heavy oak door. Apparently satisfied with what he saw, he turned to Diana. "I need to determine which parts of you have no feeling, so I can know better where to concentrate my powers."

"I feel a dull pain in the middle of my back. Above that point, I have all my sensitivity. Below that point, I feel numbness, or occasionally a stinging sensation. If I try to move my legs, unbearable pain shoots through them. It goes away if I'm still." Diana wondered how she could so easily tell him what she'd told none of her family. He was a scientist. He had to know the truth to treat her properly. Could he help it if his manner was a bit peculiar?

"It's imperative you relax the muscles for my magnetic powers to work."

"I am relaxed."

"No, you're not. You do not trust me."

"Where did you get these magnetic powers from?"

That sickening grin appeared again momentarily. "Not from any evil source, if that's what frightens you."

"I'm not afraid of you."

"I think you are. I don't know why. Is it because I'm not handsome and young? To answer your question, everyone has magnetic powers to an extent. I was fortunate in finding an instructor who trained me to magnify mine. I studied his methods faithfully. If the subject is unable to relax from the music and breathing, it's at times necessary to massage them into relaxing. If you will allow me to apply my hands to the back of your neck, I believe I can show you what I mean."

The man reached toward Diana's neck, and she instinctively drew back. "You said you were not afraid of me," he reminded her.

To prove her courage, Diana forced her shoulders up and her head down. Swinton rubbed his hands together noisily. "To warm them," he explained. "The heat can relieve stiffness as well." He placed his strong hands upon the back of her neck and began to manipulate it. "I feel a great deal of tightness in the sinews here. It radiates out to your shoulders as well."

Her neck had been aching. Diana willed herself to yield to his ministrations and began to experience an easing of the muscles in the area he massaged. Her stomach remained knotted. She felt his hands slip to the muscles in her shoulders, and they also improved. She felt so much better she began to trust the man knew what he was doing. Her head bent further forward, and her eyes closed inevitably, giving herself up to him. Her headache began to ease.

"Yes, much better," he said. One hand left her shoulder. "Can you feel this?" he asked.

Diana thought she felt a heaviness on her right thigh. "I think so."

"Good. You're getting sensation back at that point. It's working. I must relax you more."

Then Diana felt the hand on her hip slide to her bottom and squeeze. Electricity shot through her. She shrieked and sat straight up, tossing her feet to the floor.

The casing beside the fireplace burst open, and Daniel erupted from within. His hands were promptly on the man's neck. Diana's scream had deafened the charlatan and frozen him. Colin and Jeremy pulled back the heavy door and attempted to enter. They ran into Swinton as Daniel held him aloft by his hair and neck. His eyes bulged while his feet ran in the air. "Get this thing out of here," Daniel roared.

The young man's tone of command and raging mien forced a peer of the realm and a respected Member of Parliament to jump to it like a pair of lackeys. They took Swinton in hand and carried him swiftly toward the vestibule. The footman on duty opened the entry doors as he saw them coming, so in one swift move, Swinton was tossed brutally onto the front steps. The friends re-entered the house, and the doors were shut abruptly behind them.

They could hear the impostor shrieking outside, "But I cured her. You don't understand! I cured her. My things! My instrument! You can't do this. She's cured! My stipend!"

Colin turned to the butler. "Have Jenkins and Royal help you. Get his things from the library and escort him off the property. Let him know in no uncertain terms that all at parliament and my clubs will know how he's behaved here. And don't ask what I mean by that."

As they raced back to the library, Jeremy whispered, "You might wish to think that through. If parliament..."

"Bluff. No one shall hear of this. But I'll make certain he's never received again. You can help me."

Daniel was crouched on the floor in front of Diana, apologizing for being so slow. "I could only see his back from where I–"

The apology was cut off mid-sentence when Diana vomited the iron filing concoction all over her suitor. For a second, his stunned expression was all Diana saw. Then Daniel collected himself, cleared his throat, and said with a gleam in his eye, "Thank you for that blessing. I deserved it."

She laughed long and loud. He looked adorable. "I'm so sorry, my champion, but not completely. I feel so much better now. That brew was nauseating."

"Obviously, my delicate orchid. I consider it an honor that you shared it with me."

She smiled mischievously as she had not smiled at him in many months. Then Diana's melodious laughter rang out once more, and Daniel joined her with his own warm, full-throated laugh.

Simultaneously their eyes widened, and they stopped laughing. She was sitting upright!

## CHAPTER TWENTY-SIX

Colin and Jeremy marched back to the library to explain themselves and ask what the experimentalist meant. They were greeted with the sounds of two people giggling and the glorious sight of Diana sitting upright with her feet on the floor.

"Diana," Colin shouted. He clamped his eyes shut, then opened them wide. He clapped a hand to his chest. A smile began and grew across his face. "You are vertical! Is that quack responsible for this?"

"In a way. I moved to cast-up my accounts. His iron potion was disgusting. I could no longer hold it. I wasn't conscious I was sitting until Daniel noticed."

"How do you feel?"

"Better than lying down. My lower extremities hurt less."

"Hurt less?" Colin sat on the edge of the chair facing his sister. His stupefied expression was comical. "But, you hadn't complained of pain there. The doctors said it would be a good sign if you began to ache below your injury."

"They did? My feet and legs have been killing me for weeks."

"We often asked if your pain had traveled. You always denied it."

"Cora said it would upset you and Eden more to know I was in agony. She said Eden could lose the baby. She said the pain was a sign my nerves were dying, and when they were dead, the pain would end. It has lessened since the move, so I thought..."

"That woman will be turned off and without a reference! She may find her own way home. She was explicitly told to alert us if you complained of the slightest twinge. What of Judith? Did she know?"

"I hid it from her. She seems to tell you everything."

"I hate to intrude, but might someone ring for a maid?" Daniel sheepishly indicated the condition of his clothing. "I'm afraid to move and make this mess worse."

Colin glanced at the pale grey slime covering Daniel's cravat and weskit and nodded to Jeremy. Jeremy walked to the bell pull and rang for a servant.

"Forgive me, Daniel, for failing to notice," the earl said.

"Understandable."

Turning back to his sister, Colin told her, "I came to apologize for bringing that charlatan into your sphere. However, if his concoction made this happen, I'm overjoyed that I engaged him. Understand, this entire debacle was against my reason, but I've been frantic to bring about your good health in any possible way."

"I thought it was what you wanted. I thought at least I could please you in this by giving it a try. It was an opportunity to make up for my stupidity."

"We are a pair, are we not? I was desperate. You seemed to have lost hope. When I told you of Jeremy's idea, your face lit up. I thought it was what you wanted. It's been torture to see the light go out of your eyes, especially because of something I did..."

"You! It was I who disobeyed when I..."

"We'll talk later."

"But Colin, if it happened, it was meant to be..."

Colin raised a hand to indicate quiet; the house steward had appeared behind a maid.

Mr. Perrin entered and shifted on his feet as he spoke. "Forgive me, my lord, but her ladyship wishes to convey she must speak with you instantly."

"Very well. See to this mess, tell Eversley's man to lay out fresh garb for him, and bring the night nurse to my study in half an hour's time." Thinking Eden in hard labor, Colin took the stairs two at a time.

******

He charged through the open door of his wife's chambers and halted. She looked perfectly well and calm, her customary sweet smile in place. She was propped up in her lying-in bed of straw against a half dozen pillows. Her fullest, most opaque, long-sleeved cotton nightgown clad her modestly, while the white quilted counterpane pulled up over her swollen belly hid her feet. Her glorious mahogany tresses played over the bedding like dark winding brooks. She was dazzling.

"You sent for me, my love?" he said.

"My spies tell me there was a ruckus downstairs. How is Diana? What happened?"

Colin exhaled and wagged a finger at her. "All in due time. I thought you might be in pain. How do you get on?"

"As you see me–impatiently awaiting the expected event. I did feel a twinge or two, but it was so long ago, I begin to think it was my imagination."

Colin avoided the ominous presence of the birthing chair in the center of the room and shifted a pile of aired and folded linen placed on his favorite seat. He rolled the chair to the edge of his wife's temporary bed and described in detail the events of the previous hour, including Diana's "blessing" of Daniel with the contents of the vile mixture. A strained expression gripped her face, and Colin took one of her hands in his.

"Poor Diana," Eden said, "to have to go through all of this above everything else. Thank heaven, she's improved, and so greatly, it seems."

"She's had an extreme trial for one her age and protected state," Colin said. "Yet she's rallied. I always thought her a brave girl, but this season she's revealed her reflective qualities. I declare, I believed she merely reacted to circumstances. She's deeper than I imagined." He hesitated to go on as he observed his lovely wife. "While I'm confessing, I must admit to you, sweetness, why I've been such a peevish old bear of late. I accuse myself of frustration, anger, and feelings of utter helplessness–with you receiving the consequences in my conduct too many times. All my brilliant plans for the Lords this year have not only failed but exploded in my face. Nothing goes right. I control nothing. It is unmanning to know that. And the constant thought that Diana's condition was worsened by me has caused me to make some poor choices."

The fingers of Eden's hand contracted tightly in Colin's. He searched her face and found nothing untoward. He squeezed her fingers in answer.

"You've had much on your plate, my love. Yet you're right, you know," she said. "You're not in control: you never have been and never will be. Only the author of life controls destiny. It's a good thing, for he has the superior view. Consult him more before you make plans. Determine his will, then act. You're wrong about being helpless. God waits to help you, but you must ask for it. Do you attempt to change the world alone? Could this be the problem?"

Colin hung his head. "You know me well. A full day can go by without my giving a thought to God, except perhaps to blame him or ask him why without waiting for an answer. I'm too taken up with the cares of this world."

Eden's grimace silenced him. She blew out a breath and said quickly, "You're about to find out how little you command events. The author of life has decided to bring new life into the world. Send Rivers for the *accoucheur*!"

Colin leapt from the chair and moved to the door in one sweep as he nimbly avoided slipping on the straw-strewn floor. To the footman leaning in wait in the hall, he cried, "Rivers–get Worth!"

******

Colin sat on the edge of the chair next to his countess' temporary bed with a soft rag infused with Hungary water, mopping her face. She'd been lifted from the birthing chair back to the straw bed after the delivery to facilitate nursing the newborn. Eden had undergone so many variations of expressions in the last two hours, he'd been amazed. An actress might have paid money to study his wife in labor to add to her repertoire. The nurses had shooed at him, and the *accoucheur* tried warning him and then ordering him out of the room, but he wouldn't budge. They made it obvious they resented his presence in their private domain. When the white-slime-covered, violet-hued, squalling child was delivered, pronounced a boy, cord cut and tied, lauded, washed, wrapped, and handed to Eden to nurse, she asked Colin to go down and announce the birth and relieve his sister's mind. "I know Diana will imagine all sorts of awful things happening which are not true."

"Are you disappointed it is a boy?" Colin asked his spouse. "I know the ladies love to spoil their daughters."

"Aaron would have been disappointed if it was a girl."

"I see. I shall be but a moment," Colin said as he rose to leave.

Eden allowed the tiniest moan to escape, and her husband was back at her side. She smiled weakly and handed the baby to a nurse. "The pressure is relieved somewhat, but the cramps have not yet stopped." Her belly was still distended.

"It's the placenta: Nursing your baby stimulates its expulsion," Mr. Worth said. Glaring at Colin over his spectacles, he added, "You may not care to witness this."

The nurse approached with a pan and towels. Eden spoke, "Please go now. The afterbirth is not pretty. I'm fine. Tell Diana all is well."

When Colin had left, the doctor leaned down to apply his ear to Eden's belly. She was surprised at that.

"I was uncertain before, but now–there is yet a faint second heartbeat," the doctor said. "Above a hundred and forty beats, if you put any stock in that predicting a girl. A twin prepares to exit the womb!"

Downstairs, Colin announced the glorious news to Diana, Daniel, and Jeremy as they took part in the last of a high tea. Diana was still sitting upright with her feet firmly on the floor. She'd been trembling and too weak to attempt rising. Jeremy took it upon himself to order sandwiches, tea, and any sweet Diana formerly craved. The collation proved beneficial to the spirits of all. Diana, especially, found herself ravenous. Since Daniel soon attended Oxford, Jeremy had regaled them with some of his exploits there.

"I want to see Eden," Diana demanded of her brother the instant she saw him. It could be the last time she saw her alive. "I want to share my good news with her."

"I let that cat out of the bag a few hours past."

"Colin, I want to see Eden–now."

Colin raised a brow but yielded. Diana could be mulish, and this delicate moment of joy should not be spoiled with her threatening antics. "As you wish. But expect to be indulged this way for a week or two only. Then it's back to me ordering you about and not vice versa."

Colin arranged for Diana to be carried in a well-pillowed Bath chair up the stairs by four footmen. When they arrived in Eden's room, the young mother, who was positioned in the birthing chair, let out a moan and began panting like a cat. Colin ordered the servants to take Diana out, but his sister shouted, "No. I want to stay!"

"Yes, Diana, stay. I'm delighted to have you here," Eden soothed. "You were too young to understand last time, but now, it's good that you be here. It's better that you know what happens than that you imagine and worry and wonder."

Diana was wheeled to an adjacent corner where she could be out of the way but close enough to talk to Eden and observe. Colin stood next to her. The footmen hastily retreated. The spicy aroma of the tureen of caudle on the night table next to her delighted Diana's nostrils. The window was open to let in fresh air, though a fire danced on the hearth. Before the birth of Lord Aaron, both Eden and Colin had religiously read to each other the *Treatise on the Theory and Practice of Midwifery* by W. Smellie, M.D. They insisted many of the authors' novel ideas be put into practice in the delivery of their first child. Eden said they were natural and made sense. She had recalled the births of some of her siblings. The windows were covered, and every possible entrance of fresh air was stopped up for fear of letting in diseases. It made it impossible to breathe. Aaron had proved an easy birth, taking only six hours. He'd been the healthiest of children, so Doctor Smellie must have known what he was writing about.

One of the nurses suspended a ring over Eden's belly to observe the way it swung. The thread holding it was a hair from Eden's head. The nurse told Diana, "This ring should be her ladyship's wedding ring, but she won't let us remove it. It sways back and forth again, sure sign of a girl."

"I'm glad we provided several sets of clouts and pilchers," Eden said, glancing toward the cradle. "The ring said the same a few hours ago, and it was a boy."

"Perhaps it predicted this one instead," the nurse said.

"Oh, Oh." Eden's moans were soft. "I'm excited to meet this little stranger I never expected to know. I pray he or she enters this world in perfect health."

"In this case, you were right to ignore the advice about special diets to avoid having the baby get too large," Mr. Carter said. Diana's doctor had learned of the second arrival and insisted on intruding into the birthing room as well.

Observing the goings-on from her corner, Diana noted Eden seemed in no more pain than she herself had been experiencing these months. She listened to the encouragements of the doctor, the nurses, and the male midwife as he crouched before Eden. They were thrilled. When Eden appeared too weary to continue, the *accoucheur's* soothing voice assured her it was almost over, and then she could have that cup of tea and long rest she so wanted.

A nurse cried, "The head is crowning! I see dark hair on it, lots of it!"

Eden rallied.

The other nurse chimed, "With all that hair, it must be a girl. And there's a caul! Good fortune for the infant!"

Diana would never forget the sight and sound of the new little human pulled headfirst from her mother and flailing her tiny arms. She fought the nurse and wailed at the insult of the last few hours and the strange sensation of air in her lungs. She squinted at the light invading her eyes.

Colin bent over the cradle and picked up the first twin, who seemed distressed to hear his womb mate's voice. He held the baby close to him and peered into his eyes. "Be tranquil, young man. She'll be cosseted as much as you. Probably more."

When the *accoucheur* pronounced the baby a hale and hearty girl child, Diana ventured to say, "God has provided one for Colin, one for Aaron, and one for Eden. Now you'll not need to make any more."

Eden and Colin glanced at each other archly. "No, we will not *need* to," Colin agreed. Even biting his lip could not conceal his deeply dimpled grin.

## CHAPTER TWENTY-SEVEN

Jeremy blinked. Was it morning already? It was odd to wake abruptly when he was so comfortably ensconced in the downy mattress of his bed at Chadilaine. His hosts kept this room ready for his visits. It overlooked the man-made lake. The navy blues and stripes of the walls and fabric were masculine. The scent of the lavender-infused bedsheets usually greeted him when he awoke. Yet this morning, there was a different, more pervasive scent. It was sweet, floral, lemony. Jeremy stretched and yawned. He pushed himself to a sitting position. He felt lifted somehow. *What was that scent?* He knew it, but... Ah yes, Cassy. There she was. She stood by the window, backlit in a flowing lilac gown.

"Good morning, beautiful," Jeremy said.

"A glorious morning to you, my own," Cassandra's sultry voice answered.

"Is it too early to go down for breakfast, yet?"

Cassy laughed quietly. "I don't bother about that, Jeremy. I wish to tell you something."

"I'm all ears, love."

"It saddens me to see you still mourn me."

*Mourn her?* It dawned on Jeremy that his wife had died three years since. His heart stopped. He swallowed. He mustn't chase her away by fear. "I never want to sadden you, Cassy. What should I do?"

"I'm deliriously blissful in this place, sweetness. You're not happy where you are. The words were: 'Till death do us part.' We are parted for now. The Creator has given me this one visit. I'll not return. Don't look for me. Don't long for me, Jeremy. It does neither of us any good. Remember happy times, but don't wish them back again. Make new memories. Live your life fully–that will bring me joy. It will bring Sandra joy, as well. You need another partner, a good woman, to make you whole and happy on Earth. There's a perfect partner for you here at Chadilaine. She deserves to be happy too. You can make her happy, Jeremy, as you made me happy."

"Of whom do you speak?"

"You know who I mean. I must go now. Don't call me back. Love is eternal, Jeremy, but your heart is big enough to love more than once.

Goodbye."

"Wait, Cassy, I need to tell you..."

"I know how very much you love me, Jeremy. You didn't need to tell me in words. You told me every moment we were together. You told me in your eyes, in your smile, in your hand at my back when we walked, when we danced. In each joke you shared with me. Each time you showed me your newest magician's trick. When you loved our daughter with your whole heart and all your energy, you let me know that you loved me endlessly. When you shared your concerns for the laws of our country. Your love taught me how to truly love, taking the good with the bad, gently correcting blunders and praising good attempts. Do not talk to me of love, Jeremy. Your love surrounded me on Earth. But there's infinite love here that far surpasses anything there. It's utterly selfless, authentic love you can warm yourself in; you can swim in; you can float in; you can laugh in. It beckons me to reciprocate, and I want to. It draws me to its core. It fills me. Please don't call me back, Jeremy. Don't try to keep me here. Allow me to live in his eternal love."

Jeremy blinked back brine, and in that moment, she was gone. As morning sunshine slid behind the curtains onto the floor, he jumped out of bed and drew the draperies back to let in the rest of the light. The warm rays fell upon his form. While he stood there, he felt his body glow with the light. He ran to the tallboy chest, opened the top drawer, and drew out his journal and pencil. Sitting in his nightgown, Jeremy recorded the conversation he'd just had. It would be for him alone. Perhaps years from now, he would show it to Sandra. As Jeremy wrote the last word, he felt revitalized. He couldn't be sad, no matter how hard he tried. He couldn't make himself long for what was not. He wouldn't try to. This would make Cassy happy. He'd start life anew with fervor. Now. This day. First, he would have breakfast!

******

Eden's mother, Mrs. Barrett, came late the next afternoon to Eden's room to describe the christening that had just been held for the twins in the chapel on the estate. Eden stayed abed by physician's orders. She was in no mood to challenge them. She relished the rest.

The nurse and her assistants brought the twins in their christening dresses along with Aaron in his Sunday suit for Eden to coo over before they were whisked away to change into more practical clothes. Mrs. Barrett heartily approved the twins' names–Grace and Seth–as being appropriate biblical names. She fussed over the babies, commenting on their perfect features, their good behavior in the chapel, and the delicate stitches and embellishments of their wardrobes. When offered the opportunity to hold one of the wee ones, though, Mrs. Barrett declined for fear her trembles could cause her to drop it. But she did stroke their fuzzy heads.

She spoke excitedly about helping to plan a party for the day Eden was churched. As she chatted, she stated she felt she was right to warn them about bringing Diana out this year. "I sensed she was too young and impetuous even at seventeen. I could never have foreseen the tragedy that did occur." Mrs. Barrett dipped her chin and cast a brief accusing glance toward Eden. "I regret I felt the need to leave a note for Lord Edmunds, but you did not appear to give credence to my doubts about Diana's maturity."

Eden recalled the many times her mother had encouraged her and her sisters to marry young, could she truly have changed? Seeming to read her daughter's mind, Mrs. Barrett said, "We were in a far different situation, Eden, a desperate one. Diana's is superior. She can have her choice. My girls had little choice. They had to grow up fast. Diana has been allowed to be a child. She's also been encouraged to think independently. She will not be a biddable charge in London society. Even now."

"I think she's changed, Mother, and for the better."

"Change in people is slow."

Too tired to argue, Eden nodded and leaned back against her pillows. Her mother recognized the close of the visit. "I'm an irritating burden to my children, who would have me go to my reward sooner than later. I, too, wonder what causes the Lord to delay."

"No, Mother..." Eden began.

"I know it to be true. Your father was the dreamer. That left me to be the rational one and the one to discipline. No one appreciates the pragmatic parent. I did my best."

******

Soon after Mrs. Barret left with her companion, Colin poked his nose around the door.

Eden greeted him. "Do you recall receiving a warning note from Mother?"

His eyes narrowed and he hesitated. "A note... from your mother?" *Could she mean the note?* He placed fingers to his temple as if trying to recall.

"She mentioned leaving a note for you here at Chadilaine in April. She said she wrote to warn that if Diana was brought out this year, there were certain to be repercussions."

"Odd thing for your mother to do. But I dimly recall such a note before we left for London. Why do ask?"

"You're so apt to save everything, I thought it best you destroy the note lest Diana come across it. If she were to do so, it could cause discord between Mother and her."

"I recall crumpling it and tossing it in the trash container under my desk at the time. I imagine the servants have emptied it since. I didn't recognize your mother's handwriting, though." *No lie so far.* "Why would she write such a thing?"

"Yes, her hand is not what it was. Rheumatism and trembling make it hard for her to write. She was worried Diana was still a wild gamine. She thought Diana's headstrong character was sure to cause awkward escapades before the season was over."

"She wasn't far off. I should have heeded it."

"Impossible to predict what your sister might do. Yet, I think Diana's awful situation has honed her character. I only bring myself to say this now because she's progressing so well."

"Thank God for that." *What a facer!* The meddling old lady had written the note. Why should it bother him so? He'd been completely wrong about the author of the message. He'd jumped to conclusions. He didn't care to think of himself as one who did. He blamed an innocent... *no, cannot call Bradley innocent.* If Eden's mother hadn't left that message, he would not have kept so sharp an eye out, and he would not have employed the foundling home boys as he had. He was forever indebted to the irritating woman. He must look on her with greater charity and take better care of her from now on–at a distance.

******

When the parlor maids tidied up in Colin's study, they brought the outdated newspapers into the servant's hall for the butler, Mr. Greyson, to read. He was the one who noticed the possible Bradley reference in one of the police reports. He read aloud to those present in the servant's hall. "This Courier article states, 'the freshly murdered red-haired girl found among other corpses in a small warehouse not far from Anchor Road on Halfpenny Hatch has been identified as a light skirt last known to be kept by a certain recently deceased army officer of the bon ton.'"

The staff listening recognized the address as near Lady Diana's accident. The butler read further silently in case there might be something mentioned that an innocent scrub girl should not hear. He went on to comment, "It seems the girl was wearing a green ribbon around her neck braided with strands of gold and black hair. One of the medical students at the mortuary recognized it and her. Took a bit of ribbing he did for knowing her that personally." The staff smiled half-heartedly at the side comment, but they were silent, except for a single "Oh" escaping from

Judith. This news was too alarming to discuss openly immediately. It needed to be digested. Had Lady Diana been in more peril than had been supposed?

At the first opportunity, Judith asked Mr. Grayson if she might take some old newspapers home to her Pa to read. When the butler agreed, she retrieved a few, making sure The Courier was among them. That evening after her brother and sister were safely abed, she went back to the kitchen table where her father sat drinking a steaming cup of tea. He seemed to be growing younger by the day. His life of worry had eased. He had plenty to eat, and it had filled in wrinkles and erased the gaunt hollows in his cheeks.

"You're lookin' more relaxed, Pa. It looks good on ya."

He sat back and crossed his hands over his belly. "Plantin' flowers is a sight more rewardin' than plantin' corpses."

Judith showed her father the place where the article had been circled in pencil. She could read but poorly. Her father had been taught well as a boy. He read the whole to her, guessing at a few of the larger words.

"That neck ribbon the paper describes is the one Lissa Carmody wore," Judith said. "Her ma braided it herself from strands of her own hair and Lissa's pa's hair before they died. She told Lissa to wear it 'round her neck, and they would always be with her. When I last seen Lissa, she wouldn't look me in the eyes, but she did wave and nod as she passed. Later I thought I saw her with Major Bradley."

Judith's father glanced at her forlorn expression. "Don't worry, girl. She's in a much better place now."

"And her a light-skirt? You don't think she's in a worse place?"

"No. The Lord judges fair. That girl had a good heart. She fell into bad hands. She did what she must to keep safe and stay alive. She didn't know no better way. I should have taken her in, but when she needed us, I weren't thinkin' straight meself. All I could wrap my brainbox around were your ma dyin' and me havin' to provide for you three, an' Lily bein' a babe, an' your brother needin' medicine. Lissa's life weren't her choosin'; it were her cross forced upon her. She carried it as best she could."

Judith nodded. It was a relief to hear someone agree with her private hope.

## CHAPTER TWENTY-EIGHT

Diana sat hunched forward in the sun on a bench by the lake with Judith by her side. Judith pulled her redingote tighter against the late October air. Diana snapped her copy of *The Mirror of Graces* closed and laid it on her lap. She stretched her arms and scrunched her eyes closed. Upon opening them, her glance lit on a wooden structure. "I intend to climb into my treehouse very soon to survey the snowy grounds. I always feel natural and free and at home up there. It used to be my hiding place when I needed solace."

Judith gazed at her hands curled in her lap. "You might want to save the adventures 'til after your birthday ball. Don't want to be gettin' scrapes or fallin' out of the thing. Looks to me to need some patching of rotted wood."

"Perhaps your father could determine its reliability." Her train of thought led to the improvement of Judith's previously sickly siblings. "I saw your brother and sister helping him pluck the dead flowers along the lane. Your sister's hair has gotten so full and shiny. Your brother sat on a sled that your father pulled behind him. What do the doctors say about Toby?"

Judith bit a thumbnail and hung her head even lower. "They say it's the consumption. Warm weather or sea air might help, but he's too far gone and so little, we mustn't expect him to live much longer."

"I'm sorry to hear that. I'm surprised your father had him out in the cool air, though it was mid-day."

"Toby begged Papa so pitifully to take him along, my father couldn't say, 'No.' " The hefty maid wiped a sleeve on her nose. "Pa said he'd feel more than awful if Toby were to die tomorrow and him not getting' to go out in the sun, and feel the breeze on his face, and smell the sweet petals like he so wanted to."

Diana grasped one of Judith's hands and gave it a squeeze. She wasn't certain what she could say. Surely nothing that could help. Yet it would be wrong not to speak, would it not? While she hesitated, Diana noticed the trim, buckskin-clad figure of Matthew strolling toward them on the lane that began at the Dower House. As he approached, he tipped his high-crowned beaver and asked, "May I join you, young ladies, if I promise to be brief and leave you to your secrets?"

"Stay as long as you please. Your company is always welcome, Matthew."

"Glad to hear it, but I come to say I'll soon be absent."

"Where do you go?"

"I've arranged for my hideaway cottage by the sea where I'll be attended by an Indian Sage and a beefy boxer who should be able to slowly wean me from ..." Matthew slid his eyes toward Judith. "...bad habits. The boxer offers a system of slow stretching and massaging of the muscles, which he promises will ease pain and lengthen the muscles so I can walk normally. He holds that favoring the injury is the worst thing one can do for it. It makes even more sense to me now after seeing how greatly you've improved. I apologize, Lady Diana, for this means I must leave before your birthday ball and will be unable to attend."

"There'll be other parties, Matthew, for years to come. Go to your retreat instantly and heal. I absolve you."

Mathew complimented Diana on how hard she'd worked at getting her strength back and getting up on her feet. "Your walking has improved incrementally. I could never imagine your healing being so rapid. It's nothing short of a miracle. Yet a miracle you have had a hand in."

"Doctor Carter said much of the pain I had was due to remaining stiff and still all those months and not eating enough variety of foods. I blame myself for putting so much faith in the words of the night nurse, Cora. If I'd simply told my doctors in London the truth–that I felt burning in my feet–they would have ordered the massaging and light movement sooner. I've learned my lesson there. I swear never to base my actions on the comments of a single person again. At least I'll try never to."

"Someone once told me that to 'try' is to give yourself leave to fail; one must 'do' or 'not do.'

"Sounds profound, but difficult in practice."

"Quite right! Change is hard."

Diana smiled up at her brother-in-law. "I'm attempting a change in character as we speak, one which is most trying for me."

"Can I be of help?"

"Possibly. If you ever notice me attempting to control fate, call it to my attention."

A grin invaded Matthew's expression. "And here I am trying to change by beginning to govern my fate."

Diana shifted forward on the bench. Her face grew radiant as she tried to explain her experience. "If I've learned anything from this accident, it is that trusting God with your future life is very freeing. You begin to calmly anticipate the next bend in the road. You allow yourself to enjoy life right now–to be amazed by it, amused by it, engrossed in it. You no longer consider time spent in contemplation as wasted! To give God permission to control your life is to be honest with yourself. It's to admit you are imperfect and your intelligence is limited. One as proud as I has a hard time with that. It took months of pain to drain pride out of me. I still work on filling that space with humility and thankfulness. I feel like a new person, one filled with joy, hope, love for mankind. I hope I don't sound like a fanatical madwoman to you."

"You sound like one in love with life."

"Rather, I'm in love with God, and he is life itself and love itself."

Noticing Lord Eversley approaching from the manor, Matthew told Diana. "It's good you are properly chaperoned today, Diana. I see a suitor approaching. I look forward to continuing this conversation at a future time." He beamed at Diana and indicated with a lift of his chin the path Daniel followed. As the younger man drew closer, Matthew teased him, "Sent down already?"

Daniel grinned. "Hardly. I return to my studies tomorrow. Thought I'd ride up and see the invalid."

"No invalids here," Matthew said, eyeing Diana. He nodded to Daniel, tipped his hat to the ladies again and winked at his sister-in-law, then strolled toward home.

After chatting briefly with Judith, Daniel reached in a greatcoat pocket and produced a newspaper-wrapped loaf of bread. "The swans look hungry, Judith," he said, offering the bread to her.

Judith took the offering, agreed the birds looked ravenous, and gamboled off toward the lake to feed them, her laughter trailing behind her.

"What brings you away from university and all the way to Chadilaine, Daniel?"

"You. What else? And why formal?"

"No good reason. Sit. I do not care to crane my neck."

"But it displays that slender column to advantage when you do."

Diana patted the space next to her forcefully.

"I come to declare myself," he said, slumping onto the bench, a knee touching hers most tantalizingly.

"Declare yourself what?" she teased, her eyes laughing at him.

"You make this difficult."

"Good."

Daniel attempted to stand, saying, "I'll return when you're more conciliatory."

Diana grasped his coat and yanked him back down. Her expression was instantly repentant. "I'll be good. I promise."

"I shall say this badly because Judith may return at any moment. I love you desperately and want you for my wife, but I should complete my studies. I've much maturing to do, and when I've determined who I am and what I believe, you may not approve the person I've become. I want to secure your allegiance yet allow you the freedom to reject me if you feel you couldn't be happy with me as my imminent self. Your happiness is my delight. I offer you a secret understanding which you can discard at any time in the future without social censure."

Diana blinked at him. "If I understand correctly, you offer me a secret engagement to be revealed or cast-off sometime in the far future at my discretion."

"Exactly. Is it too peculiar?"

"Unique, original, and the only way which could induce me to accept at this point in my life."

Daniel furrowed his brow and tilted his head. "Did you say, 'accept?' "

"I did. Now kiss me quickly before Judith turns around."

"Oh, I do not think..."

Diana clutched his face firmly in both her hands and leaned in to press her lips to his. They were wonderfully warm and soft. She felt the strength of his hand instantly supporting her neck. He didn't draw back and neither did she. Heat rose in her face and neck. Her heart pounded in her ears. Every bone in her body melted.

Daniel broke them apart first. "We must not, Diana. We're not formally promised."

Diana breathed in puffs. Her mouth still prickled, and her heart beat hard against her ribs. "Still, it was very nice, and I've been longing to see what it was like." Diana glanced toward the swans. "Judith still looks at the lake." She reached for him again, but Daniel grasped her hands and held them away.

He stood and stepped back. "You've no idea what that did to me, Diana. We must control ourselves."

"Why?"

"If you insist on this behavior, I must declare my intentions to your brother this instant."

"But..."

Daniel's stern expression let her know he'd brook no argument.

"Help me up. I need your arm to walk back," she said.

Daniel bent to take her elbow and lift her to her feet. She stumbled against him and he enfolded her close. The top of Diana's head fit neatly beneath his chin. He allowed her to linger against him. She felt the rise and fall of his breathing in tandem with her own. The spiced scent of his soap assailed her nostrils. She felt him lift an errant lock of her hair between a thumb and forefinger to stroke it.

"Daniel..."

"This must be the very last one until we are wed," he said, tilting her face up to receive his kiss. All sound disappeared. All thought suspended. They melted together as one. They breathed as one. It was warm and peaceful and joyful there. It was heaven. No one ever wants to leave heaven.

Then Judith cleared her throat–loudly–quite near them.

Daniel straightened and looked Judith's way. She was engrossed in studying the ground. "Did you want something, Judith?"

"No, milord. Not now. But if I see anything going on again, I'll have to report it to my employer."

"Thank you, Judith."

"Daniel," Diana said, "I was about to say I'm most pleased you love me and want me as your life's partner. Know that I will always love you. But, though I do want to promise my heart and my hand to you, I'll not press you to make our understanding public. I've tried to determine God's will in our lives. So far, I believe he would like us to fulfill each other, but to go slow in our betrothal so we can get to know his design for us. I think this partnership is God-ordained, but we need to give it time. Do you think we should tell the family and ask them to keep it secret?"

"I don't know about that. It's a temptation for me as well as you, but there will most probably be unforeseen repercussions if we do. Let's not resolve on that for the moment." Daniel reluctantly released Diana from the circle of his arms and turned to her abigail. "Judith, Lady Diana will need your arm to get back to the manor. I intend to go for a brisk stroll in the opposite direction."

As Lord Eversley paced away from them, Judith asked, "Why do you need my arm, my lady? Has something gone amiss? You moved quite nimbly at dance lessons this morning. Perhaps the exercise tired you?"

Diana watched Daniel's energetic pace until the path he took turned into the wood and he disappeared. He didn't cough or exhibit signs of difficulty breathing. She smiled broadly. She might just get that waltz she'd so anticipated when the season began.

As Diana and Judith entered the house, Hope bounced up to them.

"Diana, just the one I was looking for. I've thought of a wonderful ploy to play at your birthday ball. You announce that because it's your evening, the usual parade into supper by precedence is suspended. The ladies may choose their own partner. Then we'll not be stuck making conversation for the entire meal with some old married windbag. Do not look shocked, Diana. It says in the Morning Courier that The Countess L– did the same thing at her birthday ball."

"A shrewd political family must not depart from protocol in such a disgusting way, Hope. Moreover, it's to be a select group, and I've invited no bores."

Hope flounced away, calling over her shoulder, "It was merely a suggestion."

Diana watched her go. *And a fascinating one, at that.*

## CHAPTER TWENTY-NINE

Diana peeked into the dining room and approved the decorations. She'd asked that a faux river be made to wind down the middle of the supper table with ferns and stones arranged about it and Chinese goldfish swimming in the water. Everything was ready. She closed the door when she heard visitors entering the hall. Matthew's voice startled her. He came with his entourage to surprise Diana. She adjusted her mother's shawl about her shoulders and straightened her spine. Beaming, she went to greet her brother-in-law. "What a brilliant surprise! I didn't expect you to be able to attend. You look elegant, Matthew. And you've brought your friends as well. Then we shall have more males than females, and that means my party will be deemed a success. Welcome!"

Matthew introduced Diana to a small, exotically dressed, bright-eyed, elderly man and a tall, burly bear of a man with a gentle expression. "The best friends I've ever known," he added.

"Enchanted," Diana said.

"We're here for the weekend only. I had an idea I need to approach Judith's father with. I thought to ask if he might allow his little ones to stay with me awhile at my cottage. The warm sea air is greatly beneficial for the lungs. And the view is stunning."

"What a generous scheme," Diana said. "I know I always loved exploring along the seashore. We gather in the ballroom soon. Colin has some mystery going on in there. I must go up and allow my lady's maid to apply finishing touches before we begin."

As Matthew approached the ballroom with his allies, he heard the name Miss Hope Barrett mentioned in hushed tones. He halted to eavesdrop.

Sir Barry spoke to Lord Dawson. "Do you not fear she will cause scandal?"

Dawson murmured, "I'll secure her and take her to my seat in the North and never bring her back into society again. She'll be good for breeding with those wide hips. And as young as she is, she can give me a great brood of pups in case an epidemic occurs."

Matthew marched through the doors, breaking the two men apart with his body. His associates followed him through the opening. Matthew thought to tell Hope what he heard. He disapproved of her machinations but would not wish so callous a mate on anyone, especially a sister who might invite him to her home for Easter parties and such. He hesitated, knowing she disdained advice in any form. If he tried to hint her away from the suitor, spite could drive her toward him the more. He would wait a bit and intercept her only if she seemed to prefer the cad.

When he saw Dawson approach Hope, he resolved to do the brotherly thing and warn the nasty lord off with stories of insanity in the blonde children of their family. No, that would be circulated and keep her a miss for life. Perhaps a disease or a mishap that had caused sterility? He would have to consider this fully. He must choose a defect for Hope that would frighten the unworthy lord away without frightening off more suitable potential beau. Was that possible? It was an odd dilemma.

******

Colin and Eden stood together by a large, shrouded object perched on a sturdy easel. They awaited Diana's entrance. The guests had been announced and greeted by the Ashton family before Diana left prior to the start of the party. Announcing that all were to assemble in the ballroom for the unveiling of Diana's birthday gift, Colin and Eden had led the way. When Diana entered the lofty doorway of the room, Jeremy, with little Sandra in his arms, announced, "Ah, here's the birthday girl now, and 'She walks in beauty, like the night...' "

The company turned as one to look toward the doors and spontaneously applauded the vision. Diana was spectacular. Head held high on her slender columned neck, she floated across the floor in a cream silk evening gown embroidered in pale hues of blue and violet and overlain with silk gauze. She had allowed her shorter hair to be curled and intertwined through a slender tiara of seed pearls and tourmaline. A fresh spray of wild orchids from the orangery had been tucked into the comb. Artfully draped low over her arms was her mother's shawl. She beamed at the company and walked straight to Colin's side. "What have we here, dear brother?"

"As if you cannot guess. We all wait for you to unwrap your gift." Colin handed her the cord, which would cause the cloth to fall from the painting.

Diana tugged the cord, and the guests applauded the wonder revealed. Diana radiated her approval to Daniel. She laughed aloud at the fox's wide eyes peeping from its hiding place near her riding skirt. Diana opened her fan and made the sign with it to "come here" to the artist. Daniel promptly obeyed.

At the door, Jeremy Blake started to hand Sandra to her nurse to be taken upstairs. The little girl noticed Diana's first portrait now hung at Chadilaine. Her child's sweet, loud voice echoed in the hall: "Mama?" Diana turned to see little Sandra in her father's arms pointing at the painting. "No, sweetheart, that's a painting of Lady Diana," Jeremy said. "You see: her hair is the color of summer honey, and her eyes are emerald green."

The child squinted. "Not Mamma?"

Jeremy furtively sought his best friend's eyes. Colin avoided his. Eden smiled insincerely. Jeremy's brow wrinkled. The guest's eyes were turned on him. He chuckled and shrugged, handing Sandra to her nanny. "I've been showing Sandra a portrait of her mother we have at home. She doesn't recall how my late wife looked, and now she thinks paintings of all beautiful ladies wearing court dress are called, 'Mama.' " The guests tittered and nodded, agreeing Lady Diana was indeed as beautiful as little Cassandra's mother had been. Eden's eyes exuded appreciation to her husband's friend. He nodded to her and breathed a sigh.

The moment passed. The company moved toward and marveled at Diana's presentation portrait, commenting it had caught her to perfection. Many asked who the artist was and whether he might consider a commission from them. None received a satisfactory answer.

Diana began the ball by announcing, "Since it is my birthday and all here are friends, I declare formality and precedence dispensed. It shall be ladies' choice all evening. Ladies will choose their partners for the dances, and their first choice shall be the one they process in to supper with." Female friends had been pre-warned to be near the one they wished to sit by. Hope was left out of the circle of awareness. Neither had Faith been told for fear her honest heart would disclose the secret to Hope.

Faith, in her white silk dress, conspicuously left her group to glide a few steps and grasp the arm of Mr. Jeremy Blake with a strong grip. "You are my choice of partner for the evening," she announced for the world to hear. She looked happy, deliriously happy–blissful.

Jeremy flinched as her touch charged him with electricity. His glance fell. He caught his breath. His chest lifted. He looked full in her face and beamed. "Miss Barrett. You look a radiant angel. Doing your good deed by favoring an old crone with your excellent company?"

The corners of her mouth slowly lifted high. Her bright eyes approved heartily of all she read in his face. She wrinkled her nose at him.

Matthew still pondered his dilemma about his sister when a perfectly lovely raven-haired young miss took hold of his arm and smiled up at him. He beamed at her, placed a gloved hand on her hand, and led her to the dance floor, hoping his leg would behave long enough to endure a few dances at least.

When Diana took Daniel's arm, it was a simple task. He was already at her side when she made the announcement, and she grasped his gloved forearm possessively.

As the other ladies swiftly clutched the arm of their favorites, Hope was stuck with an older lord to whom she would not normally give the time of day.

The musicians struck up the waltz, which Diana had chosen as the first dance of the evening, lest Daniel be fatigued later. He grinned at her. "I, uh, am delighted to have this opportunity to show you I've been practicing the waltz at home for this very prospect."

The sweethearts paraded confidently to the top of the room.

*FINIS*

If you enjoyed this book, please rate it, and leave a brief review at http://amzn.to/36kdKx2

A line or two will go a long way to help get this story into the hands of those who would enjoy it. Thank you, Dear Reader, ahead of time.

You can learn more about the author and her books, read her blog, and sign up for her occasional newsletter and raffle prizes at:

**https://elainelyonsbach.com**

Your e-mail address will never be shared, and you can easily unsubscribe at any time at the bottom of the newsletters.

www.ingramcontent.com/pod-product-compliance
Lightning Source LLC
Chambersburg PA
CBHW032008240626
47153CB00003B/1169

*9780578592398*